COMRADES IN ARMS

War heroes, heartbreakers...husbands?

The close friendship between Lieutenant Colonel
Jack Trestain and Major Finlay Urquhart was forged
in the heat of Waterloo's battlefield.

Famed for their daring and courage, these are
Wellington's most elite soldiers, but now they're
facing their biggest challenge yet—falling in love!

If you enjoy

The Soldier's Dark Secret

you won't want to miss the second instalment
of this fabulously intense and dramatic duet
from Marguerite Kaye!

Look out for Finlay's story

Coming soon

D1148582

THE SOLDIER'S DARK SECRET

Marguerite Kaye

Published in Great Britain 2015
by Mills & Boon, an imprint of Harlequin (UK) Limited,
Eton House, 18-24 Paradise Road, Richmond, Surrey, TW9 1SR

© 2015 Marguerite Kaye

ISBN: 978-0-263-24765-7

Harlequin (UK) Limited's policy is to use papers that are natural,
renewable and recyclable products and made from wood grown in
sustainable forests. The logging and manufacturing processes conform
to the legal environmental regulations of the country of origin.

Printed and bound in Spain
by CPI, Barcelona

Born and educated in Scotland, **Marguerite Kaye** originally qualified as a lawyer but chose not to practise. Instead she carved out a career in IT and studied history part-time, gaining first-class honours and a master's degree. A few decades after winning a children's national poetry competition she decided to pursue her lifelong ambition to write, and submitted her first historical romance to Mills & Boon®. They accepted it, and she's been writing ever since. You can contact Marguerite through her website at: www.margueritekaye.com

Books by Marguerite Kaye

Mills & Boon® Historical Romance
Mills & Boon® Historical Romance *Undone!* eBooks

Comrades in Arms

The Soldier's Dark Secret

Armstrong Sisters

Innocent in the Sheikh's Harem
The Governess and the Sheikh
The Sheikh's Impetuous Love-Slave (Undone!)
The Beauty Within
Rumours that Ruined a Lady
Unwed and Unrepentant

Castonbury Park

The Lady Who Broke the Rules (Undone!)

Stand-Alone Novels

Never Forget Me
Strangers at the Altar

**Visit the author profile page
at millsandboon.co.uk for more titles**

Chapter One

England—August 1815

The small huddle of women and the bedraggled children who clung to their skirts stared at him as one, wide-eyed and unblinking, struck dumb and motionless with fear. Only the compulsive clutching of their mother's protective fingers around the children's shoulders betrayed the full extent of their terror. He was accustomed to death in combat, but this was a village, not a battlefield. He was accustomed to seeing enemy causalities, but these were civilians, women and young children...

Jack Trestain's breathing became rapid and shallow as he tossed and turned in the throes of his recurring nightmare. He thrashed around on the sweat-soaked sheets. He knew he was dreaming, but he couldn't wake from it. He knew what was coming next, but he couldn't prevent it unfolding in all its horror.

His boots crunched on the rough sun-dried track as he walked, stunned, around the small village, his brain numb, unable to make sense of what his eyes were telling him. The sun burned the back of his neck. He had lost his hat. A scrawny chicken squawked loudly, running across his path, making him stumble. How had the mission turned into such a debacle? How could his information, his precious, carefully gathered knowledge of the enemy's movements, have been so wrong?

It was not possible. Not possible. Not possible. The words rang in his head over and over. He was aware of his comrades' voices, of orders being barked, but he felt utterly alone.

The cooking fires were still burning. From a large smoke-blackened cauldron the appetising aroma of a herb-filled stew rose in the still, unnaturally silent air. He had not eaten since yesterday. He was suddenly ravenous.

As his stomach growled, he became aware of another, all-pervading smell. Ferrous. The unmistakable odour of dried blood. And another. The sickly-sweet stench of charred flesh.

As the noxious combination seared the back of his throat, Jack retched violently, spilling his guts like a raw recruit in a nearby ditch. Spasm after spasm shook him, until he had to clutch at the scorched trunk of a splintered tree to support himself. Shivering, shaking, he had no idea how long the girl had been looming over him...

It was the fall that woke him. He was on the floor of his bedchamber, clutching a pillow. He had banged his head on the nightstand. The ewer had toppled over and smashed. The chambermaid would think him one of the clumsiest guests she'd ever encountered. His nightshirt was drenched, the contents of the jug adding to his fevered sweat. His head was thumping, his jaw aching, and his wrists too, from clenching his fists. Wearily, Jack dragged himself to his feet and, opening the curtains, checking the hour on his pocket watch. It was just after five. He'd managed to sleep for a total of two hours.

Outside, morning mist wreathed the formal lawns which bordered the carriageway. Opening the casement wide, he leaned out, taking ragged breaths of fresh air. Damp, sweetly herbaceous air, not the dusty dry air of far-off lands, that caught in your lungs and the back of your throat, that was so still all smells lingered, and you carried them with you on your clothes for days afterwards.

Jack swallowed hard, squeezing his eyes tight shut in his effort to block out the unwelcome memory. Slow breaths. One. Two. Three. Four. Open your eyes. Moist air smelling of nothing but dew. More breaths. And more.

Dammit! It had been two years. He should be over it by now. Or if not over it, he should have it under control. He'd been coping perfectly well in the army—more or less. He'd been dealing with it—mostly. Functioning— on the whole. He hadn't fallen apart. He'd been able to control his temper. He'd even been able to sleep, albeit mainly as a result of exhaustion brought on by a punishing schedule of duties. Only now, when he was free of that life, the very life that was responsible for creating his coruscating guilt, it was haunting his every waking and sleeping moment.

Dear God, he must not fall apart now, when it was finally all behind him. He had to get out of the house. He had to get that smell out of his head. Exercise, that's what he needed. It had worked before. It would work again. He would *make* it work again.

His forearm had finally been released just yesterday after weeks in a cumbersome splint. Jack flexed his fingers, relishing the pain which resulted, his toes curling on the rug. He deserved the pain. A damned stupid thing to do, to fall from his horse, even if his shoulder had just been torn open by a French musket. Quite literally adding insult to injury.

Take it easy, the quack had advised yesterday, reminding him that he might never recover his full strength. As if he needed reminding. As if it mattered now. 'As if anything matters,' Jack muttered to himself, pulling off his nightshirt and throwing on a bare minimum of clothes before padding silently out of the house.

The sun was beginning to burn the mist away, drying the dew into a fine sheen as he set off at a fast march through the formal gardens of his older brother's estate. Jack had been on active service in Egypt when their father died, and Charlie inherited. In the intervening years, nearly all of which Jack had spent abroad on one military campaign or another, Charlie had added two wings to their childhood home, and his wife, Eleanor, had redecorated almost every single room. The grounds, though, had been left untouched until now. In a few weeks, the extensive new landscaping programme would begin, and the estate would be transformed. The lake, towards which he now made his way, through the overgrown and soon-to-be-uprooted Topiary Garden, would be drained, dredged, deepened and reshaped into something that would apparently look more natural.

He stood on the reedy bank, inhaling the odours so resonant of childhood: the fresh smell of grass, the cloying scent of honeysuckle and the sweetness of rotting vegetation laced with mud coming from the lake bed. There was never anyone around at this time of day. It was just Jack, and the ducks and whatever fish survived in the brackish water of the lake.

Divesting himself quickly of his few garments, he stretched his arms high above his head, took a deep breath, and plunged head first into the water. Though it was relatively warm on the surface, it was cold enough underneath to make him gasp. Opening his eyes, he could see little, only floating reeds and twigs, the mixture of dead leaves and sludge churned up by his splashy entry. He broke the surface, panting hard, then struck out towards the centre, his weakened right arm making his progress lopsided, forcing his left arm to compensate as he listed to one side like a sloop holed below the waterline by a cannon.

Ignoring the stabbing pain in his newly healed fracture and the familiar throbbing ache in his wounded shoulder, Jack gritted his teeth and began to count the lengths. He would stop when he was too exhausted to continue, and not before.

Celeste Marmion had also been unable to sleep. Attracted by the soft light of the English morning, so very different from the bright blaze of the Côte d'Azur where she had been raised, she had dressed quickly and, grabbing her notebook and charcoals, decided to reconnoitre the grounds of Trestain Manor before facing her hosts at breakfast. Arriving late last night, the brief impression she had had of her new patrons, Sir Charles and Lady Eleanor Trestain, was pretty much as she had expected. He was the perfect gentleman, rather bluff, rather handsome, his smile kind, though his manner veered towards the pompous. His wife, a slender and very tall woman with a long nose and intelligent eyes, reminded Celeste of a highly-strung greyhound. Lady Eleanor was a good deal less welcoming than her husband, giving Celeste the distinct impression that she was placing her hostess in a social quandary, for although Sir Charles had welcomed his landscape painter as a valued guest, Lady Eleanor seemed more inclined to treat her as a tradesperson.

'Which is perfectly fine by me. I am here for my own reasons, not to play the serf in order to placate a social snob. Lady Eleanor is really quite irrelevant in the grand scheme of things,' Celeste muttered to herself as she made her way through a magnificent but dreadfully neglected Topiary Garden.

She could hardly believe that she had finally made it to England. It had been her goal ever since January, when she had received that fateful letter. It had been a terrible shock, despite the fact that they had been estranged for years, to learn that she would never see her mother again. She had thought herself completely inured to Maman's coldness, but for a few days after learning of her death, Celeste had been left reeling, assailed by a maelstrom of emotions which struck her with a force that was almost physical.

She had, however, quickly regained her equilibrium. After all, her mother had been more of an absence than a presence in her life for as long as she could remember, even before Celeste had been callously packed off to boarding school at the age of ten. It should make no difference to Celeste that the house in Cassis was closed up, for she never visited. It should make no difference that there was now no possibility of any reconciliation. She had never understood her mother's attitude towards her, the cause of their gradual and now final estrangement, but she had long decided not to let it be a cause of hurt to her. Until she had received that blasted letter which hinted at reasons, mysterious reasons, for her mother's heartless indifference.

Celeste had tried very hard in the weeks after that letter to carry on with her perfectly happy, perfectly calm and perfectly ordered and increasingly successful life, but the questions her mother had raised demanded to be answered. Until she knew the whole story, until she knew the truth behind those hints and revelations, Maman's life was an unfinished book. Celeste had to discover the ending, and then she could close the cover for ever. It was an image she found satisfying, for it explained away quite nicely that churning feeling which kept her awake at nights when she thought of her mother. Guilt? Hardly. Her whole life she had been the innocent victim of a loveless upbringing. And of a certainty it was not grief either. In order to grieve, one had to care. And she did not care. Or, more accurately, she had taught herself not to care. She did feel anger sometimes, though why should she be angry? She did not know, but it did not sit well with the self-contained and independent person she had worked so hard to become. And so she had come to England to find some answers and close an unhappy chapter in her life.

Napoleon's escape from Elba in March earlier in the year had put paid to Celeste's original plans for her trip here. As France and Great Britain resumed hostilities, she waited restlessly for the inevitable denouement on the battlefield, guiltily aware that her impatience was both unpatriotic and more importantly incredibly selfish. She knew nothing of war save that she wished it would not happen. She cared not who won, provided that peace was made. Until Waterloo, like almost every other person of her acquaintance, she managed to close her eyes to the reality of battle. After Waterloo, the full horror of it could not be ignored.

But peace was finally declared, and that,

despite the defeat of France, was a cause for celebration. No more war. No more bloodshed. No more death. It also meant that Celeste was finally free to travel. The commission from Sir Charles Trestain to paint his gardens for posterity before he had them substantially altered had come to her by chance. A fellow artist of her acquaintance, who had been the English baronet's first choice, had been unable to accept due to other commitments and had recommended Celeste. She could not but think it was fated.

So here she was, in what she was only beginning to realise was a foreign country. Her command of the language had been the one and only piece of her heritage which her English mother had given her, though they had spoken it only when alone. As far as the world was concerned, Madame Marmion was as French as her husband.

Celeste stopped to remove a long strand of sticky willow which had become entangled in the flounce of her gown. The grass underfoot was lush and green, the air sweet-smelling and fresh, no trace of the southern dry heat of home—or rather the place she was raised, for a home was a place associated with love and affection, something which had been in very short supply in Cassis.

No matter, she had her own home now, her little studio apartment in Paris. The air in the city at this time of year was oppressive. Celeste took a deep breath of English air. She really was here. Soon, hopefully before the summer was over, she would have some answers. Though right at this moment, she wasn't exactly clear how on earth she was going to set about finding them.

A gate at the end of the neglected Topiary Garden revealed a view of a lake. The brownish-green water looked cool and inviting. Frowning, deep in thought, it was only as she reached the water's edge that Celeste noticed the lone swimmer. A man, scything his way through the water in a very odd manner, rather like a drunken fish. Coachman, gamekeeper, gardener or perhaps simply one of the local farmers taking advantage of the early-morning solitude? She could empathise with that. Solitude was a much-underrated virtue. Whoever he was, she ought to leave him to finish his illicit swim in Sir Charles's lake. Had the roles been reversed she would have found the intrusion most offensive. And yet, instead of turning back the way she had come, Celeste stepped behind a bush and continued to watch, fascinated.

He was completely naked. The musculature of his torso was beautifully defined. His legs were long, well shaped, and equally well muscled. He would make a fascinating life study, though it would be a lie to say that it was purely with an artist's eye that she observed him, peering as she did through the straggle of jagged hawthorn branches. Like his swimming, the man's face was far from perfect. His nose was too strong, his brow too high, his eyes too intense and deeply sunk. He looked more fierce than handsome. No, not fierce, but there was a hardness to his features, giving him the air of a man who courted danger.

His swimming was becoming laboured. He slowed and stopped only a few yards from where she stood, staggering slightly as he found his footing. The water lapped around his waist. His chest heaved as he began to make his way towards the bank where his clothes were draped over a branch some distance away. It was too late for her to make her escape. She could only hold her breath, keep as still as possible and hope that he would not spot her.

His torso was deeply tanned. There was an odd puckered hollow in his right shoulder where the flesh appeared to have been scooped out. His entire right arm was distinctly paler than the rest of him, as if he had spent the summer wearing a shirt with one sleeve. A scar formed an inverted crescent on his left side, just under his rib cage. A man who liked to fight or one who was decidedly accident prone? He was panting, his chest expanding, his stomach contracting with each breath. His next step revealed the rest of his flat belly. The next, the top of his thighs, and a distinct line where his tan ended.

And then he stopped. He looked up to the sky, and Celeste's breath caught in her throat as his face almost seemed to crumple, bearing such an expression of despair and grief that it twisted her heart before he dropped his head into his hands with a dry sob. His shoulders were heaving. Appalled, mortified to have witnessed such an intensely intimate moment, Celeste turned to flee. Her gown caught on the hawthorn briar, and before she could stifle it, an exclamation of dismay escaped her mouth.

He looked up. Their eyes met for one brief moment that seemed to last for an eternity. He looked both heartbreakingly vulnerable and volcanically angry. Celeste tore herself free of the thorns and fled.

Back in her room at Trestain Manor, Celeste could not get the image of the man's tortured face out of her head. Nor her deep shame at having spied on him. She, of all people, should respect a person's right to privacy, given how hard she defended her own. It took fifteen minutes for the colour to fade entirely from her cheeks and another fifteen before she was calm enough to face breakfast with her new patrons.

Praying that the man would not turn out to be one of Sir Charles's footmen, she made her way down the stairs to the dining room where one of the austere servants indicated the morning repast was being taken. The very welcome aroma of coffee was overlaid with a stronger one of eggs and something meaty. Hoping that she would not be obliged to partake of either, Celeste opened the door and stopped dead in her tracks on the threshold.

The room was dark, for the windows were heavily curtained, and despite the white-painted ceiling, the overall impression was gloomy. An ornately carved and very highly polished walnut table took up most of the available space, around which were twelve throne-like chairs. Three were occupied. Sir Charles was seated at the top of the table. Lady Eleanor was on his right. And on his left sat another man. A man with damp hair, curling down over his collar. With a coat stretched across a pair of broad shoulders. Her stomach knotted.

'Ah, Mademoiselle Marmion, I trust you slept well. Do join us.'

Sir Charles pushed his chair back and got to his feet. Celeste, her polite smile frozen, could not shift her gaze from the other guest. There was a kerchief knotted around his neck rather than a carefully tied cravat. He had shaved, but somehow he looked as if he had not.

'Jack, this is Mademoiselle Marmion, the artist I was telling you about. She's come all the way from Paris to capture our gardens for posterity before Eleanor's landscaper gets his hands on them. *Mademoiselle*, do allow me to introduce you to my brother Jack, who is residing with us at present.'

Her first instinct, as he rose from his seat, was to run. He was smiling, a thin, cold smile, the sort of smile a man might bestow on a complete stranger, but she was not fooled. Celeste clutched the polished brass doorknob, for her knees had turned to jelly as the man from the lake crossed the room to greet her. The naked man from the lake who was Sir Charles's brother. *Mon Dieu*, she had seen naked men before but what made her cheeks burn crimson was having witnessed that anguished look on his face. She had seen him naked, stripped bare in quite a different way. She felt as if she had violated some unspoken rule of trespass. Forcing herself to let go of the door handle, she met the cold, assessing look in his dark-brown eyes. What had possessed her to watch him? Why on earth had she not fled as soon as she'd seen him?

He bowed over her hand. Did he notice that her fingers were icy? 'Mademoiselle Marmion. *Enchanté*. It is a pleasure to meet you. Again,' he added sotto voce, leaving her in no doubt that he had recognised her.

'Monsieur Trestain.' Her voice was a croak. She cleared her throat. 'It is a pleasure.'

'Indeed?' He ushered her to the table, holding out the chair opposite his own for her. 'For future reference, *Mademoiselle*,' he whispered, 'I am accustomed to taking my morning swim in private.'

His tone was neutral but there was an underlying note of barely controlled fury. Celeste's hand shook as she picked up the silver coffee pot. Though she managed to pour herself a much-needed cup without spilling it, she was acutely aware of Jack Trestain watching her, expecting her to do just that. She had been in the wrong, but she did not like to be intimidated. 'I took the opportunity to explore a little of your beautiful grounds before breakfast,' she said, turning to Sir Charles.

'Excellent, I applaud your sense of enterprise.' Sir Charles rubbed his hands together. 'And did you find anything to inspire you, *Mademoiselle*?'

'Yes, do tell us, did you see anything of interest during your exploration?'

Jack Trestain's curt tone cut across his brother's gentler one. Celeste threw him a tight smile. 'The lake has some interesting views.'

'I'm sure you found it fascinating,' Jack Trestain said, returning her look unblinking, 'though perhaps you will prefer to admire the view in the afternoon sunshine, in future.'

She could not mistake the warning tone in his voice. With some difficulty, Celeste swallowed the spark of temper which it provoked.

She had been completely at fault, but this man was taking deliberate pleasure in her discomfort. She nodded curtly and took a sip of coffee to prevent herself from being tempted into a retort.

'Well,' Sir Charles said, casting a sideways glance at his brother, obviously perplexed by the animosity reverberating from him. 'Well, now. Perhaps Jack's right, the afternoon sunshine would provide the best light for capturing the views. What is your opinion, my love?'

The rather desperate look Sir Charles cast his wife intrigued Celeste. The way in which Lady Eleanor commandeered the conversation, launching into a long and detailed description of the various changes which her landscaper planned, and the possible studies Celeste could make, spoke of considerable practice in changing the subject. Jack Trestain, leaning back in his chair, ignoring the plate of ham and eggs set before him, watched with a sardonic smile on his face, obviously perfectly aware of the diversionary tactics being deployed, equally aware that he was being excluded from the conversation lest he cause further offence.

Lady Eleanor, running out of steam on one subject, switched, with barely a moment to take breath, to another. 'You are admiring our dining room, I see,' she said to Celeste, who had actually been staring down at her plate. 'It is quite a contrast to the rest of the house, you were no doubt thinking. Very true, but we did feel, Sir Charles and I, that it was important to preserve at least one of the original rooms when we carried out our refurbishment. The wall covering is Spanish Cordova leather, you know. I believe it dates from the late sixteenth century. When Sir Charles and I decided—'

'You don't look like an artist.'

Lady Eleanor bristled. 'Jack, really, I was in the middle of…'

'…delivering a history lesson,' he finished for her. 'You might at least wait until we've finished eating before you do so.'

Her ladyship looked pointedly at her brother-in-law's full plate. 'So you were, for once, planning on actually eating your breakfast, were you?'

'Eleanor, my love, there is no need to— If Jack is not hungry he need not…'

'Oh, for God's sake, Charlie, there's no need to be perpetually walking on eggshells around me.'

A long, uncomfortable silence greeted this

remark, broken eventually by Jack Trestain himself. 'I beg your pardon, Eleanor,' he said stiffly, 'I got out of bed on the wrong side this morning.'

'Happens to us all on occasion. No need for apologies, Brother—that is, I am sure that Eleanor...'

'Apology accepted, Jack,' Lady Eleanor said quickly, pressing her husband's hand.

Celeste took another sip of coffee. Jack Trestain put a small piece of ham onto his fork, though he made no attempt to eat it.

'I confess, Mademoiselle Marmion was not what I was expecting either,' Sir Charles said with another of his placatory smiles. 'Your reputation, you know, I expected someone older, more experienced.'

'I am five-and-twenty, Sir Charles.'

'Oh, please, I did not mean— One must never ask a lady her age.'

'I am not embarrassed by my age, *Monsieur*. My first commission I received seven years ago from the Comte de St Verain. I am proud to say that I have been able to support myself with my painting ever since.'

'And are your commissions all similar in nature to our own?' Lady Eleanor enquired.

Celeste nodded. 'Very similar. In France, many of the great houses were seized during the Revolution and the grounds badly neglected. The families who have managed to reclaim them employ me to paint the gardens once they are restored to their former glory.'

'While you and I, my dear, are rather contrarily commissioning Mademoiselle Marmion to paint our estate before it is enhanced a deal beyond its current state.' Sir Charles beamed, seemingly pleased by the thought of being a little unconventional.

'And you, Monsieur Trestain,' Celeste enquired, turning to his brother, 'will you be remaining here to witness this transformation?'

'I have no idea, *Mademoiselle*. Nor any notion why it should concern you.'

'Until recently, our Jack was in the military, a career soldier at that,' Sir Charles intervened hastily.

Celeste's jaw dropped unbecomingly. 'You are a soldier!'

'A lieutenant-colonel, no less,' Sir Charles said, with a hint of pride, sliding an anxious look at his silent brother.

'Indeed,' Lady Eleanor chimed in with a prim smile, 'Jack was one of the Duke of Wellington's most valued officers. He was mentioned several times in despatches.'

'And Jack has mentioned more than several times that he is no longer a soldier,' Jack Trestain said with a steely look in his eyes. 'In any event, I expect Mademoiselle Marmion is more likely to admire Napoleon than Wellington, Eleanor.'

The scars. She should have realised they were battle scars. And that also explained his animosity towards her. How many years had Britain and France been at war? Celeste pushed her chair back, preparatory to leaving the table. 'I am sorry. It did not occur to me that— I was so delighted to be here in England, so happy that hostilities between our countries had ended, that I did not consider the fact that I am—was until recently—no doubt still am in your eyes, *Monsieur*, the enemy.'

'*Mademoiselle*, please do not distress yourself,' Sir Charles said rather desperately. 'My brother did not mean— You have it quite wrong, does she not, Jack?'

'Entirely wrong. I have no objection to your being French,' Jack Trestain said in a tone that left it clear that he still objected to her having spied on him. 'I repeat, I am no longer a soldier, *Mademoiselle*.'

'But you were until recently?' Appalled, thinking back to the horrific reports she had read in the newspapers, Celeste forgot all about Jack Trestain's rudeness. 'You were at Waterloo? *Mon Dieu*, of course you were. Your arm,' she exclaimed, wondering that she had been so foolish not to have guessed.

'How did you know about Jack's arm?'

Sir Charles was frowning at her. Celeste gaped. She couldn't think of a single thing to say in explanation.

'*Mademoiselle* obviously noticed that I'm favouring my left arm at the moment,' Jack Trestain said, stepping in unexpectedly to cover her gaffe. 'Being an artist, I am sure she is rather more observant than most.'

She was surprised by his fleeting smile. The man's mood seemed to change with the wind. When he smiled, he looked so very different. He did not look as if he smiled often. He was a battle-hardened soldier. Those terrible scars. Realising all three pairs of eyes were on her, Celeste rallied. 'Yes, that's it,' she said, nodding furiously, 'Monsieur Trestain has hit the nail on the head.'

He tilted his head slightly in acknowledgement and flashed her another smile, one that lit his dark-brown eyes this time, and she felt absurdly gratified.

'Well now,' Sir Charles said, after receiving an encouraging nod from his wife, 'the day's getting on. I have a meeting with my lawyer in town at noon, Mademoiselle Marmion, but I thought I could give you a quick run through of our plans for the new gardens, just to give you an idea of where the most extensive changes will be, for it is these areas we wish to have immortalised by you on canvas, so to speak. What do you say?'

'If you are pressed for time, Charlie, then why not let me look after Mademoiselle Marmion.'

It was Sir Charles's turn to gape. 'You, Jack?'

Lady Eleanor pursed her lips. 'I am not sure that would be such a good idea.'

Her husband, however, had recovered from his surprise. 'Come now, my dear, are we not forever encouraging Jack to embark on some gainful enterprise to aid his recuperation?'

His wife looked unconvinced. 'It will take up a deal of Jack's time, and you cannot deny, with all due respect to him, he has not precisely been the most patient of men recently. Every time our little Robert asks him…'

'We have told our son not to pester his uncle. When Jack is good and ready, he will tell his nephew all about Waterloo,' Sir Charles said, rubbing his hands together and slanting his brother a nervous look. 'Jack is still recuperating from some serious injuries, my love,' he reproved gently. 'He is bound to be a little short of—of patience.'

'My point exactly,' Lady Eleanor said. 'Mademoiselle Marmion will have even more questions than Robert, no doubt, about the changes, the estate…'

'Which I am better placed than most to answer,' Jack Trestain interjected, 'having been raised here.'

Sir Charles beamed. 'An excellent point. And showing *Mademoiselle* around will give you the opportunity to see more of the countryside, for I wish *Mademoiselle* to make a few landscapes of the wider estate. You might even get a taste for country living, see somewhere close at hand that takes your fancy. I can heartily recommend it.'

This last was said with some hopeful enthusiasm, and greeted with some disdain. A bone of contention, obviously.

'Perhaps, Charlie,' Jack Trestain answered, 'stranger things have happened.'

'Excellent! That is settled then, provided *Mademoiselle* has no objection?'

Celeste couldn't fathom Jack Trestain at all. One minute he was furious with her, the next he was covering up for her and the next he was offering to put himself out for her and spend time in her company. He was volatile, to put it mildly, but he also had a delightful smile, and a body which she found distracting, and she had not found the body of any man distracting for a long time. Not since— But she would not think of that.

Realising that they were awaiting an answer from her, Celeste shook her head. 'No, I have no objection whatsoever.'

Chapter Two

'Why did I volunteer?' Jack had not been expecting this to be the first question the intriguing Mademoiselle Marmion asked him, though perhaps he should have. It was obvious she had a sharp intellect and an observant eye. Whether that was because she was an artist, as he had suggested in order to extricate her from her faux pas regarding his arm, he did not know. What was inescapable was that within minutes of meeting her she had already managed to throw his behaviour into sharp relief. He could not be entirely oblivious to the effect his erratic temper was having on Charlie and Eleanor, but his brother's softly-softly approach had allowed them all to be complicit in ignoring it.

Until now. Jack shrugged uncomfortably. 'I have been somewhat out of temper, on

account of my injuries. It is the least I can do.'
It would suffice as an explanation. It would
have to, since he didn't have a better one to
offer, being as confused by his recent behaviour as anyone. Which was something he was
reluctant to concede, since it implied there was
an underlying cause, which there was not. At
least not one he cared to admit to Charlie. Or
indeed anyone.

As an explanation, it also conveniently excluded the fact that Mademoiselle Marmion
herself had influenced his impulsive decision.
Had she been a small, balding Frenchman with
a goatee beard, would he have been so keen to
offer his services? Indeed he would not, but
that was another thing to which he would rather
not admit. Jack smiled at her maliciously. 'If
you would rather have Lady Eleanor's services
as a guide…'

'No,' she said hurriedly, just as he had known
she would, 'no, I certainly would not. Lady
Eleanor cannot decide if I am to be treated as
a superior servant or an inferior guest.'

'I'll let you into a little secret about Eleanor,' Jack said. 'She is the youngest of four
daughters of the vicar a few parishes over, and
though no one gives a fig for that save herself,

as a consequence she is inclined to over-play her role of lady of the manor. Don't be too hard on her. She makes my brother happy, which is good enough for me. Or it should be.'

'Have a care, *Monsieur*, or I might think you a sensitive soul beneath that prickly exterior.' Mademoiselle Marmion frowned. 'Which brings me back to my question. Unlike Lady Eleanor, you made your feelings about me perfectly plain at breakfast. I confess I am confused as to why you now voluntarily choose to spend time in my company.'

Unlike Charlie and Eleanor, *Mademoiselle* was not one to beat about the proverbial bush. 'You are referring to the fact that I took umbrage at your spying on me this morning,' Jack said.

She flinched, but held his gaze. 'I did not spy. My intrusion was unwelcome, I can see that, but it was also unintended. I am, however, very sorry. Had the roles been reversed, I too would have been...'

She broke off, flushing, but it was too late. Jack was already imagining her naked, scything through the waters of the lake, and Mademoiselle Marmion was clearly perfectly aware of that fact. 'Think nothing more of it,' he said quickly, trying desperately to do just that. 'Your apology is accepted, provided you do not repeat the transgression.'

'Thank you. I promise you that in future I will avoid visiting the lake in the morning.'

She smiled at him, and he caught his breath. She really was very lovely, with her white-blonde hair, and those eyes the colour of brandy. Her skin was smooth, flawless, but not the creamy-white of an English rose; it was a pale biscuit, sun-kissed and warm. Then there was her mouth. Luscious pink. Too wide for fashion, but perfect for kissing. Kissing her would be like biting into the sweet, delicate flesh of a perfectly ripe peach. The kind which grew in the heat of Spain, not the hard, bitter little fruits which were espaliered on the wall of Charlie's garden. Kissing her would be like bathing in the dry heat of the true south. Kissing her would be like a taste of another world.

Though he could not for the life of him imagine why he was thinking of kissing her. He'd had no urge to kiss anyone since—well, for quite some considerable time. 'I think we should get out into the gardens while the light is good, Mademoiselle Marmion,' Jack said brusquely. 'I'll wait here while you fetch a hat.'

'I was raised in the south of France. I don't need a hat for the pale English sun, Monsieur Trestain.'

'Then thank the Lord, that means I'm not required to wear one either. And since we're dispensing with formalities, I would prefer it if you would call me Jack.'

'Then you must call me Celeste.'

'Celeste.' Jack grinned. 'How very appropriate. An angel sent from heaven to relieve my boredom.'

'An artist sent from France to paint your brother's estate,' she retorted.

'Touché. In that case we should get down to business.'

Celeste followed Jack Trestain down a narrow path through a colourful but uninteresting rose garden. His leather breeches fitted snugly around a taut derrière that was really very pleasant to admire from behind. His jet-black hair, dry now, curled over the collar of his shirt. She couldn't help but remember the muscles, now decently covered in white cambric, which had rippled while he swam.

She cursed softly under her breath and tried to concentrate on the path. And the task in hand. Not the intriguing man ahead of her, with his powerful soldier's body. A frisson of desire made her stomach flutter. Twice today, she had experienced this sudden yearning, for the very first time since—since. She had not missed it. She had not even noted its absence, until now. Perhaps, Celeste thought hopefully, it was a sign that she was starting come to terms with the loss of her mother. Not that she'd been struggling precisely, but she had not been quite herself, she could admit that much now.

'The Topiary Garden.' Jack Trestain opened the gate with a flourish.

Celeste had passed through it this morning, but had not taken the time to study it. Now she did so with delight. 'This is fascinating. I have painted several such places before. I think it is unusual to have such a French garden attached to such a very English house, no?'

'It was first laid out about two hundred years ago,' Jack Trestain replied. 'I think it was originally designed by one of your countrymen, now I come to think about it. To appreciate the symmetry and the scale of it, you'll get a much better view from the top floor of the house, if you were thinking of making this one of your featured landscapes.'

'Absolutely I am,' Celeste said, 'and I think a view from the lake too, through the topiary with the house in the background.'

'When my mother was alive, the borders were a blaze of colour at this time of year. And the parterre too. You'll recognise the lavender that borders it, there. I was once passing through Provence when they were gathering the lavender crop. The scent of it took me straight back to my childhood, escaping down here with Charlie, playing hide-and-seek in this garden. It's well past its best now.'

'Were you in the army for a very long time, Monsieur Jack?'

'Thirteen years. My father bought me a commission when I was sixteen. Why do you ask?'

Celeste shrugged, feigning a casualness she was far from feeling. 'Were you forced to leave because of your injury? Or because there are no more wars to fight?'

'I was not forced to leave. I resigned my commission.'

His clipped tone made it very clear he considered the subject closed. The same tone he had used with Lady Eleanor at breakfast. Thirteen years was a large part of anyone's life to exclude from discussion but then, there was an equally large part of her own life she didn't ever discuss. Celeste smiled brightly. 'Then let us concentrate on my own modest commission, which I have only just started.'

Jack disguised his relief well enough, but she noticed it all the same. As they walked down another path, Celeste prattled on about other gardens she had painted, other topiary she had drawn, aware he was studying her as covertly as she was studying him. Unsettled and distracted by her own interest, unsure whether to be flattered or concerned by his, she decided that she would do better for now to concentrate on her work, and so took out her sketchbook.

The Topiary Garden was divided into two by the long gravelled path which led towards the lake. On either side, the yew hedges had been trained into the most extraordinary shapes. Despite the fact that it had not been pruned, it was still possible to distinguish peacocks, a lion, a crown, and what looked to be several chess pieces, as well as more traditional cones, boxes and cylinders. Holly bordered the low and overgrown beds which had been laid out in the shadow of the yews. No longer feigning interest, Celeste made several rapid sketches.

Looking up some time later, she smiled at

Jack watching her now with unalloyed interest, tilting her last sketch to allow him to examine it better. 'In France,' she said, 'this garden would be prized and restored, not cut down to make way for a— What was it Lady Eleanor called it?'

'A little wilderness,' Jack replied, 'whatever conceit that is. Eleanor loathes it as it is, and I have to confess, it is much darker than I remember.'

'With some remedial work, it could be very beautiful.'

'Your sketch certainly makes it look so. Perhaps you should share your thoughts with Eleanor.'

'Oh, no, that would be presumptuous. It is her garden, not mine.'

Jack ushered her towards the welcome of the shade, where a mossy stone bench was positioned under a yew which had been clipped into an arch. He had come out without a coat, and now rolled up the sleeves of his shirt. The contrast between his pale right arm and tanned left was stark. It was not only the colour, but he had clearly lost muscle.

'It must have been a very bad break to have kept your arm in a splint for so long.' Without realising, Celeste had reached out to touch him. She snatched her hand away.

'Why did you stay at the lakeside this morning?' Jack asked. 'You've as much as admitted you should have left the moment you saw me. What made you stay?'

The bench was small. His leather-clad thigh brushed hers, and his knee too, for he had angled himself to face her. 'I am an artist,' Celeste said, her voice sounding odd. 'You made an interesting subject.'

'Did you draw me, then?'

His hand covered hers, which were clasped on her lap. Her heart began to thump. 'There was no time,' she said.

'Yet you insist you were watching me purely with the eye of an artist?'

His thumb was stroking her wrist, so lightly she wondered if he was even aware he was doing it. The tension between them became palpable. Beguiled as much by her own new-found desire as by Jack's proximity, Celeste could think of nothing to say but the truth. 'I watched you because I could not take my eyes off you. I was fascinated.'

His eyes darkened. His hands slid up to her shoulders. She leaned into him as he pulled her towards him. It started so gently. Soft. Delicate. Celeste leant closer. The kiss deepened. She could feel the damp of his shirt and the heat of his skin beneath it. A drop of perspiration trickled down between her breasts, and she felt a sharp twist of pure desire.

She curled her fingers into his hair. Their tongues touched. Jack moaned, a guttural sound that precisely echoed how she felt, filled with longing, and aching and heat. Their kiss became fierce. He bent her backwards on the bench, his body hovering over hers, blocking out the sunlight. He smelt of soap and sweet summer sweat. His legs were tangled in her skirts. Only his arms, planted either side of her, prevented her from falling.

She was also in danger of falling, metaphorically speaking, from a far greater height if she was not extremely careful. Celeste snapped to her senses. Jerking herself free, she sat up. Jack's cheeks were flushed. His hair was in wild disarray. His shirt was falling open at the neck to reveal his tanned throat. The soft linen clung to his frame, revealing tantalising glimpses of the hard body underneath. She wanted more. It was good that she wanted more, but with this man! No, she must be out of her mind.

She edged a little way along the bench, shaking out her skirts. 'I hope you are not expecting me to faint?' she asked more sharply than she intended.

'Despite our extremely brief acquaintance you do not strike me as someone much given to histrionics.'

'You are perfectly correct, I am not. Even when kissing complete strangers.'

'Not quite complete strangers, *Mademoiselle*. We have at least been formally introduced.' Jack shook his head, as if trying to clear the dazed look from his eyes. 'I apologise,' he said tersely. 'I have no idea what came over me. I'm not in the habit of mauling innocent women, especially not when they are my brother's guests.'

'Your brother's landscape artist, not his guest, and I am neither innocent nor inclined to accept an apology for something that was as much my doing as yours,' Celeste snapped, unduly irked by his assumption that it was all his responsibility. She was relieved to discover she could feel this way again, but she really wished it had not been this maddening man who had sparked her back to life. She picked up her sketch pad and charcoals, trying to regain her composure. 'It was just a kiss, nothing more,' she said, because that was all it was, after all.

'Just a kiss?' Jack repeated, still looking stunned. 'Is that what you really think?'

She did not. She thought—not very clearly, admittedly—that it was the most extraordinary kiss she had ever experienced. She thought, looking at him now, that she would very much like to kiss him again, but she was not about to admit that. 'Very well,' Celeste conceded, 'an excellent kiss, though I suspect that abstinence may have contributed to its intensity.'

He flushed dark red. 'What the devil do you mean by that?'

Celeste took a step back. 'Not that it is any of your business, but I have not been inclined to kiss anyone for—for some time.'

His expression softened a little. 'Ah, you are referring to your own abstinence?'

'What else would I have implied?' Celeste said, thoroughly confused. He could not possibly have thought she referred to him? There could be no shortage of women eager and willing to kiss Jack Trestain. Then she remembered. 'Oh, you mean you have been incapacitated by your recent poor health.'

A perfectly understandable explanation, and no reason whatsoever for him to flinch as if she had hit him. Yet that is exactly what he did, before abruptly turning on his heels and marching off. Utterly confounded now, she watched his long legs cover the ground quickly, back through the gate, along the grass walk to the rose garden. He did not look back.

Celeste slumped down on the stone bench. While her mind struggled to make sense of what had happened, her body was very clear in its response. What they had shared had been much more than just a kiss. It had been an awakening, a stirring of something that she hadn't realised had been so utterly dormant.

Her last *affaire* had ended not long before she had received *that* letter. It had ended as her *affaires* always did, without tears or remorse, while it had still been mutually enjoyable, before it could degenerate into boredom, or worse still, the expectation of a future. Not that she'd ever allowed any of her few love affairs to reach that stage. Not that a single one of them had evoked an emotion even close to love in her.

Celeste began to turn the pages of her sketchbook. Love was a subject she knew little about. On the topic of being loveless however, she was something of an expert. It defined her upbringing. It defined her mother's marriage. Or it had. She snapped the leather covers shut. Ever since she'd received that *damned* letter, she'd been losing control in all sorts of odd ways. She snapped at the stupidest of things. She couldn't concentrate on her work. And now this! It was just a kiss, for heaven's sake. She was overwrought. She had not kissed anyone for a long time. Jack was a very accomplished kisser. Jack, for whatever reason, seemed to find the whole process of kissing her even more unsettling than she had. She would very much like to repeat the process of kissing Jack, if only to prove that it was just a kiss, enhanced by abstinence, just as she'd suggested. Her own.

And as for her suggestion regarding his? Why had he taken such umbrage at her perfectly reasonable assumption? Celeste rolled her eyes. Jack Trestain was an enigma, and one that she had no time to decipher.

'There you are, my love. I have been looking for you all over.'

Jack, who had been sleeping on the recessed

seat in the nook of the fireplace, woke with a start and looked around him, quite disoriented.

'Charles,' Eleanor was saying, 'I am writing to my mother. We have such a glut of plums and damsons I thought it would be a good idea to pickle some rather than simply bottle them, and Mama has an excellent receipt. How went your meeting with the lawyer?'

Jack had quite forgotten the trick of acoustics between this room and the one below. His head, resting against the fireplace, was in the precise spot which amplified the voices. He and Charlie had discovered it as boys, and had spent hours talking to each other, one of them in each room. The Laird's Lug, their Auntie Kirsty had told them it was known as in Scottish castles, a way for the master of the house to eavesdrop on his family and his servants, though Jack reckoned this one at Trestain Manor existed more by accident than design.

Charlie and Eleanor were discussing estate business now, in that domestic, familiar way Jack remembered his parents doing. His head was thumping. Serve him right for sleeping in the middle of the day, though when he slept so little at night, he had little option but to catnap when he could. While in the army, he used to pride himself on possessing a soldier's ability to sleep whenever and whatever the circumstances. Standing, sitting, marching, he'd slept, and woken refreshed. No, not always refreshed, he thought ruefully, there had been times when he'd felt perpetually exhausted. But the fact remained, until he resigned his commission, sleep had never been a problem.

Was that true? Could his insomnia have been masked by his frenetic army career? He didn't know. He did know that things had gone rapidly downhill after he left. The nightmare which had been sporadic now regularly invaded his dreams. He woke every morning feeling as if he'd been bludgeoned, his limbs weighted with stones. Precisely as he felt at the moment.

It was too much of an effort to move, so he settled back where he was, letting Charlie and Eleanor's voices wash over him. Charlie was uncommonly happy with his estate and his wife and his family. Charlie thought that if Jack could settle down as he had, raise some sheep and cows and pigs, start his own nursery, that Jack would be every bit as contented as he was. Poor delusional Charlie. He meant well, but he had no idea, and his ignorance drove Jack to distraction, though he would never wish it otherwise. He envied Charlie. No, that was a lie. Charlie's placid, uncomplicated life would drive Jack to an early grave, but he envied him the ability to love that placid, uncomplicated life.

Jack couldn't remember a time when he hadn't wanted to be a soldier. He'd been an excellent soldier, and he'd been an exemplary officer. He'd loved being a military man, he'd taken such pride in doing his duty for king and country. There had been times when that duty had required him to see and do some terrible things. Unforgivable things. While he still wore his colours, he had managed to reconcile himself to that. Now, he no longer could. Now, he was being forced to question everything that he'd loved and all that he'd stood for. There were times when he felt as if he were being quite literally torn in two. Times when he raged at the injustice of what was happening to him, times when he was overwhelmed by guilt. There was no right and wrong any more, and his world, which had been one of clear-cut lines for so long, was now so blurred that he was careering around like a compass struggling to find true north. What the hell was happening to him?

Jack ran his fingers through his hair. He ought to have it cut. Just one of many things he ought to do, and had not the gumption to attempt. Every day he swore he would try to be normal. He would take an interest in mundane things like harvests and dressing for dinner and the weather and the king's health. With increasing regularity, he failed. So many things important to Charlie and Eleanor seemed so trivial to him, and so trivial things tended to take on a disproportionate importance. Like that kiss.

Just a kiss, Celeste had said, though he could have sworn she was as unsettled as he had been by it. And then she'd made that comment about abstinence enhancing its intensity. Bloody stupid phrase. Presumptive. Though she had not been referring to him, as he'd assumed. She was no innocent, she claimed, and she certainly didn't kiss like one. He'd never experienced a kiss like it. Was that due to enforced abstinence? It had come as a surprise, certainly. He'd assumed that aspect of his life, like sleeping soundly, was beyond him, at least for the time being.

Jack leant his head back against the hearth. It should be reassuring that it was not. Reassuring that he could still—what? Experience desire, lust? He swore. Most likely the woman was right, and it really had been just a kiss, blown out of all proportion by the circumstances. No mere kiss was that momentous. He wished he hadn't run away now, like a raw recruit retreating under enemy fire. He wished he'd stayed and kissed her again, and proved to himself that it was not a one-off and that his body, unlike his mind, was not completely in limbo.

He closed his eyes and allowed himself to remember the taste of her and the feel of her and the smell of her. She was quite lovely. She was altogether ravishing. She would set any man's blood on fire. He shouldn't have kissed her. As it was, his self-control hung by a fragile thread. He was confused about many thing but the one thing he knew for certain was that maintaining his self-control was crucial. So he could not risk kissing her again. Definitely not picture her lips pressed to his, her hands…

'I wonder how Mademoiselle Marmion is faring?'

Jack's eyes flew open. The name leapt out at

him, bringing the background buzz of conversation in the room below to the fore.

Charlie was speaking now. 'I'm sure she fares perfectly well. She seemed to me an uncommonly confident woman for one of her years. Perhaps it comes from being French. And she is a successful artist too. No, my love, we need have no fear for *Mademoiselle*. Jack may be— He has developed something of a temper, but he would never behave with impropriety, I am certain of that.'

'It is not only his temper, Charles. He has a look in his eyes sometimes that frightens me.'

'The things he has experienced on the battlefield would frighten anyone.'

'Yes, but—Charles, you must have noticed, there are times when one may address any number of remarks to him, and it is as if he were deaf or asleep. I thought he was simply being rude the first time, but—it is very *odd*.'

What was it they said about never overhearing good of oneself? Snooping and listening in to private conversations had been the tools of the trade of his carefully cultivated informants, but this was different. Jack cringed.

'We can be sure of nothing with regard to your brother these days, Charles,' Eleanor continued after a leaden silence. 'He is so very changed.'

'Indeed.' Charlie's voice was wooden, a sure sign that his stiff upper lip was being called into action. No doubt he was wringing his hands.

'He rebuffed poor little Robert again yesterday. I have told the child time and again not to plague his uncle for war stories, but...'

'He is only five years old, and his uncle is a hero to him. Indeed, Jack is a hero to us all, if only he could see it. If only he could *talk* to me, but I fear...'

Jack leapt to his feet. So much for his naive belief that he had been covering his tracks. It was mortifyingly clear that Charlie and Eleanor had merely been pretending not to notice his odd behaviour.

I'm sparing you, he wanted to roar at Charlie. *I'm preserving all your sad, pathetic illusions about me*, he wanted to tell him. He wanted to shake his brother into silence. He wanted to be sick, because he loved Charlie, and he even cared about Eleanor, dammit, because Eleanor loved Charlie too. He wished to hell, for Charlie's sake, that he *could* sit down with Robert and tell him tales of derring-do. He wished that it was true, that he really was the hero mentioned by Wellington in despatches, but it was not the case. Heroes didn't have stains on their soul.

Jack crept from the room. He might not be a hero but he had survived. He would continue to survive. To live, to be truly alive though, that was quite another matter. An aspiration for the future, perhaps. In the meantime, it was a question of enduring.

Chapter Three

Next day, Celeste set to work in the walled garden, the morning sunshine sending fingers of light creeping along the western border. She knew from the landscaper's plans which Jack had shown her that the oldest of the succession houses and the pinery were to be demolished and replaced with modern structures which could be more efficiently heated. There was a charm to the original buildings which she had started to capture in charcoal, the paper pinned to a large board propped on a portable easel.

She had not seen Jack since he so abruptly left the Topiary Garden. He had not appeared at dinner, nor breakfast. According to Lady Eleanor, this was not unusual behaviour, as Jack often skipped meals. Sir Charles had reminded his wife that the remains of his late-night snacks were regularly found by the kitchen maids, so there was no need to worry that Jack had no appetite whatsoever. Which meant that they clearly were worried, and equally clearly set upon pretending to the source of their concern that they were not. Celeste was not, after all, alone in thinking Jack Trestain's behaviour decidedly contrary.

She pinned a fresh sheet of paper on to her easel. She would not speculate as to the cause. She found him intriguing. She found him interesting. She found him very attractive. All of these, she took as positive signs of her own return to normality, but she would not allow herself to dwell on the subject any further. She had more than enough issues to occupy her thoughts without adding Jack Trestain to her list.

She picked up her charcoal, decided to adjust her perspective and set to work.

Half an hour later, deep in concentration, Celeste did not notice Jack's arrival until he was behind her, making her jump, squiggle a line across her drawing, drop her charcoal and swear rather inappropriately in French. 'You gave me such a fright. Look what you've made me do.'

'I didn't mean to startle you, but you were miles away.'

'I was concentrating on my work.'

Jack was looking at her drawing, but Celeste got the impression he was thinking about something else. She had not misremembered how attractive he was. Nor the strength of her reaction to his physical proximity. Her skin was tingling as if the space between them was charged, like the atmosphere prior to a lightning strike. 'What do you think?' she asked, in an attempt to restore some semblance of normality. She was on sure ground discussing art.

He blinked. 'I think I should apologise for my abrupt departure yesterday.'

Celeste too kept her eyes on her drawing. 'I was actually referring to my sketch, but since we are on the subject, I fear we were at cross purposes yesterday. When I said— When I mentioned abstinence— I know nothing of your circumstances. I was speaking for myself.'

'You may as well have been speaking for me,' Jack admitted ruefully. 'I have not— It has also been some time since I...' Their eyes

met briefly, then flickered away. 'I was therefore rather taken aback.'

'As was I.' This time their gaze held. Celeste
smiled faintly. 'I am sure that was the reason
for the— It explains why we allowed ourselves
to become somewhat carried away.'

Jack touched his hand to the squiggle Celeste
had drawn, tried to rub it out, then stared at the
resultant smudge. 'Stupid thing for me to get so
aerated about. It was, as you pointed out, just
a kiss. We're adults, not flighty adolescents.'

'Yes, exactly.' She nodded determinedly to
disguise her disappointment. She should not be
disappointed. He was agreeing with her, after
all. 'Most likely we would be disappointed if
we—if we repeated the experience.'

It came out sounding like a plea to be proved
wrong, and for a moment, Jack looked as if he
would comply. 'Most likely,' he said as he took
a step towards her. She could feel his breath on
her cheek. He smelled of grass and sunshine.
Her heart was beating hard again, making it
difficult to breathe. She stared into his eyes,
mesmerised. The gap between them impercep-
tibly, tantalisingly narrowed. Their lips almost
touched before they both leapt back as if they
had been singed by a naked flame.

Celeste snatched her sketch from the easel and tore it in half. 'I don't know what is wrong with me today. I am struggling to find the correct perspective for what should be a simple sketch.'

Jack hesitated, then threw himself down on a wooden bench, his long legs sprawled in front of him. 'I doubt either Charlie or Eleanor will care which angle you choose, provided you deliver something that closely matches reality. I'm sure the drawing you have just torn up would have proved perfectly satisfactory.'

'Not to me,' Celeste said indignantly. 'I would have known I could have depicted the scene in a more accomplished manner. You may consider what I do to be a trivial endeavour. My paintings don't save lives or win wars or—or whatever it was you did when you were a soldier, but they are still very important to me.'

'I'm sorry, I didn't mean to patronise you.'

His smile was disarming. Celeste bit her own back, refusing to be so easily won over. 'But you did none the less.'

'I did,' he conceded.

He dug his hands into his pockets. 'You know, life in the military is not as exciting as you might think. There's far more time spent marching and drilling than waging war. And in the winter, when the campaign season is over, there's a deal more playing cards and making bets and drinking than doing drill.'

'When I am between commissions, I still paint,' Celeste said. 'Not landscapes, but people. I am not so good at portraits, but they are mine, and so it is not like work, you know?'

'Are you often between commissions?'

'In the beginning, regularly.' She chuckled. 'As a result, I was much thinner and not so well dressed as I can now afford to be.'

'No less pretty, though, I'd wager, if I may be so bold as to offer a compliment to compensate for demeaning your sense of professional pride. Did you always aspire to be an artist?'

'I am never going to exhibit at the Académie des Beaux-Arts, and I have no ambition to do so. I am not the type to try to break all the rules and to starve in the process, spending my last sou on paint rather than a baguette. I have a modest talent. I was fortunate enough to study with some excellent teachers in Paris, and I needed to find a way of supporting myself, so...' Celeste shrugged.

'Your parents then, they are dead? You said

you needed to support yourself,' Jack explained when she raised her eyebrows at the question, 'so I assumed…'

'Yes. Both dead.' Celeste stared down at her hands, frowning. Despite spending a good deal of time thinking about it, she had not the foggiest idea how to begin the search for answers which had brought her to England. She needed help, but her ingrained habit of trusting no one save herself inhibited her from seeking it. Not that, as a foreigner, she thought morosely, she had the first idea of where to start seeking.

'Penny for them?' Jack was looking at her quizzically. 'Your thoughts,' he said. 'You were a hundred miles away again. I fear I'm boring you rather than distracting you.'

'No, it's not that.' Perhaps she could ask him just one simple question to get her search underway? She really did have to make a start because there, tucked away at the back of her sketchbook, was a letter containing a puzzle she needed to solve in order to draw a line under the past and get on with her life.

'Jack?'

He looked at her questioningly.

'Jack, if you—if you needed to find something. Or someone. How would you go about it? I mean if you did not know where this person lived, or—or who they were, precisely. Are there people one can employ to discover such things?'

'You mean to track down someone who has gone missing?'

She had his attention now. All of it. Though he was still lounging casually on the bench, though his expression was one of polite interest, his eyes were focused entirely on her. Celeste shifted uncomfortably. 'Not missing precisely. Not anything at all, really. I'm speaking hypothetically.'

She risked looking up, and wished she had not. 'Hypothetically,' Jack said, openly sceptical. 'Well, hypothetically, you could employ a Bow Street Runner.'

'Is that what you would do?'

He smiled. 'Good grief, no. Speaking hypothetically of course, I am more than equipped to solve the problem for myself, but we're not talking hypothetically, are we?'

Realising that she was clenching her hands so tightly together that the knuckles showed white, Celeste hid them under her painter's smock. She ought to look him in the eye, but she was sure if she did Jack would know she was lying. She was not a good liar. She was good at keeping silent. She was very good at hiding her feelings, but she was a terrible liar. 'It doesn't matter,' she said. 'Forget I asked.'

She could have bitten her tongue out, realising only at the last moment that telling Jack Trestain something didn't matter was a sure-fire way of alerting him to the fact that it did, though he said nothing for so long that she began to hope he had done just as she asked. At least she was a step further forward. She had no idea what a Bow Street Runner was, but she could find out. She prepared to get to her feet. 'I should…'

'Sit down.' His grip on her arm was light enough, but one look at Jack's face, and Celeste thought the better of resisting him. 'Who exactly is it you're trying to trace? A lover? An errant husband, perhaps?'

'I have no husband, errant or otherwise, and as to a lover— No, not since before— Since— It has nothing to do with affairs of the heart.' She sounded defensive. She was getting upset. And Jack was not missing any of it. 'It is nothing,' Celeste said. 'I regret raising it.'

Jack gave her a neutral look. 'You know, you'd be taking pot luck by employing a Runner. Some of them are excellent chaps, but some— Frankly, I wouldn't trust my sister alone with them. Not that I have a sister. Have you? Or a brother? Is it a sibling you're seeking?'

'I am not so fortunate as to possess either,' Celeste said repressively.

Jack nodded. 'So, it's not your parents or a husband or a sibling you're trying to trace. Who then?'

He was not going to give up. Celeste shook her head and folded her lips.

Once again, Jack failed to get the message. 'Now I come to think about it, you weren't clear if it was a person or a thing. Is it stolen property then, jewellery? Or the family silver?'

'*Mon Dieu*, Jack, I wish you would leave the matter alone!'

'You ask me for advice but now won't tell me why. Don't you trust me, Celeste, is that it?'

'I don't trust anyone. I find it is safer that way.'

'That, if I may say so, is a fairly bleak philosophy.'

'You may, since I suspect it is also yours.'

He looked quite taken aback. 'Irrespective of the veracity of that statement, you would admit it is a philosophy which makes finding your missing person or whatever the hell it is rather problematic.'

'I told you, I was merely speculating.'

'And I told you, I don't believe you,' Jack said, his tone conciliatory. 'Look, it's obviously important to you, whatever it is. It's clear you need help, and I assure you, you can rely on my discretion.'

All of which was most likely true, but it was such a big step to take. Celeste wrapped her arms around herself. What should she do?

'If it's difficult for you to tell me, imagine yourself faced with a complete stranger.'

'Why are you so keen to— Of what possible interest is it to you?' Celeste cursed under her breath and jumped to her feet. 'You wish to know? *Vraiment?* Very well then, I will tell the truth and shame the devil. I have come to England to find out why my mother killed herself! Are you happy now?'

Jack's face was a picture of shock. Celeste, even more shocked than he at her impulsive admission, sucked in great breaths of air.

'I'm sorry,' Jack said after a brief silence. 'Celeste, I'm so very sorry.'

He reached out, as if he would put his

arms around her. For a brief moment, she was tempted to accept the comfort of his embrace, and that shocked her almost as much as her blurting out the shameful truth to a man she barely knew. She pushed him away, rather too roughly, though she was beyond caring about that. Then suddenly quite drained, she sank on to the bench beside him.

Suicide. Jack could think of no subject more guaranteed to engage his attention and his sympathy. He clenched his fists. He would try his damnedest to help this woman. That would, at least, be something.

Beside him Celeste was pale, angry and on the verge of tears, though she seemed absolutely determined not to cry. She was looking at him very warily too, most likely already resenting him for forcing her to blurt out something so private and shocking.

'You can trust me,' Jack said once more. 'If I am able to help you, I will.'

'Why would you?' she demanded baldly. 'You're virtually a stranger.'

He pondered how to answer this without arousing her suspicions. It had cost her a good deal to ask for help, which made him wonder that someone so beautiful and so attractive and so talented should be so bereft of confidantes. 'A stranger with too much time on his hands, and not enough to occupy his mind,' he said, which had the benefit of being true. 'A stranger who has had some experience in such matters,' he added, which was, tragically, also true.

'What experience? Jack? I said what experience?'

He realised some time had elapsed since Celeste had posed the question. He dragged his mind back, with some relief, to the present and managed a dismissive shrug, as if he had been merely assembling his thoughts. 'When a man is battle-weary, an extreme melancholy can make him think death offers the only release. No one can persuade him that the melancholy will eventually pass. In extreme cases, the man becomes so desperate as to take matters into his own hands as your mother did. Soldiers are trained not to show their feelings, and very often in such cases, the outcome is totally unexpected and, to those left behind, wholly inexplicable. Like you, they are left with unanswered questions.'

'And how do these bereaved families set about gaining answers?'

They didn't, was the honest answer, in most cases. Jack could no more explain it than the poor unfortunates who took their own lives could. All he could offer was platitudes. He looked at Celeste, no longer distrustful but hanging on his words, the faintest trace of hope flickering in her eyes. He could not bear to douse it with a cold bucket of truth. If he could somehow help her, if he could find the answers for her that he had been unable to provide for others, then perhaps it would help atone. A little. Even a little atonement was better than none. 'Perhaps it would help,' he prevaricated, 'if you could tell me the circumstances of your mother's death first. It must have come as a terrible shock.'

'We were not close.' Perhaps recognising the defensive note in her voice, Celeste made a helpless gesture. 'I live in Paris. My mother lived in Cassis, in the south. I received her letter in January this year. She was already— It was already— I—my mother was already dead. Drowned. She drowned herself.'

Celeste blinked rapidly. Though he could not see, for they were obscured by her smock, Jack was willing to bet that her hands were painfully clasped. Yet there was a defiant tilt to her head, as if she was daring herself to submit to whatever emotions ensnared her in their grasp.

As a soldier, he was well versed in the art of managing grief. An iron will and rigid self-control had vital roles to play in combat. In battle, you put the living before the dead. It was why other soldiers got so uproariously drunk afterwards. It was why they sought out brothels and taverns, to laugh and to lose themselves, because they could not cry, but they could counter death with a lust for life, and they could later blame their tears on an excess of gin.

But Celeste was not a soldier, and the dead woman was her mother, not a comrade. Though like a soldier, she seemed determined not to crack under the strain. Instinctively, he knew any attempt to comfort her would not be welcome. Jack sat up, putting a little distance between them. 'This letter— You said *her* letter? Do you mean…?'

'Yes, my mother wrote to me to inform me she was about to commit suicide. It was, in essence, a letter from beyond the grave.'

Unable to stop himself, Jack reached for her hands. As he had suspected, they were tightly clasped. He covered them with his own. She stiffened, but made no attempt to repel him. He felt a sharp pang of sympathy. It was not just grief she was holding on so tightly to, but a hefty dose of guilt. Anger at her mother's act shook him. He bit back the words of blame, knowing full well they were irrational and un-deserved, and unlikely to cause Celeste anything but pain. 'Dear God. I am so sorry.'

'There is no need. It was a shock. I admit it was a shock, but once I had recovered from that, I read the letter in the hope that it would at least provide some sort of explanation for what, to me, was an incomprehensible act.' Now she did pull her hands free. '*Mais non*, nothing so straightforward from my mother. I should have known better than to have expected her to change the habits of a lifetime. It was more of a riddle than an explanation, sent in the full knowledge that by the time I received it, she would not be available to help solve it.'

Her anger simmered, the heat of it palpable. 'Celeste, she would not have been thinking rationally. To take such drastic action, she must have been very desperate,' Jack said, knowing the words were utterly inadequate, though none the less true.

'I don't doubt that. Though not desperate

enough to ask for my help.' Her lip quivered. The tension in her shoulders, the gaze fixed on her lap, made it clear that sympathy was the last thing she desired, but the raw pain was there, hidden under a mask of bitterness and anger. 'That letter...' She stopped to take a calming breath. 'It is not only that there is no explanation. That letter raises a list of questions I wouldn't even have known to ask.'

Questions. Such cases always raised more questions than answers. Answers which were so rarely found and which allowed guilt to flourish amid the uncertainty. Jack had written countless letters to the loved ones of his men who died in battle, emphasising the glory, and the valour and painlessness of death. Lies, all lies, but beneath the glossing over of reality lay one inalienable truth. They had died doing their duty for their country. Their death had a purpose.

The others, though, the families of those thankfully rare cases where death had been self-inflicted, they had no such truths to console them for what he had once, God forgive him, thought the most heinous of crimes. He searched for Celeste's hands once more, gripping them tightly. 'This letter, it's a great deal more than most have in such circumstances. Will you tell me what she said, and then I will be able to see how I might be able to help you?'

She considered it, looking at him earnestly, but eventually shook her head. 'Not yet. I can't.' She slipped from his grasp, getting to her feet with an apologetic look. 'I appreciate you sharing your experience of what is a painful and delicate subject. And for being so careful of my feelings. I do not discount your offer to help—it is most generous, but I must consider it carefully. The emotions involved are intensely private. Do you understand?'

Much as he wished to, he resisted the temptation to press her, because he did understand that, only too well. Jack got wearily to his feet. 'I have no other demands on my time or my services, so please take as much time as you need.'

Following a sleepless night, Celeste felt wrung out like one of her painting rags after washing. In the end, she had decided to trust Jack. She could not imagine having the conversation they'd had yesterday with a complete stranger, and she could not expect that a complete stranger would have demonstrated the tact or level of understanding Jack had of such matters.

It was not really such a leap of faith when she laid it out logically like that, to trust him. But it was not logic which ultimately convinced her. It was only after he had left her, when she had recovered from the dull ache precipitated by speaking of her mother's death, that she realised how difficult it must have been for him to talk so sensitively on such a delicate matter. Soldiers were men of war. Soldiers were tough, and brave and bold. English soldiers were famous for their courage and their staunchness in the face of adversity. They did not cry. They did not fear. They most certainly did not have a conscience. Or so she'd thought. Assumed, she corrected herself, because until she met Jack, Celeste thought shamefully, she hadn't actually thought about it much at all.

She remembered the reports in the newspapers after Waterloo. Death on the battlefield was neither clean nor quick. It was no wonder that the men who fought suffered from—what was it Jack had called it?—an extreme melancholy after witnessing all that horror and suffering. Was Jack suffering from that too? There had been moments yesterday when she thought he spoke from personal experience. But then he did, she reminded herself, thinking of the letters he'd mentioned having to write. The point was he understood and that was why she could trust him.

'May I come in?'

As if she had summoned him, the man himself stood in the doorway of Celeste's temporary studio. Dressed in a pair of tight-fitting pantaloons which showed off his long legs to good effect, and a coat which enhanced his broad shoulders, his cravat was neatly tied, and his jaw freshly shaved.

'You look very—handsomely dressed,' Celeste said, taken by surprise once more by the force of the attraction she felt for him. The clothes of an English gentleman not only accentuated his muscular physique, but they also, somehow, accentuated the fact that the man wearing them was not always a gentleman. In fact he was just a little bit dangerous. And, yes, a trifle intimidating too.

'Which is a polite way of saying I look a lot less shoddy than normal,' Jack said, closing the door behind him. 'You, if I may say so, look as ravishing as usual. And believe me, I have seen my fair share of beauties. A perk of the job, working on Wellington's staff.'

'So his reputation, the French press did not exaggerate it?'

'I doubt it possible.'

Celeste smiled, but the sight of the letter sitting where she had lain it in preparation made it a forced affair. She picked it up, but despite her resolve, found herself surprisingly reluctant to hand it over. 'Are you still— Your offer to help, is it still open?'

'Of course. I want very much to—'

'Only I would not wish to presume,' Celeste interrupted, 'and it occurred to me that perhaps you offered only because you felt a little sorry for me.'

'No. I understand what you are experiencing, that is all, and I wish to prevent you from— Is that the letter?' Jack said, holding out his hand.

'Yes.' Celeste still kept a firm grip on it. 'I don't know what people commonly write in such missives...'

'Most do not write anything,' Jack said, 'as far as I am aware. Or they merely reassure their families that they love them.'

'Well, in that one regard my mother has followed the custom,' Celeste said acerbically, 'though it is the one thing I know for certain to be a lie.' A brief silence met this remark. She flushed, annoyed at having betrayed herself. 'It is more of a puzzle than it is a confession,' she said, gazing down at the letter again. 'I admit it has me baffled. What we need is someone to make sense of it—what on earth have I said to amuse you?'

'Not amused, so much as taken aback, I am sorry,' Jack said, his expression once more serious. 'It's just that solving puzzles is—was—my stock in trade. I have a certain reputation as an expert in acrostics. My brother would be shocked at your ignorance, for he mistakenly delights in my minor fame.' He took her hand. 'Celeste, I was Wellington's code-breaker.'

She looked at him in bewilderment. 'I'm sorry, but I truly am ignorant of these things.' She broke off, staring as the implications of what Jack had said finally dawned on her. 'Code-breaker? Do you mean you were a spy?'

'After a fashion, though not, I suspect, in quite the way you are imagining. Not so much cloak and dagger as pen and paper. Information,' Jack clarified. 'Contrary to what civilians believe, wars are not won on the battlefield. Obviously, the battlefield is where matters are finally resolved, but getting there at the right time, in the correct field positions, having the men and the horses and the artillery all lined up, and knowing your enemy—his strategies, his positions, his plans, his firepower—that's what wins or loses a war. Having a retreat planned if required. And knowing what you're going to do if you break through his ranks— those matter too. You've no idea how many battles are lost when a commander in the field gets too far ahead of himself, or finds himself in retreat when no organised withdrawal has been planned.'

'You are right, I have absolutely no idea.'

Jack laughed. 'Put simply, information is what an army thrives on. My role was to assimilate that information to allow the generals to plot their campaigns and I did that by cracking codes, by piecing together different snippets from different sources and assembling them in an order that made sense. Solving puzzles, in other words.'

'And that, I am pleased to say, does make sense.' Without giving herself the chance to rethink the decision again, Celeste handed Jack the letter.

'Thank you. May I read it now?'

Her nerves jangling, she nodded. Jack sat down on the *chaise longue* which she had positioned in front of her easel. Unable to watch him, she busied herself, opening her precious box of paints and making an unnecessary inventory of the powders and pigments in their glass vials, of her brushes and oils. Behind her, she could hear the faintest rustle of paper worn thin by her many readings. A squeak, which must be Jack's boots as he shifted in his seat. Another rustle. He was taking an age. He must have gone back to the beginning. She wondered if she should set about stretching a canvas, but immediately abandoned the idea. Her hands were shaking. She began to rearrange her paints again.

'I'm finished.'

Celeste whirled around, dropping a vial of cadmium-yellow which, fortunately for her and the floor covering, landed softly on a rug without breaking. Cursing under her breath, she snatched it up and put it back in her box before joining Jack on the sofa. 'What is your verdict?'

'I think you must have been shocked to the core when you read this the first time.'

She gave a shaky laugh. 'It was certainly unexpected.'

'Unexpected!' Jack swore. 'You had no inkling of anything it contained?'

'No. I told you we were not close. *En effet*, my mother and I were estranged.' She was aware of Jack's eyes on her, studying her carefully. It made her uncomfortable, for while she refused to become emotional, she suspected that emotional is precisely what anyone else would be under the circumstances. She gazed resolutely down at her hands. 'As to the man I believed to be my father, he was always distant. From the beginning, I sensed he resented me. At least now I know why.'

'You were not his child.'

'So it would seem,' she said with a shrug.

'You're very matter-of-fact about something so important.'

'I have had eight months to become accustomed to it.'

Jack eyed her doubtfully. 'But you're not accustomed to it, are you? Despite your mother's positively begging you not to pursue the questions she raises, here you are in England, doing exactly that. It obviously matters a great deal to you.'

Celeste's hackles rose. 'I am curious, that's all,' she said. Even to her, this sounded like far too much of an understatement. 'Well, would not you be?' She crossed her arms. 'You said yourself only yesterday, people—the ones who are left behind—desire answers. Even when we are advised from beyond the grave not to pursue them. Do not tell me that you would have folded the letter up and forgotten all about it as my mother bids me, Jack Trestain, because I would not believe you.'

'No, I wouldn't do that, but neither would I be sitting here pretending that it was merely a matter of satisfying my curiosity either. For God's sake, Celeste, it's your mother we're talking about, not a distant aunt,' Jack exclaimed. 'She drowned herself. She made sure that this letter wouldn't reach you until she was dead. She then alludes to some tragedy in her past being the reason, and caps it all with the revelation that the man you thought all your life was your father is not actually your father, and fails to inform you of the identity of the man who is."

Jack held the letter out at arm's length. '"Though I write this with the heaviest of hearts,"' he read, '"knowing that I will never see you again, I am thankful that at least this time I have the opportunity to say goodbye." Your mother's opening words. What about the fact that she denied *you* the opportunity to say goodbye to her? Aren't you upset about that?'

Celeste didn't want him to be angry on her behalf. If anyone was entitled to be angry with her mother it was she, and she was not. In order to be angry she would need to care, and she did not. She didn't want Jack to care either. She wanted him to treat this as an intellectual exercise, devoid of emotion. Like breaking a code. 'You said yourself, she was most likely not in a rational frame of mind. At the end of her tether. Perhaps even a little bit out of her mind. There is no point in my becoming upset. It achieves nothing. Besides, I've told you, we were not remotely close.'

'And if you say that it doesn't trouble you often enough, you think I'll eventually believe you.'

Celeste flinched. 'I don't care what you believe. Next, you will be telling me that my mother loved me despite a lifetime's evidence to the contrary.'

'That is exactly what she claims in her letter.'

'Yes, from beyond the grave, safe from any

challenge to the contrary. How am I to believe it when I have nothing, no evidence at all, to support it? All my life—all my life, Jack!—she pushed me away. And now this. I don't believe her. How can I believe her? Of course I don't believe her. *C'est impossible!*'

Celeste jumped to her feet, turning her back on him to stare out at the long, bland stretch of lawn, struggling desperately to get her unaccustomed flash of temper under control. 'You have to understand,' she continued in a more measured tone, 'it was similar when I was growing up. Always, my mother managed to find a way of refusing to answer questions. *Why have I no aunts or uncles? Why must we never speak English except when alone? Why have I no grandparents or even a cousin, as all the other children at school have? Why are you so sad, Maman? Why does Papa hate me?* At least now I have the answer to that last question. Papa was not, in fact, my *papa* at all.'

Tears filled her eyes. Celeste swallowed hard on the jagged lump in her throat, staring determinedly out at the lawn. 'I have endured a lifetime of silences and rejection, so really that letter was in essence one final example. Don't tell me that she loved me, Jack. I know what she wrote, I don't have to read that letter again to see the words dance in front of my eyes, but that's all they are. Just words.'

'If it doesn't matter, if it truly doesn't matter, then why then are you so intent on digging up the past?' Jack put his hands on her shoulders, forcing her to turn and face him. 'You do realise that what you discover might be hurtful.'

'Not to me. My hurt is all in the past. All I am doing is filling in the blanks, the missing pieces of my mother's history. I want to understand why she behaved as she did. I want to know who my real father is. I think I am entitled to know that, but I do not want to meet him, or indeed my mother's family. I'm not expecting anyone to kill the fatted calf and welcome me into their home. I am aware that I am most likely a bastard. Knowing is sufficient for me.'

'Your mother's history is your history too, Celeste. You might be better off not knowing it. Sometimes it's better to leave the past behind you.'

'Or bury it so deeply that you can pretend it never happened, that it can no longer harm you?' She pulled herself free of his hold. 'But what if the ghosts refuse to stay buried, Jack? What if they continue to haunt you?'

His face paled. 'What the devil are you implying?'

She had not meant anything in particular. Intent only on silencing his relentless probing, it seemed she had inadvertently struck a raw nerve. It would be dangerous to push him further but it was time to let him sample a little of his own medicine. 'I have no idea why my mother went to such extremes to make me hate her, but I do know that I need to find out why. I need to understand. I need answers, Jack, while you—you seem so very determined to avoid asking the questions.'

'What questions?'

There was no mistaking the icy tone in his voice, but she ignored it. She was becoming very interested indeed in how he would respond. 'What is it that prevents you eating and sleeping? What is it that makes you stop in the middle of a conversation and—and disappear? As if you are no longer there. What is it that makes—?'

'What is it that stops you from crying, Celeste? What is it that prevents you from admitting that your mother's death affected you? Ask yourself those, more pertinent questions.'

Jack turned towards the door. Furious, uncaring that she had now achieved her objective, Celeste grabbed his arm. 'You see, you are running away from the truth. Why won't you talk about it?'

'Take your hands off me. Now.'

She had gone too far. She knew it would be insane to push him further, but she knew with certainty that was exactly what she was going to do. Celeste tilted her chin and met his stormy eyes. 'No.'

She half-expected him to strike her, but he made no such move. Instead, he pulled her towards him until they stood thigh to thigh, chest to chest. She was still angry, but her body responded immediately to the contact with a shiver of delight. 'I am not afraid of you,' Celeste said, tilting her head at him.

'I know,' Jack said. 'It's part of your appeal.'

Chapter Four

Jack's blood stirred at the first touch of her lips on his. He pulled her tight against him and kissed her more deeply. She returned his kiss with equal fervour. He'd been half-expecting her to slap him. He had kissed her merely to turn the tables on her. Now she was turning the tables back on him, just by reciprocating.

He had been angry. Nay, furious. Now his temper had vanished, burst as easily as a bubble by her touch. A gust of longing twisted his gut. He had not felt desire for such a long time. He could not recall ever feeling desire like this. Nothing to do with abstinence. Everything to do with this woman.

His fingers were shaking as he flattened his hand over her shoulder. This was not what he had intended. She was looking at him, her eyes wide open, watching him. Not afraid of him, though there was something there in her eyes he recognised. Yearning. Yes, and fear of the intensity of that yearning. He ought to stop. She should insist that he stop. He slid his hand down to cup her bottom and kissed her again. He needed, wanted, more. His body demanded it.

Her breathing quickened with his. Her fingers strayed into his hair. Her mouth was on his cheek, her lips warm, soft, little flicks of her tongue on his jaw, the corner of his mouth, licking along his lower lip, nipping, licking, until he could no longer stifle a moan of desire, and she gave an answering sigh.

He abandoned himself to her kisses, to the heat of her touch, to the fever of passion which had him in its iron grip. Their mouths locked. Their tongues thrust and tangled greedily. His hands were on her back, her bottom. Her fingers roamed wildly over him, his back, shoulders, tugging at his coat, clutching at his flanks.

He was achingly hard. He cupped her breasts, frustrated by the layers of her clothing, the impediment of her corsets. He dipped his head to kiss the soft swell of her cleavage, inhaling the sweet smell of her, relishing the shudder of her breath, the rapid beat of her heart, knowing that he had done this to her, that she was doing the same to him.

Their kisses grew ragged. His thirst for her was not remotely quenched. His coat was hanging off by one arm. He shrugged himself free of it, pressing her against the wall of the studio. She moaned, tugging his shirt from his pantaloons, flattening her hands on his back. Her skin on his. He hadn't thought he could get any harder. His erection throbbed. A long strand of her white-blonde hair had escaped its pins to lie against the biscuit-coloured skin of her bosom.

He had never wanted any woman this much. His erection pressed into her belly. He slid his hand inside the neckline of her gown to envelop the fullness of her breast. When he touched the hard peak of her nipple she cried out, the distinctive sound of a woman on the verge of a climax. He felt the answering tingling in the tip of his shaft that precluded his own. Shocked, he pulled himself free, hazily aware that she was pushing him away.

What the hell? It was no consolation at all to see his own question reflected in her face. He couldn't think of a damned thing to say. He could, unfortunately, think of a hundred things he wanted to do. Needed to do. Urgently. Jack swore long and hard under his breath. *Breathe. Don't think about it.* But he couldn't take his eyes of her. She hadn't moved. Head and shoulders against the wall. Eyes closed. Breathing slowly. Measured breaths like his. Hands curled into fists like his. Cheeks flushed with desire, no doubt as his were. That long tendril of hair lying across her breast. He reached for it, caught himself, took a step back and tumbled against the leg of a table.

Celeste opened her eyes. Jack pushed his hair back from his face. They stared at each other for a long moment. Then she stood up, tucked the strand of hair behind her ears, straightened her shoulders. '*Bien*, at least now we know that it was not a product of circumstances, that kiss in the Topiary Garden.' Her voice was shaky, but she made no attempt to avoid his gaze.

'The one you insisted was just a kiss,' he said.

'As I recall, you agreed with me.'

'Because I thought I had exaggerated its effect on me.'

'And what about this time?'

He shook his head. 'No. It would not be possible to exaggerate how that just felt. Frankly, it was almost too much.'

'For both of us,' Celeste said wryly.

Would another woman have denied it? It didn't matter. What mattered was that she did not. It made his own instinct to pretend nothing had happened, or to pretend nothing so— so— No, he would not try to quantify it, and he would not try to deny it. 'Do you regret it?' Jack asked as he self-consciously tucked his shirt back into his pantaloons.

She had been rearranging the neckline of her gown, but at that she looked up. 'Why should I?'

There was an edge in her words that took him aback. He had asked her, he realised now, purely because it was the sort of thing he thought he ought to ask. He knew he ought to regret his actions, but he could not. He was too elated to have the proof that it had not been a fluke, his reaction to that first kiss. Elated to know that whatever was wrong with him, lack of desire was no longer an integral part of it. Frustrated—hell, yes, he was frustrated. But he was also— Yes, he was also still a little bit afraid of the reaction she had provoked in him. And more than a little afraid of the consequences if he had not stopped.

'I have never been one of those women who pretend they have no desires of their own.' Celeste's voice cut into his thoughts. 'Nor am I the kind of woman who pretends that such physical desires represent anything more significant, Jack.'

'You're warning me off. There's no need, I assure you. At this moment in time, my only ambition is to get myself through the day—' He broke off, realising too late what he'd admitted, remembering, suddenly, why he had kissed her in the first place. And now he'd given her the perfect opening to start again.

But to his surprise, her expression softened. 'Yes,' she said. 'That is how I have felt since—since.' She blinked rapidly, and forced a smile. 'It is a good thing, this—this—between us, because now I know that I am recovering myself— No, that is not the correct expression.'

'Slowly getting back to normal?'

'Yes. That is it. That is what this is, yes? We are both adults. We are obviously well suited as regards—kissing,' Celeste said, flushing. 'We need not pretend it is anything else, no?'

He was most likely imagining the pleading

note in her voice. It was most likely his male ego that wanted to believe she was much more confused by what had happened between them than she appeared. As confused as he was? 'You're right,' Jack said with a conviction he was far from feeling.

Celeste nodded. 'Yes. It makes sense, what I said.'

It did. Perfect sense. So it was pointless wondering why she sounded as unconvinced as he. 'So,' Jack said in a bracing voice that made him cringe, 'talking of getting back to normal, perhaps we should concentrate on these questions your mother has raised. Do you have any other clues, save the letter?'

If she noticed anything odd in his voice, she chose not to comment on it. 'A couple of things. There is this, for what it's worth, which is not a lot.' Celeste unclasped the locket from her neck and handed it to him. 'It came with the letter. My mother always wore it. I don't think I ever saw her without it.'

Jack turned the oval locket over in his hand, examining it carefully. The metal was slightly tarnished so it was difficult to tell, but it looked like it might be gold or, more likely rose-gold, a cheaper alloy. It was embellished with a fleur-de-lis design. Around the rim were laurel leaves set with clear stones and in the centre was set a larger blue one.

'It's just a trinket,' Celeste said dismissively, 'though a pretty one.'

'I'm no expert,' Jack said, 'but the design is very fine, most intricately worked. See these hinges? They are very high quality indeed and not at all commonplace. I think it may be more valuable than you think.'

In fact, he was pretty sure that the smaller stones were diamonds, and that the blue stone was a sapphire. As a consequence the locket was more than likely commissioned, and indeed, on the back he noted tiny symbols, probably the goldsmith's mark. Which might make it, and the owner's name, traceable. But he could not be certain, and so, as was his custom, he kept his own counsel rather than raise Celeste's hopes prematurely. 'Do you mind if I open it?' he asked.

'If you wish.'

She shrugged, but he was becoming attuned to her many permutations of shrug, and Jack knew this one for feigned indifference. When he eased open the catch, he could understand why. Inside were two miniature portraits, one on each side. The first, of a flaxen-haired child, was obviously Celeste. The second, facing it, was of an older woman, her pale hair pulled tightly back from her forehead. Aside from the eyes, which were blue, the resemblance between mother and daughter was very strong, but when he said so, Celeste frowned.

'Do you think so?'

He was surprised by the uncertainty in her voice. 'She is unmistakably your mother, and clearly the source of your own beauty.'

Celeste touched the miniature with the tip of her finger. 'She was beautiful. I had forgotten.'

'May I ask her name?'

Celeste snatched her hand away. 'Blythe.'

'They seem to me to have been painted as a pair,' Jack said. 'I'm no expert, but...'

'No, you are right. Both are by my mother's hand.' She had herself firmly under control again, and spoke in that cool way of hers he'd initially mistaken for detachment. 'Unusually, actually, for she mostly painted the landscapes around Cassis. The fishing boats, the *calanques*—the limestone cliffs and inlets which punctuate the coast. I have never seen another portrait painted by her.'

Which made this pair all the more touching, Jack thought. He was tempted to say so, but hesitated, remembering her reaction earlier, when he had pushed her on her feelings. And she had pushed him straight back. A salutary lesson, he reckoned, in how not to go about extracting information. 'Cassis,' he said instead. 'The village where you grew up?'

Celeste treated him to one of her shrugs. The feigned indifference once again. 'Paris has been my home for many years.'

'I remember, you said you were sent there to school when you were—ten?'

'Yes. And stayed on to study art.'

'You were very young to be sent so very far from home.'

'It was a very good school.'

She would not meet his eyes. Another sensitive subject. 'You mentioned there was another clue?' Jack said, once more deciding that the best policy would be to bide his time.

She handed him a small packet of stitched muslin. Inside was a man's signet ring. 'I found it when I went to Cassis to close the house up after—after,' Celeste said. 'I was taking Maman's paintings down. This was sewn to the back of her favourite canvas. It must have been there for years. I have no idea what it sig-

nifies. It clearly does not belong to my mother.'
She leaned across him to peer down at the ring.
'The markings, I thought perhaps were a family crest. That might lead us somewhere,' she
said, looking at him hopefully.

'It looks to me more likely to be a military
crest. I'm not sure of the regiment. I would
need to check.'

'Military? Why on earth would my mother
have such a thing in her possession?'

'It's a good question.'

'As if we don't have enough questions already. Do you think you can help, Jack?'

He studied the ring with an ominous sense
of foreboding. 'I can try.'

The next morning, a soft breeze blew up as
Celeste walked with Jack along a path which
led from the far end of the lake, over a gentle
rise to an ancient oak, underneath the spread of
which was a wooden bench. The view was prettily bucolic, bathed in the golden early-morning
light. They stood on top of the hill while Jack
pointed out the spire of St Mary's Church some
five miles away, where Lady Eleanor's father
was the vicar, and closer, the many-gabled rooftops of Trestain Manor. Golden fields of half-

harvested wheat contrasted with the dark-green tunnels of hops, while the low, thatched roofs of the farm buildings and cottages contrasted with the distinctive, conical roofs of two oast houses where the hops were roasted.

Celeste was entranced, her charcoal flying over page after page of her sketchbook, while Jack, seated on the bench under the tree, filled her in on some of the history of what she was drawing. He was back to his usual garb of leather breeches and boots, a shirt without either waistcoat or coat. The sleeves of his shirt were rolled up. The skin of his right arm was already turning golden-brown. She would like to draw him like this, his long, booted legs stretched out in front of him, his hair falling over his forehead, the curve of his mouth in a lazy smile. That mouth, the source of such intoxicating kisses.

Desire knotted in her belly. She had never before tumbled so perilously close to completion after a few kisses. The rapidity of her arousal had caught her completely unawares. When he had touched her nipple...

Celeste inhaled sharply. Even now, the memory of it was enough to heat her. And to frighten her. All very well to thank Jack for bringing her body back to life as she more or less had, rather embarrassingly, yesterday, but he had brought it to a place it had never been before. Her claim that abstinence had somehow attenuated what Jack's kisses did to her felt faintly ridiculous now. In her whole life, she had taken four lovers, and there had been two years between the first and second, yet she knew with certainty that none had made her feel the way Jack did.

The natural conclusion, that it was not circumstances but this man, this very particular man, was what had kept her awake last night. Clearly there was something, some force, some element, some quirk of nature, which made their bodies so well matched. This explanation, she should have found comforting, but for some reason, she did not. If it had not been so reasonable, she would have been inclined to dismiss it as wrong.

'Is *Mademoiselle* ready to partake of breakfast now?'

Celeste jumped, staring down at blankly her half-finished sketch. Her charcoal was on the grass beside her. How long had she been daydreaming? At least with her back turned to him, Jack would not have noticed. Or if he had, he had decided not to comment, she thought with relief. There was nothing worse than being asked what it was one was thinking, for it was inevitably something one did not wish to share. It had been unkind of her to mention those lost moments of Jack's yesterday. Call it daydreaming, call it disappearing, as she had, wherever they were, they were private. His and his alone.

She gave him an apologetic smile as she joined him on the grass, leaning her back against the bench. 'Thank you.'

He quirked his brow but said nothing, pulling the hamper they had brought with them out from beneath the shade of the tree before spreading a blanket out. There was fresh-baked bread, butter and cheese, a flask of coffee and some peaches. 'Picked fresh this morning, and though they are ripe,' he said, sniffing the soft fruit, 'I don't expect they'll be anything like what you're used to. Our English sun is just not strong enough.'

Celeste stretched her face up to the sky, closing her eyes and relishing the heat on her skin. 'It is a good deal warmer than I expected. I don't think I have seen a drop of English rain yet.'

'You will. One merely has to wait a few days.'

Jack handed her a cup of coffee. Celeste tore off a piece of bread, burying her nose in the delicious, yeasty smell of it. 'Another myth. I was told that the English cannot bake good bread, but this is most acceptable.'

'A high compliment indeed from a French-woman.' He handed her a slice of cheese and laughed when she sniffed that too, wrinkling her nose. 'Try it, you might be surprised.'

She did, and was forced to admit that, like the bread, it was excellent. 'Though it breaks my French heart to do so,' she added, smiling over her coffee cup.

'But you're half-English, are you not?'

'I suppose I am, though I don't feel it. I think one has to be part of a country before one feels any sense of belonging. All this,' Celeste said, spreading her arms wide at the sweeping view, 'it feels so alien to me.'

'Maybe that's because you're a Parisian.'

Celeste laughed. 'When I first arrived in Paris, I felt such an outsider. It was as if everyone but me knew a secret and they were all whispering about it behind my back. Even after fifteen years, I'm still not considered a genuine Parisian. I don't have that *je ne sais quoi*, that air about me. To the true Parisians, I will always be an incomer.'

'I know exactly what you mean,' Jack said. 'Paris, it's always seemed to me, is a city that only reveals itself at night, and even then, you have to know where to look. I always sense the best elements are just round the next corner, or along the next boulevard. In Paris, I always feel as if I'm on the outside looking in. It's not like London at all.'

'I have never visited London. I hope to go there before I return to France.' Celeste broke off another piece of bread and accepted a second piece of cheese which Jack cut for her. 'You have been away from England a long time,' she said. 'Does it still feel like home?'

He paused in the act of quartering a peach. 'Charlie wants me to buy an estate and settle down. I never did share his love for country life, though he seems to have conveniently forgotten that.'

'Perhaps it would be different if you had been the eldest son, if Trestain Manor belonged to you and not to your brother?'

Jack laughed. 'Lord, no, I'd be bored senseless. It was always the army for me, so it's as well I'm the second son and not the first.' He handed her the peach. 'What about you? Have you never thought of going back to live in your fishing village?'

'No.'

'Don't you miss it? I used to miss all this,' Jack said. 'Even though I wouldn't want to live here, it's my childhood home.'

Celeste stared at the quarter of peach in her hand. 'The house in Cassis was where I lived. It was never a home.' Her voice sounded odd, even to her own ears. She was, yet again, on the brink of tears for no reason. It was Jack's fault. All she wanted him to do was help her unravel the mystery of her mother's past, but for some reason, he persisted in linking that past with her own. He seemed to have the knack of inflaming her emotions as well as her body. She set the peach down. 'Paris is my home,' she said, as if repeating it would make it more true. Not that it needed to be more true. It was true.

She thought of the house where she had grown up. The distinctive creak of the front door. The very different creak of the fifth stair which had a broken tread. The way the floors always seemed to echo when she walked, signalling her presence too loudly. She tried to close her mind to the memories, but they would not stop flowing. It was Jack's fault. This was all Jack's fault.

On her last visit, after receiving the letter, she had packed up every one of her mother's paintings. They lay in crates now, stacked in a corner of her Paris studio. She couldn't bear to look at them but nor could she bear to dispose of them. The rest of the house she had left as it was.

She shook her head. She was aware of Jack, sipping his coffee, pretending not to study her, but the ghosts of the past had too strong a claim on her. Her mother on the cliff top painting, her hair covered by a horrible cap, her body draped in shapeless brown. Her mother's face, starkly beautiful in the miniature inside her locket, strained and sad. Her mother's paintings were all of the coast and the sea which took her. The sea which she had abandoned herself to, without giving Celeste a chance to save her. The beautiful, cruel sea, which her mother had chosen to embrace, rather than her own daughter.

The pain was unexpected. Nothing so clichéd as a stab to the heart; it was duller, weightier, like a heavy blow to the stomach. *At least this time I have the opportunity to say goodbye*, her mother had written, so certain that Celeste cared so little she would not wish to do the same. With good cause, for Celeste had made it very clear, after Henri died...

A tear rolled down her cheek. Her throat was clogged. She couldn't speak. She was filled with the most unbearable sadness. *What was wrong with her!* She never cried. Had never cried. Now, hardly a day went by where she teetered on the verge of stupid, stupid tears.

In the distance, the chime of St Mary's heralded noon. She dabbed frantically at her eyes with her napkin. She never carried a handkerchief.

'Celeste?'

Jack! It was his fault for dredging all this up. His fault for making her so on edge. She jumped to her feet and snatched up her sketchbook. 'I have the headache,' she said. 'I have no more paper. I need to rest. I need more charcoal.'

She was fleeing, just as Jack had, after that first kiss, and she did not care. All that mattered was that he did not stop her. She barely noticed in her anxiety to escape that he made absolutely no attempt to do so.

Chapter Five

'So this is where you're hiding.'

Celeste forced herself to turn around slowly. Jack stood hesitantly in the doorway, dressed in his customary breeches and boots. She willed the flush of embarrassment she could feel creeping up her neck not to show on her face. 'It is safe to come in,' she said. 'I am not going to descend into a fit of hysterics or stamp my feet or even run away again.'

He strode over to her, his relief obvious. 'I'm sorry, Celeste,' he said. 'It was not my intention to cause you upset yesterday.'

'Cassis was not a happy place for me when I was growing up,' she said carefully. 'I don't like to talk of it or even think of those days. *En effet*, I never do. It is in the past where it belongs.'

And she would make sure it remained there. It sounded contrary, considering the accusations she had flung at Jack yesterday, but their cases were not the same, she had decided after another sleepless night. She had come to terms with her past, he had not. What she needed to concentrate on now was dealing with her mother's past. Which was a separate issue.

Slanting a look at Jack, she was not surprised to catch him studying her, but she was relieved when he nodded his acceptance, albeit reluctantly. 'Charlie,' he said, turning his attention to the portrait she had been examining. 'Aged about five, I think. What brings you to the portrait gallery?'

'I was interested to see how the estate had been depicted previously, to avoid the risk of replicating any existing works.'

'Ah, so you're here purely in the name of artistic research and not at all out of curiosity?'

Celeste smiled. 'Naturally.' She turned to the next work, a family portrait, which showed a youthful Jack and Charlie sitting at their parents' feet. 'You looked much more alike as children than you do as adults. You both take after your mother rather than your father, I fancy.'

'So my mother was forever saying. It was a

matter of pride to her that Charlie and I bore the McDonald countenance and not the Trestain visage,' Jack said, reaching out to draw the outline of his mother's face on the canvas with his finger. 'She was a Scot, and verrrrry, verrrry proud of the fact,' he said in a ham-fisted attempt at a Scottish burr.

'You miss her?'

'She died when I was in Spain, about six years ago. But, yes, I do miss her. She wanted me to join the Scots Greys, but my father put his foot down on that one. Nevertheless, she always claimed that my fighting spirit as well as my nose came from her side of the family. Here she is, a good deal younger, in her wedding portrait, with my maternal grandfather.'

Celeste eyed the picture of the fierce man in Highland dress. He looked very much like Jack did when he was angry. 'Would you have had to wear one of those skirts if you joined the—the...'

'Scots Greys. No, only the Highland regiments wear kilts.'

'*Tant pis*. That is a pity. It would suit you uncommonly well, I think,' Celeste said. 'You have the most excellent legs for it.'

'You speak merely as an observant artist, of course?'

She felt herself colour slightly. 'Naturally. Is there a picture of you wearing your regimental uniform?'

Jack rolled his eyes. 'In full ceremonial dress, no less, looking like I've a poker up my—looking as if I've swallowed a poker. Charlie commissioned it when I was promoted. Here, take a quick look if you must.'

He put his arm around her shoulders and steered her to the far end of the small gallery, where the portrait, in its expensive gilt frame, was hung to take best advantage of the light. 'Your brother must have spent a small fortune on this,' Celeste said, raising her brows at the artist's signature. 'A full-length study. He is obviously very proud of you, Lieutenant-Colonel.' She waited for Jack's customary glower at any mention of the army, but to her surprise it did not surface.

He looked very forbidding in the portrait. His hair was cropped much shorter, barely noticeable under the huge crested helmet he wore with its extravagant black horsehair tail. He stood very tall and straight, his hand resting on the hilt of his sabre, his face looking haughtily off into the distance. The scarlet coat was extremely tight-fitting, showing off his broad shoulders and narrow waist, the high, braided collar framing his jaw. White breeches and long, glossy black boots drew attention to his muscular legs. 'Which regiment did you belong to?'

'Dragoons,' Jack said abstractedly. 'Of course we didn't wear those ridiculous helmets or the white breeches when going into battle. What do you think of it?'

'As an artist? It is a technically flawless work. As a viewer, it speaks unmistakably of authority. It depicts you with a—a certain hauteur. I think I would be just a little bit intimidated by the man in the portrait. I would of a certainty obey his orders unquestioningly. If I was one of his men, that is,' she added quickly.

Jack laughed. 'I doubt you would follow even Napoleon's orders.'

'No, I would have made a very bad soldier. But you, you look—*bien*—exactly what you were, a high-ranking British officer, used to unwavering obedience and with the air of a Greek god, gazing down on us mere mortals.'

'Good grief, you make me sound like a pompous ass.'

'No, not pompous, supremely confident. Very sure of yourself.'

'I suppose I was.'

Jack was staring at the portrait as if it were of a stranger, just as she had stared at the miniature of her mother only the other day. She was still struggling to equate the beautiful woman in the portrait with the Maman in her mind's eye. Art could obscure reality as well as portray it. Which was the real Blythe Marmion? Which was the real Jack Trestain? Had the regal, commanding officer in the portrait ever existed? Jack was asking himself the same question, judging by the expression on his face.

'This likeness was taken less than three years ago,' he said. 'I left the army less than three months ago, yet it seems as if a lifetime has passed. I struggle to recognise myself. I can barely remember being the man in the portrait. I thought, you know, that if I re-enlisted, I might— I was fine then. Seeing this—I can't imagine it now.'

He turned away, heading across the room to the farthest point away from the portrait. *I was fine then.* For the first time, he had admitted that he was not fine now. *What had happened to him?* More than ever, she longed to know, but Celeste bit back the questions she was desperate to ask, the answers she would have demanded only a few short days ago. Memories were painful things. Memories were private things. Some memories, as she had learnt only yesterday, were too painful to be shared.

It was like Pandora's box, her memory. Every time the lid creaked open a fraction, it became more and more difficult to close. Things she wanted to forget wriggled free. Things that reminded her she had not always been the person she was so proud of now. She did not want to be reminded of that person. She would never again be that person.

And Jack? With Jack it was very different. The soldier in the portrait had been a respected and admired officer, one mentioned in despatches, whatever that meant. The man he had become was fighting a different battle now. He had his demons, just as she had her ghosts. No doubt she was just a foolish artist, but she admired this man's bravery a great deal more.

She rejoined him in front of another full-length painting. 'And who is this remarkable specimen?' Celeste asked him brightly.

'This is my father's brother, also called

Jack,' he replied. 'As you can see, aside from our name, we have precious little in common.'

The man was fat, fair and flamboyant in a claret-velvet suit, gazing winsomely out at the viewer, a silver jug in one hand, a book in the other. 'Household Accounts,' Celeste read in puzzlement. 'How very strange. Usually when a man holds a book in a portrait it is to symbolise his learning.'

Jack smiled wryly. 'In this particular case it symbolises his notorious thriftiness. This next lady now, my Aunt Christina, is my mother's youngest sister, known as Auntie Kirsty. She is married to a real Highland laird and lives in a genuine Highland castle. Charlie and I used to love visiting them. It was a real adventure for us. My mother hated it up there, for it was freezing cold, winter and summer, and Auntie Kirsty is one of those women who hasn't much of an opinion of soap and water. Frankly,' Jack said, grinning, 'Auntie Kirstie smells exactly like her deerhounds when they've been out in the rain. But she's one of the best fishermen I've ever come across, and she can shoot better than almost any trooper I've ever trained. You can see the castle in the background there, and this dog here, that's Calum, her favourite deerhound of the time, though most likely long gone.' His smile faded. 'I've not been there in many years.'

'Now you are no longer tied to the army, you could visit her, if you wished.'

'No. Auntie Kirstie is almost as bad as my mother was for basking in my exploits.'

'You mean she was proud of you?'

'They all were, and I was arrogant enough to think I deserved it.' Jack reached out to touch his aunt's face, the same gesture he'd used on the portrait of his mother. 'I considered myself a good soldier.'

'And the Duke of Wellington agreed,' Celeste reminded him.

'Yes, he did, but it all depends on your perspective.'

He spoke not bitterly, but resignedly. His expression was bleak, the despair not so marked as on that first, unguarded day at the lake, but it was manifestly still there in his eyes. She longed to comfort him, but how? The more he said about the army, the more she realised his relationship with it was complex, perhaps impossible for anyone who was not a soldier to understand. He loved the army, he clearly had loved being a soldier, but he spoke of those days as if it were a different person. As if it was not him. As if he would not allow it to have been him. And so perhaps they were kindred spirits after all.

The door to the portrait gallery burst open, and a small whirlwind of a boy came hurtling in, making a beeline for Jack. 'Please will you take me fishing, Uncle Jack?'

'Robert, make your bow to Mademoiselle Marmion,' Jack said, detaching the grubby little hand which was clutching the pocket of his breeches. 'This, *Mademoiselle*, is my nephew.'

'How do you do?' The child made a perfunctory bow before turning his beseeching countenance back to his uncle. '*Will* you take me fishing? Only Papa was supposed to take me but I think he has quite forgotten, and even though Papa says he always caught the biggest fish when you were little...'

Jack laughed. 'Oh, he did, did he?'

Robert nodded solemnly. 'Yes, and Papa would not lie, Uncle Jack.'

Jack dropped down on to his knees to be level with the child whose eyes were the exact same shade of dark brown, Celeste noted, as his own. 'No,' he said, 'you are quite right. Papa would not lie.'

'But you mustn't feel bad, because he told me you were the much better shot.' Robert patted Jack's shoulder consolingly, making Celeste stifle a giggle. 'Papa said that when you were only six, which is just a little bit bigger than me, you shot a pigeon this high up in the sky,' he said, standing on his tiptoes and stretching his arm above his head. 'Only Papa said that it was very naughty of you, because you weren't supposed to have the gun, and Grandpapa was very angry, and he gave you a sound whipping, and Papa too, even though *he* did not shoot the gun, and I think that's not fair. Do you think that's fair, Uncle Jack, do you?'

'Well, I…'

'Though maybe,' Robert continued, having drawn breath, 'maybe,' he said, plucking at Jack's shirt, 'Papa was whipped because he is the *eldest* and did not show a good example? That is what he said I am to do, when Baby Donal is older. So maybe you would not have stolen the gun and shot the pigeon if Papa had told you not to?'

'Perhaps,' Jack said, his eyes alight with laughter but his expression serious, 'though I was a very naughty boy when I was your age. I tended not to do as I was told, I'm afraid.'

Robert considered this, his head on one side. 'Is that why you are not a soldier any more? Did you disobey orders?'

Jack sat back on his heels, the light fading from his eyes. 'I did not, but I wish to God I had.'

Celeste caught her breath at this, but Robert had already moved on. 'Uncle Jack, will you tell me about the time when you told the Duke of Wellington about that great big fort, and he said that it was a ruin, but you knew better. And there was a big battle and—and will you tell me, because when Papa tells me, he gets it all mixed up and forgets the regiments, and it is not the same as when you tell it.'

Jack winced. 'Robert, the war is over now.'

'But you were there and you saw it with your own eyes,' the child continued, heedless.

'Robert…'

'Robert, I think perhaps your uncle…' Celeste interjected.

Robert stamped his foot. 'It is not fair! Why must I not ask you? Why won't you tell me, when you have told Papa?'

'Because Papa is a grown up. Because it was a long time ago,' Jack said.

'Well then, why will you not tell me about Waterloo? That was not a long time ago.'

'Robert,' Jack said, getting to his feet, obviously agitated, 'I think it is best...'

'But I only wanted to know what it was like,' the child said, grabbing at his uncle's leg, his face screwed up with temper, 'because Steven, who is my best, best friend in the whole village, his papa fought under Sir Thomas Picton at Waterloo in the Fifth Infantry, and I said that you were much more important than even Sir Thomas Picton, and Steven said you could not be...'

'Enough, child, for pity's sake!' Jack's roar was so unexpected that Robert stopped in midflow, his jaw hanging open. Celeste, who felt as if her heart had attempted to jump out of her chest, was also speechless.

Jack pointed at the door. 'Out! You would test the patience of a saint. No war stories, today or ever. Have I made myself perfectly clear?' He glowered at the child.

Robert's lip trembled, but he held his ground. 'I hate you.' He stamped his foot again. 'I *hate* you,' he said and burst into tears, storming from the room, violently slamming the door behind him.

Shaken, white-faced, Jack slumped on to the sofa which was placed in the middle of the room and dropped his head, pinching the furrow between his brows hard. He rubbed his forehead viciously, as if he were trying to erase whatever thoughts lurked behind it. 'I frightened him,' he said starkly. 'He's five years old, for goodness' sake, and I yelled at him as if he'd turned up on the parade ground without his musket. What the hell is wrong with me?'

'Jack, I don't think he was so very frightened. It seemed to me he was more angry than afraid.'

'What blasted difference does it make? He ran away, bawling his eyes out, and that was my fault.' Jack jumped to his feet, his fists clenched. 'I've never upset a child like that before. What on earth is happening to me?'

'Jack, I—'

'No, don't say another word.' He rounded on her. 'You! That is what is behind this. Ever since you— As if I didn't have enough on my mind without having to lie awake thinking of you and your damned kisses and your damned questions. *Why can't I eat? Why can't I sleep? Why do I—* What did you call it?'

'Disappear.' Her voice was no more than

a whisper. His anger was not directed at her, but it terrified her, the depths of his anxiety. Though he loomed over her, she stood her ground. 'Jack…'

He threw her hand from his arm. 'Don't pity me. I neither require nor desire your pity, *Mademoiselle*. I want—I want…' He flung himself back on to the sofa and dropped his head into his hands. 'Hell's teeth, I don't know what I want. I'm sorry. I'm better left to my own devices at the moment. Best if you leave.'

Celeste turned to do as he bid her, remembering her own desire yesterday to retire to her bedchamber and lick her wounds, but then she stopped, and instead sat down on the sofa beside him. 'I don't feel sorry for you, Jack. I don't know what I feel for you, to be honest, but I know it's not pity.'

He did not look up, but he did not turn away either.

She wasn't sure what it was she was trying to say. She was reluctant to say anything, especially if it was an unpalatable truth, but she knew she couldn't leave him like this, bereft and seemingly lost. 'You were correct,' she said, though it made her feel quite sick to admit it, 'when you said that Maman's death was— That it meant more to me than I thought. You were right.'

Jack lifted his head. Celeste had to fight the urge to run away. She dug her feet into the wooden floor. 'I blamed you yesterday for what I was feeling. I thought, if it hadn't been for you, I would not be feeling—' She broke off, raising her hands helplessly. 'I don't know what. Something, as opposed to nothing.'

'I'm sorry. I had no right to pry.'

'No more than I did, but it didn't stop me either. I am sorry too.'

'I never used to have such a foul temper, you know.'

'*Moi aussi*, never. Perhaps there is something in the air at Trestain Manor.'

Jack's smile was perfunctory, but it was a smile. 'I don't know what Charlie is playing at, telling Robert those stupid stories, making it sound as if war is some great adventure.'

'Isn't that what you thought at that age?' Celeste asked carefully.

'Precisely.' He ran his fingers through his hair. 'And now I know better.'

'Jack, Robert is just a little boy. He doesn't need or deserve to have his illusions shattered at such a tender age. Why not indulge him a little? What is so different, really, from telling him the kind of stories you once told your brother?'

'I only ever told Charlie the kind of things he wanted to hear.'

'Exactement.'

He was silent for a long time. Finally, he shook his head, pressed her hand and got to his feet. 'I need some fresh air, and you are probably wanting to get on with your work. I'm going to try to manage an hour on horseback without falling off.'

'But your arm...'

'Will recover faster if I use the blasted thing. I'm not made of glass. Besides,' Jack added with a grin, 'you've no idea how embarrassing it is for an officer of the Dragoons to fall from his horse. If any of my comrades knew, I'd never be allowed to forget it.'

The next day, as Jack had predicted it would, it was raining. Not the kind of polite, soft rain that Celeste had imagined would fall in an English summer, but a heavy downpour rather like the kind of summer storm in Cassis that turned the narrow streets into raging torrents. Gazing out of the windows of her studio, it was as if the sky consisted of one leaden grey cloud that had been sliced open. Water poured from the gutters on to the paths, cutting new channels into the flower beds. The branches of the trees bent under the weight of the deluge.

Celeste shivered, wrapping the shawl she had fetched after breakfast more tightly around her, for the flimsy sprigged-muslin gown she wore was no protection against the cold, damp air. She looked longingly at the small fireplace, imagining the comfort of a fire. In August! She doubted that the hardy Lady Eleanor would think it necessary.

It was too dark to work, and too wet to go outside. Sir Charles, fretting about the harvest, was planning on a tour of the closest farms, though when his wife had quizzed him on what he thought could be achieved, other than a thorough drenching, he had been unable to supply her with an answer. Lady Eleanor was to spend the morning in the kitchen making jam. A task she and her sisters used to look forward to every year when they were growing up, she had told Celeste over the breakfast table. She hoped to pass her receipts on to her own daughters, when they arrived, but in the meantime, she would be sharing the task with cook. She did not ask Celeste if she wanted to join them in the kitchen.

'And I am glad she did not, for I know nothing at all about making jam or pickles or any of these things the English take such pride in,' Celeste muttered to herself. The truth was, she thought, looking despondently out at the garden, she knew almost nothing about French cooking either. Frowning, she tried to recall if she had ever seen her mother in the kitchen, and could not. They had always had a cook. Her mother planned the meals, she recalled, writing out the menus for the week in the book in which she kept painstaking household accounts, but, no, not once could Celeste recall her actually shopping for food or preparing it. Then, at school, the kitchens were out of bounds, and in her Parisian garret, she could make coffee, but nothing more substantial.

She leafed through her sketches, which were laid out on a large table set against the wall. She didn't even like jam, but when Lady Eleanor talked about sharing the task with her sisters, Celeste had felt quite envious. There had been a softness about her ladyship too, as she speculated about a time when her yet-to-be-born daughter would join her in the kitchen.

Celeste cast her sketches aside and returned to the window. Was there nothing, no small domestic task she and her mother had shared?

Painting. Yes, there were the painting and drawing lessons, though there were so many that, to Celeste's frustration, the memory was blurred. She could remember spending hours and hours trying to draw a cat. She could remember struggling to hold her brush in the correct manner. She could remember painting endless bowls of fruit. But her memories were all of her hand, the paper, the paints, the result. She could not recall what her mother had said of any of her work. Could not remember a single occasion when her father—Henri, she corrected herself—had passed any opinion at all on her talent. In fact she could not remember him being present at all.

Outside, the rain was easing. Sir Charles would be relieved. The grass looked much greener, almost too glossy to be real. The trees too looked freshly painted. They reminded her of the idealised pictures in a storybook that her mother used to read to her. She had forgotten that. Returning to the sofa, she sat down and closed her eyes. Her mother was reading the story, her finger pointing to the words so that

Celeste could follow along. The book was in English. Where had it come from? Had it been her mother's as a child? The pages had been worn. The book contained several stories, each beautifully illustrated. An expensive book.

Celeste screwed her eyes shut tighter and tried to recall her mother's voice, but though she could see the pictures so clearly, she couldn't hear any accompanying words. Frustrated, she tried to recall other times. Sewing. Her mother had taught her to sew. Not the practical kind that she had been taught at school, but embroidery. Yes, yes, another memory swam into view. She was sitting on a stool at her mother's knee. 'When the first course is served at such a grand dinner,' Maman was saying, 'one must turn to the right, so I had to wait until the second course to speak to him.'

Celeste's eyes flew open. She stared around the room, as if her mother might appear from behind the easel. Her voice had been so clear. '*Mon Dieu*, of all the things, I remember that most useless piece of advice!'

'What most useless piece of advice would that be?'

'Jack.' Celeste jumped to her feet, clutching her shawl. 'You startled me.'

'Sleeping on the job?'

'I was not sleeping,' she said indignantly, 'I was thinking.' She eyed his wet hair, sleeked back on his head, with astonishment. 'You have surely not been swimming in this?'

'Why not?'

She wrapped her arms around herself, giving a mock shudder. 'It is freezing.'

'Nonsense, a little summer rain, that's all. You'll be asking for the fire to be lit next.' She must have looked longingly at the empty hearth, because Jack burst out laughing.

'If you think it is cold now, you should try enduring an English country winter. Which you will not be required to do, since once your business here is concluded I assume you will be anxious to return to your life in Paris.'

'Of course I am.' And she was. Everything she had achieved had been hard-earned and she was looking forward to picking up the threads of her life.

Jack put the leatherbound folder which he had brought with him down on the table next to her sketches. 'Celeste, have you considered the possibility that whatever we manage to uncover about your mother's past might change things, maybe even change your life, the one you're so keen to reclaim, irrevocably?'

She pursed her lips, shaking her head firmly. 'I thought I'd made myself plain, I have no ambition to claim any family, legitimate or not, if that is what you mean. Clearly, my mother's family disowned her. Equally clearly, my father's family disowned both my mother and me. Frankly, being the unwanted child of one man means I have no wish to repeat the experience as far as my father is concerned, and as to my mother—again, no. Her family rejected her. My mother rejected me. You see the pattern, Jack. Whatever we find will allow me to regain my life, not destroy it.'

She spoke carefully, but coolly. The barriers were well and truly in place once more, but still Jack felt uneasy. She was fragile, she had admitted that much yesterday. He wanted to spare her pain, but he had not that right. All he could do was help her, and hope that the price she paid was worth it.

Jack opened the folder. 'In that case,' he said, 'let us set to work on getting you the answers you need. First things first. Let's take stock of where we are and what we know.'

Chapter Six

Jack took out her mother's letter from his folder, and laid it out alongside a sheet of notes he had made following a detailed analysis of the contents. 'Are you ready for this?' he said.

Celeste nodded, ignoring the fluttering of nerves in her stomach.

'So, to the beginning—or the beginning as we know it. Your mother married Henri Marmion in 1794.'

Again, she nodded.

'At the height of the Terror then, when the bloodletting in the aftermath of the Revolution was at its peak,' Jack said. 'I think that must be significant.'

Celeste frowned. 'I cannot see how. My father—Henri—he was not a member of the aristocracy. He was not a politician, or indeed a man of any influence. Besides, we lived in a tiny fishing village, not Paris, or any other important city. We were just an ordinary family.'

Jack tapped his finger on his notes. 'You were four when this marriage took place. Do you remember anything from the time before? Anything at all,' he asked. 'Sometimes the most insignificant details are the ones that matter most.'

Celeste shook her head. 'I was thinking only this morning, just before you arrived, how little I can recall of my childhood. An English storybook. Painting lessons. Setting the stitches on a sampler. Maman telling me the etiquette for polite conversation at a dinner party, though why she should think it important to instruct me in *that* I cannot imagine.'

'What's your earliest memory?' Jack asked.

'That is easy,' Celeste said with a smile. 'I found a shell on the beach one day, a huge pink shell, the kind that you put to your ear and can hear the rush of the sea. I remember it was too big for me to hold with one hand. I must have been five, perhaps six. What is yours?'

'That's easy too. Charlie had a toy horse, a wooden one on wheels. He called it Hector. I was forbidden from riding it because I was

too little, which Charlie delighted in reminding me, so of course that made me all the more
determined. I managed to climb up on Hector,
and Charlie caught me and pushed me off, and
I split my forehead open on the marble floor.
I still have the scar. Here,' Jack said, taking
her hand.

It was very faint, right in the middle of his
forehead. She ran her finger along it, feeling
the tiny notches where it had been stitched, and
could not resist pushing back his hair from his
brow. It was silky-soft. She snatched her hand
away. 'Your first battle scar,' she said. 'Sadly,
not your last. How is your arm today?'

Jack shrugged. '*That* wound is healing.'

And so he edged a tiny step closer to admitting there was another, deeper wound. Celeste
bit her tongue. Trust, she was learning, was a
skittish beast, so she turned the subject to a
different sort of animal. 'Hector is a peculiar
name for a horse. What age were you when
you stole it?'

She was rewarded with a small smile. 'I
didn't steal it, I borrowed it. I had to use a stool
to climb up on to the saddle, and my legs didn't
touch the ground. Three, perhaps?'

'Is it odd, do you think, that I can remember nothing from such a young age?'

'I don't know, but in my experience, people actually take in a great deal more than they can recount. Memory works in different ways for different people. For some, smell is the most evocative sense. I tend to remember things in the form of patterns. As an artist, for you it might be colour. There are tricks that can help flesh out a memory that I used in my days of gathering information professionally,' Jack said.

'You mean when you were interrogating enemy agents?'

'Lord, no, I mean when I was debriefing our chaps after a reconnaissance. No thumbscrews or rack, in case that's what you're imagining either. Simply a case of relaxing the subjects' minds before gently directing their thoughts. We can try it later if you like.'

'No,' Celeste said firmly, 'I will keep my thoughts to myself, thank you.'

Jack raised a quizzical brow, but turned his attention back to his notes. 'I can't help but feel that your mother's marriage to Henri Marmion must be connected somehow with the Terror.' He picked up the letter. '"Without Henri, I do honestly believe we would have perished. I doubt you will believe him capable of heroism, but back in those dark days, that is what he was. A hero." She is convinced that both your lives were in danger. That's too much of a coincidence, don't you think?'

It was hard to disagree with Jack's logic, though difficult to conceive of it being true. Celeste nodded, this time reluctantly.

'Good, then that is our starting premise.' Jack pulled out another sheet of paper. 'So, what else do we know? First, your mother was English. Second, she gave birth to you in France in 1790, so she must have gone there at some point before. I don't suppose you know your place of birth?'

'I'm afraid not.'

'Or your mother's maiden name? Is there a certificate of her marriage to Henri Marmion?'

She shook her head again. 'The number of things I don't know are considerably greater than the number that I do. I don't even know where they were married, so church records aren't available as a source of information.'

'Then you won't know if she was married previously?'

'You need not spare my blushes. I have already said I must assume that I am illegitimate,' Celeste said brusquely. 'That is the only explanation for my mother's insistence that she had no family—everyone has family, hers obviously disowned her, and since she was a woman—' She broke off, struck by a sudden flash of memory. 'My mother once said to me that a woman's reputation was all she had. In her letter she wrote that the love she had for the man who sired me was the source of her downfall. The implications are clear enough.'

'Sired? You speak of your father as if he means nothing to you?'

'I obviously meant nothing to him. I am merely reciprocating his indifference.'

Jack picked up the letter again. '"Your father would have loved you, of that I am sure,"' he read. '"He too would have been proud of you."'

Celeste crossed her arms. 'That is the kind of soft soap a mother would write to console a bastard child, don't you think?'

Jack made no reply.

'You think that I am callous.'

'I think,' he said carefully, 'that perhaps your father never knew of your existence. "Your father *would have* loved you" is what your mother writes. *Would have*, implying he was for some reason prevented from having the opportunity to do so.'

It had not occurred to her to interpret her mother's words thus. A veteran of parental rejection, she had assumed that this was yet another case in point. Would her father have loved her? It didn't bear thinking about. 'It is hardly relevant,' Celeste said, steeling herself, 'since he is in all likelihood dead.'

Jack consulted the letter again. 'Your mother mentions "tragic consequences" resulting from the "impossible choice" she had to make?'

'Tragic can only mean a death. I think we must assume it refers to my natural father.' Saying it aloud brought a lump to Celeste's throat.

'Talking of fathers, tell me what you know of Henri Marmion.'

'I don't see what Henri has to do with anything.'

Jack sighed. 'Then it's as well you asked me to read this letter, because it's perfectly plain to me that he must have loved your mother a great deal. Think about the circumstances for a moment, Celeste. Your mother is in dire straits of some sort. She's alone, with an infant child and no family, in a strange country. By 1794, simply the fact that she was English would have put her on a list of suspicious characters, and it would have been impossible for her to escape France. To marry her was to take an enormous personal risk, and Marmion not only married her, but it sounds as though he cut himself off from his own friends and family in order to keep you both safe. A man doesn't do that unless he's deep in love or perhaps deep in debt.'

'He was a schoolteacher. He was a very educated man, but he taught at the village school. He could read and write Greek and Latin, he could quote so many of the Classics, but he—he hid his erudition. I could never understand it. One of the many things I could never fathom.'

'Did he ever mention his family?'

'Not that I remember, but then Henri rarely talked to me. I think he came from Cahors, in the south-west. I don't know how I remember that. His accent, perhaps.' Celeste shook her head, as if doing so would clear the tangled web that her past seemed to have become. 'He was so distant. I can't imagine that he was capable of love. I never saw any sign of affection between them. Besides, my mother claims to have loved my natural father. She made her choice for love, according to her letter.'

'Celeste, do you not think that makes Henri Marmion's behaviour more understandable rather than less so? To love, and never to have that love returned, would that not make a man distant? To see the evidence of his wife's true love in the form of her child—her only child—would that not eventually turn a loving husband into an embittered one?'

Celeste dropped her head on to her hands. 'Stop it! You are turning everything upside down. I don't know! *Dammit, I am not going to cry again.*'

She jumped to her feet, thumping her fist into her open palm, and paced over to the window. 'You know, I could count on the fingers of one hand the number of times I cried before I came to England. Even before boarding school, I learnt that tears were futile, and at school—well, you learn very quickly that it is better not to show weakness. And now I seem to be weeping constantly. Eight months since my mother died, and only now am I beginning to appreciate that she really is gone. It doesn't make sense.

'You can never understand, you with your

idyllic childhood here, growing up knowing how much you were loved, you can have no idea what it was like for me. Those miserable days at school, those cold little notes Maman wrote to me there about the weather, and the fishing, and—and nothing about her. Nothing about missing me. She didn't love me, I have known that for a long time.'

'I think she did.'

She jerked her head round to look at him. 'How can you possibly say that?'

'The locket. Worn round her neck every day of her life. Her only possession treasured enough to leave to you. Containing portraits of you and her, so close they are almost touching when the clasp is closed. A mother and her only daughter. Just because she never demonstrated her love doesn't mean it wasn't real. That locket tells me it was very real.'

Celeste dropped her head on to the cool of the window glass. When Jack put his arms around her waist, she resisted the urge to lean back into the comfort of his arms. She did not deserve comfort. This time the urge to confess outweighed the shame of what she must say. 'I had not seen her for a year before she died. The last time—the last time…'

She kept her eyes on the garden through the window glass which was misting over with her breath. 'Yesterday, when I said that she didn't give me a chance, it was a lie. Just after Henri died, Maman came to Paris. She told me that now she had done her duty by Henri, she wanted to heal the rift between us. I—I—I was angry with her. I told her that she had made her choice when she sent me off to boarding school at his behest. She did not protest very much. I presumed that the offer was more of a token than— No, I won't make excuses.'

Celeste turned around, facing Jack unflinchingly. 'I sent her packing. I could not forgive her for choosing Henri over me. When I was ten years old, I begged Maman not to send me away, but she chose to do what Henri wanted. Because she owed him our lives, she did as he asked, the letter says. Perhaps if I'd given her a chance that day in Paris, she would have explained it to me, but I did not. We were estranged for a long time but that last year, our estrangement was my fault alone. I feel such guilt. You would not understand such guilt. There is a part of me, you know, that thinks I deserve to suffer now. A part of me that thinks I do not deserve answers. Jack, I don't want you to be under the misapprehension that I'm an innocent victim.'

'Celeste, for God's sake, you had a lifetime's experience of her not explaining. You can't be thinking that what she did is your fault.'

'Can't I?'

'No.' Jack gave her a gentle shake. 'No. You don't know if it would have made any difference. You cannot know for certain if she would ever have trusted you enough.'

'Yes, I have tried to tell myself that. I am not a martyr. I have tried.' Celeste shook her head wearily. 'For months, trying, pretending, and until I came here it was working—I thought. But now I can't pretend.'

'Celeste, I repeat, it's not your fault.'

'Jack, you can't know that any more than I can. You don't understand...'

'I understand a damn sight more than you think.'

'Those soldiers you told me about, yes, but they were not your family. You were not directly responsible.' She bit her lip hard enough to draw blood. 'Perhaps this dark secret of Maman's would have sent her to her grave regardless of what I did. But there is the possibility that she might have confided in me if I had given her one last opportunity. It's possible that she might still be alive today as a result.'

'Speculation is pointless, it changes nothing.' Jack's tone was harsh. His fists were clenched. 'You can dig up the skeletons of your mother's past. They might be gruesome, or they might be nothing at all, but whatever they are, they cannot alter what happened. It was her act, not yours. You can't let the guilt destroy you.' His eyes went quite blank. 'You can never know if it would have made a difference. There are so many imponderables. If you had kept your mouth shut. If you had not been so determined to see for yourself. If you had not spilled your guts. If you had not—'

He broke off, staring at her as if she were a spectre. His expression frightened her in its intensity. 'You will never know, but if you keep asking, one thing is for certain. You will tear yourself apart. That much, I most certainly understand.'

Celeste stared at the door as it slammed shut behind him. She sank down on to the sofa. She felt as if she were seeing her life through a shattered mirror. Everything she thought she knew about herself had become distorted. The barrier which her mother had erected between them was bizarrely, in death, beginning to break down. In doing so, it was not only destroying Celeste's idea of her mother, it was destroying her notion of herself.

She curled up, squeezing her eyes closed, but the tears leaked out regardless. Was she tearing herself apart for no purpose? No, she had a purpose. She had to know. And when she did, she would bc healed, not broken.

And as for Jack? *If you had kept your mouth shut. If you had not been so determined to see for yourself. If you had not spilled your guts.* He had clearly been talking about himself. What had he been so determined to see? What did it mean, to spill his guts? Had he been ill? Or did he mean he had talked? Given away secrets?

'Non,' Celeste muttered. Jack was no traitor, on that she would stake her own life. Then what was Jack? 'I could as well ask, what is Celeste,' she muttered as exhaustion overtook her.

Jack sat at the window of his bedchamber, watching the grey light of dawn appear in the night sky and replaying his conversation with Celeste in his head for the hundredth time.

Guilt. From the moment she had told him that her mother had taken her own life, Jack had known that guilt would eventually overwhelm her. He'd hoped that by helping her quest for answers, he'd postpone its onset but it was already too late. After yesterday's confession, she wouldn't be able to ignore it.

Jack was something of a connoisseur of guilt and all its insidious manifestations. Eating away at you. Keeping you awake. Torturing your dreams. Turning you inside out. He couldn't bear thinking of Celeste suffering the same fate. Celeste, who had worked so hard to escape her miserable childhood and make her own world. Celeste who was so confident, and so independent and so strong.

And now so vulnerable. He couldn't bear to think of what it would do to her, if she did not find the answers she sought. But then he already knew. Guilt would consume her. *As it was consuming him?*

Feeling his chest tightening, Jack pushed open the window and gulped in the fresh air. Outside, the sky had turned from grey to a hazy pink. It was time for his early-morning swim. Pulling off his nightshirt, Jack grabbed his breeches and shirt. As he pulled the window closed, he noticed a flutter of white in the garden below. Celeste, hatless as usual. Her hair was piled carelessly on top of her head, long tendrils of it hanging down, as if she had not even bothered to look in the mirror. Her gown was cream coloured, with short puffs of sleeves and a scooped neck, accentuating the golden glow of her skin.

She was barefoot. He could see tantalising glimpses of her toes as she walked. The deep flounce of her gown was already wet with dew. She paused, lifting her face to the pale sun, closing her eyes. Had she slept? What was she thinking? She was so very lovely, and she looked so very fragile.

She made for the path which would lead her to the lake. Jack watched as she reached the gate, hesitated, then turned away. Giving way to a sudden impulse, he headed out of his bedchamber, descending the stairs three at a time, and ran out into the garden.

'Celeste!'

'Jack.' His bare feet left a line of footprints in the damp grass behind him. He was dressed in only his leather breeches and his shirt. His hair was in disarray and he hadn't shaved.

'I'm going for my swim.'

'Then that is the signal for me to make myself scarce.'

He smiled, pushing his hair back from his face. 'Actually, I wondered if you would care to join me?'

He looked tired. He looked devastatingly dishevelled. He looked as if he had just risen from bed. He made her think of rumpled sheets and tangled limbs. Their tangled limbs. 'Join you?' Celeste repeated, dragging her eyes away from the tantalising glimpse of chest she could see at the opening of his shirt.

'At the lake. To swim. Assuming you can swim, that is?'

'I was brought up on the coast. Of course I can swim,' Celeste said, and then the significance of his offer struck home. The lake at this time of the morning was Jack's private domain, his sanctuary. For him to offer to share it with her was hugely significant. 'No, I would be intruding. After the last time…'

'This is different. I am inviting you as my guest.'

He tucked a strand of her hair behind her ear. His smile made her insides flutter. She was weary of questioning and analysing her thoughts and motives. The urge to just *be*, to surrender to a whim was irresistible. 'Then I accept your kind invitation,' Celeste said. 'I am extremely flattered, since I know how important your privacy is to you. I would very much like to join you for a swim. I should warn you though, I am rather good.'

Jack laughed. 'I am not so very shabby myself,' he said, opening the gate for her. 'I've come on a bit since you last saw me in action.'

'I remember thinking that you swam like a fish that had drunk too much wine.'

'Not so much now. Perhaps one small glass of Madeira.'

The path to the lake was narrow and dark. The earth was cool against her bare feet. She had not swum for so long. She loved the water. She had not allowed herself to miss it. Now, seeing the glint of the lake in the early morning sunshine, Celeste felt her spirits rise in anticipation. The water was a strange colour, nothing like the sea. Golden and greenish, with a hint of brown. She stretched her arms high above her head, lifting her face to the warm English sun, and laughed with delight.

Jack pulled his shirt over his head. His muscles rippled. She caught her breath. He really was magnificent to look at. 'I think I'd best retain these,' he said, indicating his breeches.

Celeste had been so intent upon the swim, she hadn't considered the delicate matter of attire. In Cassis, she had always swum naked. She loved the feel of the ocean on her skin. But in Cassis, she had always swum alone. She had never swum in the company of a man, and this man— She dragged her eyes away again.

'Changed your mind?'

Celeste shook her head. 'Go in. I will follow you but don't look.'

Jack laughed. 'I never make promises I can't keep,' he said, turning his back and beginning to wade into the water.

She watched him dive, and then swim strongly towards the far side. He barely laboured at all. His strength had all but returned. Celeste went behind the very hawthorn bush where she'd hidden that first day, and began to undress, quickly removing her gown, her corset and her petticoats. She was left wearing only her pantaloons and camisole. It was not an ideal outfit for bathing but she could not countenance the alternative.

She picked her way across the pebbles into the shallows of the lake. Jack was at the far side again, swimming steadily. The water felt warm on her toes, the mud oozed around her feet in a not unpleasant manner. She waded in and gasped as the cool water soaked through her thin camisole and met her skin. Jack turned and began to head back towards her. Hurriedly, Celeste waded out, until the water was waist high, and then she dived into the cool water with relish and began to swim. It was not at all like the waters of Cassis, this English lake, but there was still that marvellous feeling of freedom. She struck out more strongly, heading for the opposite bank, kicking her legs behind her, and just before it became too shallow, she turned and began to swim back, passing Jack on the way.

She swam until her muscles protested, and then she turned over and floated, her eyes closed, careless of the mud and twigs and leaves tangling in her hair. For the first time since Maman had died, she felt relaxed, weightless, free. It was all still there, but it could wait. It could all wait. Rolling over to make her way back to shore, she saw Jack standing waist deep in the water, watching her.

She waded towards him. 'I think I have most of your brother's lake in my hair.'

'Did you enjoy that?'

'Oh—so, so much.' Celeste beamed at him. 'I had forgotten how swimming— It makes you forget everything.' Her smile faded. 'Is that why you…?'

'Yes. And for this.' Jack indicated his arm.

Celeste touched the puckered skin gently. 'Does it still hurt?'

'Not really.'

Sunlight danced on the water and in her eyes. Droplets of lake water clung to the rough smattering of hair on Jack's chest. Her camisole was plastered to her body like a second skin, making it completely transparent. Her nipples were hard and puckered with the cold, and clearly visible. Jack's eyes were riveted on them. She did not feel embarrassed. In fact she felt emboldened. Desire twisted inside her. Jack's eyes met hers. She stepped towards him. His arms went around her waist. His chest was surprisingly warm. It was not like before. No flare of anger to propel them towards each other. This time it was slow, a different kind of heat. She tilted her head. Sunlight dazzled her eyes until Jack's head blocked it, and his lips met hers.

Different. He tasted of lake. Cool. Tentative.

Like a first kiss. A gentle tasting, the sweetest of touches. Slow. A kiss with no purpose but to kiss. And to kiss. And then to kiss again. She wrapped her arms around his neck. He pulled her closer. Kissing. Only kissing. Her arousal was languid, melting, none of the fierce flames of before. She could kiss him for ever. This was the kind of kiss that would never end. Lips and tongues in a slow dance. Hands smoothing, stroking. Skin clinging, damp, heating.

Jack traced the line of her throat with butterfly kisses. He kissed the damp valley between her breasts. His mouth sought hers again, and their lips clung, still slowly, but deeper now. She kissed the pucker of his musket wound. She flattened her palms over the swell of his chest. His hands covered her breasts, making her nipples ache. The sweetest of aches, the gentlest but most insistent tugging of desire, making her sigh, and then making her moan.

She'd thought it was too much before. But this was too different. The dazed look in his eyes, his lack of resistance when she disentangled herself, told her he felt it too.

'Thank you,' she said gently, 'for the swim.' She began to wade ashore. She had hauled her gown over her wet undergarments and was wrapping the rest of her clothing into a bundle when Jack re-joined her. They walked slowly back to the Manor together in silence, words for once superfluous.

Chapter Seven

'A very proper, very English young lady.' Celeste repeated, looking blankly at Jack. They were in the studio, where she had been laying out her preliminary drawings to allow Lady Eleanor and Sir Charles to make their final selections, before she began the task of painting the actual canvases. 'You think that my mother was of genteel stock?'

Jack nodded. He had taken a seat across from her at the table. In the two days which had passed since their early-morning swim, they had both been careful not to mention it or the kiss which had followed. Though as far as Celeste was concerned, it hung in the air, almost palpably, every time she looked at him.

She shuffled a bundle of rejected sketches,

quite unnecessarily. 'What makes you come to this conclusion?'

Jack tapped his pencil on the notebook in front of him. 'A number of little things. Hasn't it ever struck you as odd, for example, that the wife of a school teacher would employ a cook?'

'I've never given it much thought. It's just how things were.'

'Then there's this school you attended in Paris. It sounds as if it was a good one.'

Celeste frowned. 'The girls were from good families. Titled, mostly, or very wealthy. Or both. That was one of the problems I had to deal with, being neither.'

'You mean you were bullied?' Jack's hand tightened on his pencil. 'I don't know why, but I assumed that sort of thing was confined to boys.'

'If you mean fighting, then it most likely is. Girls are more subtle,' Celeste said grimly. 'It doesn't matter, I learned to hold my own. Besides, I cannot believe it was really so grand a school,' she rushed on, having no desire to recall how effective the bullying had been. 'We were not permitted a fire except in the dead of winter and then never in the dormitory. And the bedΔsheets were almost threadbare. It was hardly luxurious.'

'Which confirms my point,' Jack said with a tight smile. 'My so-called exclusive prep school had dormitories that would have delighted a Spartan. Such privations don't come cheap. Then there is her knowledge of dinner-party etiquette. And the comment about—what was it—a woman's reputation. Your mother could draw and paint, but she couldn't cook. Could she sew?'

'She taught me to embroider.'

'Precisely.'

Jack looked pleased. Celeste was unconvinced. 'I never thought much about my mother's origins. Why should I, when Maman was so determined that she had none? She would have preferred me to believe she had been baked like dough in an oven.' Blind baked, Celeste added to herself, a brittle pastry with a hard crust.

She pushed back her chair and went over to her favourite spot at the window. Was she being unfair? Maman had been cold, distant, aloof. Certainly stern, and yet at other times she had looked...

Just as Jack had done that first morning at the lake.

Despair? Anguish? Whatever label one put on it, it was obvious now that her mother had indeed suffered. And she, Celeste, had been oblivious to it. All the signs had been right in front of her nose, and she had not noticed them. She shook her head in disgust at herself. 'I have been an idiot! For an artist, quite the blind woman. Thinking I was the poor little schoolgirl, when really it was a case of all the other little schoolgirls being so very rich.'

Her fingers went to the locket around her neck. 'That's another thing,' Jack said almost apologetically. 'I doubt very much that your locket is a trinket. In fact I think you'll find it's made of diamonds and sapphire, not glass. There's a maker's mark. I'll show you.'

Celeste took the locket off obediently. There it was. She looked at the portraits inside, painted in such a way that her mother gazed across at her. Lovingly? Her mother, who had claimed in her last letter, that she had always loved her. Was this locket proof as Jack said? Celeste found this almost impossible to believe.

Almost? She touched the miniature of her mother with the tip of her finger, an echo of

Jack's gesture with his own mother's picture in the portrait gallery, she realised. But his had been one of unmistakable affection and love. Was hers?

She looked up, smiling faintly at Jack. 'You have given me a great deal to think about,' she said, snapping the locket shut.

A rap on the door heralded the arrival of her patrons. Celeste quickly made the final touches to her arrangement of sketches, ensuring the ones she favoured were most prominent, but when the door opened, it was to reveal Lady Eleanor alone.

'My husband sends his apologies, *Mademoiselle*, he will be unable to join us this morning, but he desired me to make some preliminary selections from your work. I trust this is satisfactory?'

Without waiting for an answer, her ladyship made straight for the table where the sketches were laid out and began sifting through them. Jack cast Celeste an eloquent glance, and began unobtrusively to push the preferred drawings towards his brother's wife.

'Of course, these are just very rudimentary sketches to give you an idea of what the finished work would look like,' Celeste said, 'but I hope they are sufficient to allow you to make some decisions on the sequence in which you would like me to paint the formal gardens.'

Lady Eleanor examined the sketches carefully. It had always amused Celeste to witness her patrons' reactions at this stage. Seeing their estates spread out before them on paper almost always made them view their properties afresh, made them somehow grander, more magnificent, which in turn added to their own sense of consequence.

Lady Eleanor was no different. 'I must say, I had not appreciated the epic sweep of the estate. You have managed to cover a great deal of ground in a very short time.'

'Thank you. Monsieur Trestain has been most helpful. He has an excellent eye for the most pleasing views.'

'Well, it is comforting to know that he has managed to occupy himself gainfully,' Lady Eleanor said pointedly. 'I expect you, *Mademoiselle*, being a—a woman of the world are rather more equipped to deal with Jack's outbursts than a child. Robert,' she continued, addressing Jack directly, 'was sobbing his little heart out the other day after his encounter with you.'

Jack blanched. Celeste felt her fists curl. 'If you do not mind me saying,' she said, 'when Jack refused Robert's request in a perfectly reasonable manner, it was the child who threw the tantrum, not Jack.'

'Celeste.' Jack held up his hand to quiet her. 'I am very sorry if I upset Robert, Eleanor.'

'My son, like all small boys, is obsessed with all things military,' her ladyship replied, her stiff manner giving way to a plaintive one. 'He would hang on your every word for a first-hand account of Waterloo. Your brother tells me I must try to stop him bothering you, but Robert is such a naturally inquisitive little chap.'

'He reminds me very much of Charlie at that age,' Jack said. 'Mad keen on fishing.'

'And equally eager to hear his uncle's account of what is our nation's greatest victory. No disrespect intended, *Mademoiselle*. Really, Jack, is that too much to ask? Frankly, I'm at a loss to fathom you these days. I remember a time when you were more than happy to sit up until dawn, regaling Charles with your exploits. I know you are still recovering from your wounds, and that we must all make allowances for your—your— For the anguish you are suffering at having witnessed the deaths of so many of your comrades, but…'

'Is that what Charlie thinks it is?' Jack shook his head when Lady Eleanor made to answer. 'No matter. I am sorry to have upset him, but I cannot— The days of my boasting of my army exploits are over, Eleanor, but I am more than happy to take Robert fishing instead.'

'But I do not see…' Making an obvious effort, Lady Eleanor bit back her remonstration. 'That is kind of you, Jack.'

'It is nothing. I do care for the boy, you know, regardless of how it may appear.' Jack picked up some of Celeste's sketches. 'In the meantime, let us concentrate on your selections. Look at this study of the Topiary Garden. Do you not think that it is a great shame to have it cut down? When you see it afresh like this, through *Mademoiselle*'s clever eye, it really is quite lovely and wants only a little tidying up to bring it back to its former glory.'

'Rather more than a little tidying up,' Lady Eleanor replied, 'and it is so very gloomy.'

Jack picked up another view of the Topiary Garden. 'Look at this, though. Mademoiselle Marmion was telling me that though she's painted some of the grandest estates in France, the Trestain Manor Topiary Garden is one of the finest examples she has ever seen.'

Lady Eleanor looked doubtfully at the sketch. 'Really? I had no idea. Is this true, *Mademoiselle*?'

'Why, yes,' Celeste replied, intensely relieved that Jack had managed to turn the subject. 'In France, the art of topiary is much admired. The best examples attract admirers from all over the country. I think that your garden, with only a few changes, could do the same.'

'You would be leading the way for England,' Jack said. 'Your good sense in preserving the garden will be appreciated by generations of Trestains to come. Think about that, Eleanor.'

Her ladyship did, rewarding Celeste with a tight smile. 'I wonder, *Mademoiselle*, if it is not too much trouble, if you could perhaps give me the benefit of your artistic eye and suggest a few enhancements. I can then discuss them with Sir Charles and our landscaper. Awarding you full credit for your contribution of course.'

Celeste nodded, slanting Jack a complicit smile. Lady Eleanor continued to sift through the drawings, laying a small selection to one side which, Celeste was pleased to note, contained most of her own favourites.

'These are really very good, *Mademoiselle*,' she said, sounding as if she meant it. 'I am most pleased. Sir Charles will make the final selection tomorrow. You will excuse me now, I must go and speak to cook. Your Aunt Christina's long-awaited annual gift of a haunch of prime Highland venison has finally arrived, Jack. Something of a family tradition, *Mademoiselle*,' she added by way of explanation. 'Every year we have a special banquet when it arrives. We will be celebrating the occasion tonight.'

Jack shifted uncomfortably, looking not at all enamoured by the prospect.

'Your brother,' Lady Eleanor said, 'will be very much gratified by your presence. I believe that your aunt, in the accompanying letter, was most eager for you to partake of the beast, and particularly requested that Charles give her an account of the dinner—for it seems she has no hope of a letter from you.'

'I have had my arm in a splint these past two months, Eleanor, in case it has escaped your attention.'

Her ladyship turned to Celeste, ignoring this

remark. 'Mademoiselle Marmion, I will entreat you to use any influence you have with Jack. Is it really so much to ask that he joins us *en famille* for a special dinner sent all the way from Scotland by his favourite relative?'

Celeste, taken aback by Lady Eleanor's consulting her on any subject save art, found herself shaking her head.

'You see? Mademoiselle Marmion agrees,' her ladyship said, turning back to Jack.

'I don't think...'

But Celeste's role had, it seemed, been played. 'It is not as if we are even holding the usual grand banquet,' Lady Eleanor said. 'Not a single guest. Not even our closest neighbours. I told Charles that they would be most offended, but he said he cared nothing for any guest save you. So I take it you will not be letting him down?'

'Oh, for God's sake, Eleanor, what a damned—dashed fuss over a bite of dinner. Yes,' Jack said, 'I'll be there. Satisfied?'

'Your brother will be, and that is what matters to me. You too are cordially invited of course, Mademoiselle Marmion. Until tonight, then.'

Lady Eleanor swept from the studio. Jack

stared at the door, his jaw working. 'It is just dinner,' Celeste said tentatively. 'Though I am surprised Lady Eleanor thinks me worthy of your aunt's precious venison.'

Jack grimaced. 'Obviously, she assumes that your presence makes the chances of my attendance more likely.'

Celeste coloured. 'Have we been indiscreet?' Her colour deepened. 'You do not think that someone saw us at the lake the other morning?' It was the first time either of them had mentioned it. She wished immediately she had not. Unlike those other kisses, the memory of this one was not inflammatory, but bittersweet.

'No,' Jack said, 'I'm sure no one saw us. It's one of the things I like about that place, it's completely private.'

'Unless someone hides behind a hawthorn tree.'

Jack's smile was twisted. 'As with so many things, you are the exception that proves the rule.'

Their eyes met and held. He reached out to touch her cheek. She turned her head. Her lips brushed his palm.

'Celeste.' His voice was filled with the same longing she felt. He took a step towards her, then halted. 'You must be keen to get to work, now Eleanor has made some decisions. I will see you at this blasted dinner.'

Confused, frustrated, as much by her own reaction as Jack's, Celeste turned her back on the closed door and set about stretching some canvases.

Jack put the final touches to his cravat. It was not perfect, but it would do. At times like this, he missed his faithful army batman, but Alfred was happily ensconced many hundreds of miles away as the landlord of the Bricklayer's Arms in Leeds, and besides, the last thing Jack really wanted was proximity to any of his former comrades. Still, no one could tie a cravat like Alfred.

He pulled on his waistcoat. Grey satin stripes, and one of his best. Quite wasted in the country, but Eleanor would appreciate the effort he was making. As she'd appreciate the formality of his cutaway black coat and silk breeches. They were considerably looser on him than the last time he'd worn them to the now-infamous ball held by Lady Richmond on the eve of Waterloo. He closed his eyes, but it seemed a set of evening clothes, even one

with such associations, did not trigger anything other than a vague discomfort, and that
was coming from his shoes, which had always
pinched.

Perhaps he was on the mend, mentally as
well as physically? Perhaps this thing, this nostalgia, whatever the hell it was, would heal, as
his shoulder was doing, and his arm.

'Nostalgia,' Jack said viciously as he
shrugged himself into his coat. Such a soft,
comfortable little word to describe what he felt.
Was it all in his head? But the pain, the tearing blackness, the white heat of his uncontrol-
lable fury, the terror that made him run from
himself, the sweats and the shakes, and the dull
ache in his head, they were all too real.

'I am *not* mad.' He jumped as the porcelain
dish containing his cuff-links clattered to the
floor. It was not broken, thank the Lord. He
picked up the scattered links, replacing the dish
carefully. If he was insane he wouldn't recognise or understand what it was that made him
feel the way he did. And that, he understood
only too well. How could he fail too when he
lived through it again and again, almost every
night without fail?

Seated at the dressing table, a brush in one

hand, he stared at his reflection. What he didn't understand was that for two years he had functioned reasonably well. The dream had been sporadic. He'd carried on doing what he'd always done. True, there had been doubts, but none strong enough to stop him doing his duty, stop him believing that doing his duty was paramount. Only after Waterloo, when peace was indisputable, when war was over, had his symptoms escalated.

And only after Celeste arrived at Trestain Manor, had he had to cope with not only enduring the symptoms, but confronting the fact that they were in danger of ruining his life.

A flicker of rebellion kindled in his heart. He didn't want to spend his life enduring. He wanted to have his life *back*. Not the old one, that was gone for ever, but something preferable to this shadow of a life. Celeste sent his head spinning, she forced him to face a good many unpalatable truths, but she also sent blood rushing to parts of him he'd thought dormant. It frightened him, the thought of giving free reign to the passion she ignited, because he had retained such a tight grip on himself for so long, it was almost impossible for him to think about letting go.

Almost. Jack picked up his other brush and set about taming his hair. Almost was better than completely. Instead of dreading tonight, what he needed to do was to see it as a test. A possible step forward on the road to recovery.

Celeste was nervous, though she couldn't account for it. She stood clutching the obligatory small glass of Madeira wine, half-listening to Sir Charles recount a complicated anecdote which seemed to involve a miller, his wife, the village baker, a neighbouring magistrate and, if her ears were not deceiving her, a wheel of Stilton cheese. Celeste took another sip of the sweet wine and smoothed down her gown. It was one of her plainest, of russet-coloured crêpe with a deep V-shaped neckline and high puffed sleeves, the only embellishment being a corded sash tied around the high waistline. Lady Eleanor was dressed far more elaborately in lilac lace. Sir Charles was in full evening dress for the first time since her arrival. Obviously, Auntie Kirsty's haunch of venison demanded a major effort be made to mark the auspicious occasion. She now regretted her understated choice of attire.

Jack entered the salon just as Lady Eleanor was consulting the clock on the mantel for the third time. He too wore full evening dress. His hair was tamed ruthlessly, his jaw freshly shaved. The deceptively simple cut of his coat, the stark black of the silk suited him. As he strode across the room to bow over Lady Eleanor's hand, Celeste could not help comparing the two brothers, so similarly attired, and so very different. Sir Charles was probably more classically handsome, but Jack's imperfections, his austere countenance, were what made him, in Celeste's eyes, by far the more attractive of the two. She remembered thinking that first day, when she had watched him swimming naked in the lake, that he looked like a man who courted danger.

Heat flooded through her. She should not be thinking of him naked, especially not when he was bowing over her hand. Celeste dipped a formal curtsy, lowering her head to hide her flush. *'Monsieur.'*

'Mademoiselle. You look beautiful as ever.'

'And you too look very handsome.' Though now she studied him, she thought he looked tense. There was no time to pursue the cause of this, however, for at that moment Lady Eleanor's footman sounded a gong, Sir Charles took his wife's hand and led the small procession out into the hall and across into the dining room.

Jack was seated opposite her. Sir Charles led the conversation which was primarily concerned with previous haunches of venison and the large parties at which they had been consumed.

'I hope you've not deprived your neighbours of their annual treat on account of me,' Jack said to Eleanor. 'After all, it's not as if I've been able to attend more than twice in the last dozen years, while they looked forward to it every year.'

'Well, to be honest, Jack, we did not think—'

'What Eleanor means is that we thought it would be cosier to keep it to just the family,' Sir Charles interrupted hurriedly.

Jack put down his wine glass carefully. 'Cosier,' he said with a cold smile. 'I see.'

Sir Charles rubbed his hands together. 'Good. Excellent. It is— You must know, Jack, it is good to see you at the table.'

'You fret about me too much, Charlie.' Jack pushed his glass aside. 'I've heard reports in the village that it's going to be a bumper harvest. What do you say?'

His brother was no fool, but as he was,

Celeste had noted several times, most definitely a man who avoided confrontation, he was therefore happy to be diverted. Lady Eleanor's footmen brought in a procession of side dishes. Her ladyship supervised the placing of each, and the brothers chatted about crops. At least, Sir Charles talked, and Jack prompted, saying just enough to keep the conversation ticking over.

The first of the side dishes was already going cold when the door was held open by one footman, and two more entered the dining room bearing an enormous copper platter. Celeste, who was by now rather hungry, felt her mouth watering. The aroma coming from the venison was delicious. The meat looked succulent. Across from her, she caught Jack's hand curling tightly around the stem of his glass, though he quickly put it down when he noticed her watching him.

She couldn't understand what was wrong with him. The platter was placed in front of Sir Charles, who made a great show of sharpening the carving knife on a stcel before picking up the fork. Blood and juices trickled from the roast haunch as he began to carve through the charred skin.

A footman placed a side dish in front of Jack. A silver tureen containing vegetable broth of some sort, redolent with the herbs of Provence. Surprised, Celeste turned to Lady Eleanor. 'What is that dish? It smells exactly like home,' she said.

'Indeed,' her ladyship said, gratified. 'I had cook concoct it as a small gesture to make you feel welcome. I discovered it in a receipt book belonging to Sir Charles's mother. She was Scottish, you know. I believe the Scots have a great affinity with you French. The Auld Alliance, I believe it is—good heavens, Jack, what on earth is the matter?'

He had turned a deathly pale. As he pushed his chair back, he caught the dish of broth and sent it flying from the footman's hand. Jack got to his feet, clutching the table and swaying. His skin now had a greenish hue. He was staring at the venison, his eyes dark with horror.

'Dear lord, I think he is going to be ill, Charles,' Lady Eleanor exclaimed, turning rather green herself. 'Charles. Charles!'

Her husband jumped to his feet at the same time as Celeste pushed back her chair and got to hers. Jack swayed. He looked as if he was about to crumple, but when his brother tried to put his arm around him, he swatted it away and began to lurch for the door, his mouth over his hand. Celeste reached him as he clutched the handle. He pushed her to one side and threw himself out into the hallway and from there out of the front door and into the night air.

Another sleepless night, this one thanks not to his dream but to his lingering and complete mortification. Jack had not actually been physically ill last night. He was trying very hard to see that as some sort of progress, but as he had lain sleepless and sweating in his bed, he replayed the entire hideous scene over and over, to the point where he had thought himself beyond embarrassment. If the dinner had been a test, he'd failed it spectacularly.

Unable to face anyone, knowing he must eventually face them all, he had been wandering aimlessly around the grounds for hours. Exhausted, hungry but unable to contemplate eating, he was instead contemplating retiring to his bed when the sound of voices drifted out through the long French window which gave on to Celeste's studio.

'Yes, yes, these are all excellent, *Mademoiselle*,' he heard Charlie say.

His brother was giving his approval to the selection of sketches to be painted. They would all three of them be there. It was an ideal opportunity for Jack to make himself scarce, but he found himself instead positioned behind a trellis which obscured him, but also afforded a view into the studio. It was inevitable that the subject of the dinner would come up. What would their take on it be? Information was the best of ammunition after all. It seemed old habits died hard.

Charlie, unlike his wife, who had studied each of Celeste's sketches with a great deal of care, gave each a fairly cursory glance, and seemed indiscriminately happy with every one of them. Standing beside him, Celeste, looking pale, with dark circles under her eyes, was struggling to give her patron her full attention. Her gaze drifted over to the window.

Jack froze, though she could not possibly see him. It was ridiculous to be hiding here. He should join them. His feet refused to comply. He wondered fleetingly if this was how Celeste had felt that day—which seemed like months ago—when she had watched him swimming.

Charlie was looking at a view of the lake now. No, he had selected one. Now he was dithering between two views of the Topiary Garden, and Jack could see Celeste making a huge effort not to try to steer him towards the one she herself preferred. She smiled when he opted for it, and pushed the pinery sketches towards him.

'Yes. Excellent.' Charlie rubbed his hands together again, a sure sign he was nervous. 'I wonder if I may be so bold, *Mademoiselle*,' he said, 'as to enquire how you find my brother?'

Jack's hackles rose. Celeste looked wary. 'I am not sure what you mean. He has been most helpful.'

'Yes, yes. I can see that.' Charlie pursed his lips. 'It cannot have escaped your notice, *Mademoiselle*, that my brother is not quite— That he is not— That in short, he is rather out of sorts. On occasion.'

'He has been wounded. I think his arm has given him a great deal of pain. What do you think of this vista, Sir Charles?'

Charlie ignored the proffered sketch. 'It amounts to more than tetchiness, *Mademoiselle*. More than the residual pain from a wound now healed. Last night —for heaven's sake, you witnessed what occurred last night. What in the name of all that's sacred was that about, do you think?'

Celeste blanched. 'I don't know. I was as much— I don't know.'

Charlie threw the sketch down. 'The time has come to stop beating about the bush. My wife and I are at our wits' end. We have tried but we seem singularly ill equipped to help him, *Mademoiselle*, indeed I think we unintentionally exacerbate matters.'

Jack strained forward. Charlie was leaning over Celeste. Celeste, hindered by the table, was bending backwards. 'I am fain to embroil you in a private family matter,' his brother said, 'but it has struck both my wife and myself that you seem to be able to...well, to influence Jack in a way we cannot.'

'*Monsieur*, Sir Charles, I do not...'

'You do. He listens to you. Eleanor says that it was only at your behest that he finally consented to come to dinner last night.'

'No.' Celeste flushed. 'That is, I might have— But it was very wrong of me. Jack was eager to please you too, *Monsieur*—Sir Charles. He is not— He— I should not have—'

'What sparked such an extreme reaction out of the blue like that—that's what I want to know. It can't go on, that much is certain.'

Clearly agitated now, Charlie thumped his

fist on the table. Jack felt his own fists curl. Appalled, sick to the stomach and furious, he forced himself to listen.

'He used to be the most even-tempered of chaps,' Charlie was saying, 'and now one must constantly be treading on eggshells around him. He barely eats. He hardly sleeps. I don't know how many times the chambermaid has reported some piece of broken china from his bedchamber. Then there is the way he— He— Our little boy, Robert.'

'You remember, Mademoiselle Marmion was witness to one of those episodes in the portrait gallery the other day, my love.'

'Lady Eleanor, I really do think that your son—'

'I hate to say it,' Charlie interrupted again. 'It pains me a great deal to say it, but I must protect my child from upset or worse. Last night, you will admit, *Mademoiselle*, that Jack was quite out of control?'

'He was— I admit he was not himself.'

Celeste! It was like a punch in the gut. Jack closed his eyes, only to find himself immediately swamped with the smell of that damned soup and the ferrous tang of bloody meat and scorched flesh. He swayed, clutching at the trellis for support. He opened his eyes. Deep breaths. More.

It was as if he was watching a play, the voices booming and fading, his own vision wavering. Celeste was wringing her hands. Charlie was tirading. Celeste was shaking her head. Jack shook his like a dog after a swim.

'We don't know,' Charlie was saying. 'That's the nub of it, we simply don't know. My brother is not the man he was. I hoped we could help him. Fresh country air, good food, that sort of thing. But he is getting worse. We don't know what he will do next, and I'm not sure we can afford to wait and see. I would suggest he see a medical man, one who specialises in matters of the mind, but…but dear God, I cannot contemplate having my brother confined.'

Confined? Stunned, Jack wondered if he'd misheard.

'Confined!' Celeste went quite still. 'Sir Charles, are you saying that you believe Jack— Monsieur Trestain is—is of unsound mind?'

Silence greeted this remark. Jack waited, every muscle clenched so tight his jaw ached. Charlie shuffled his feet. He rubbed his hands together. He cast Eleanor an anguished look. Then he sighed. 'I must confess with a heavy heart that I fear it may be the case,' he said, and Jack, with a growl of fury, launched himself through the French doors and into the studio.

Lady Eleanor screamed. Sir Charles froze in mid-sentence. Jack's expression was thunderous and extremely intimidating, but instead of cowering, Celeste caught herself at the last moment and stood her ground.

He looked wild. His eyes were stormy. His fingers were furling and unfurling into fists. 'I am of a certainty *not* mad, Charlie.'

'I didn't say—'

'You did.' Jack took a menacing step towards his brother. Sir Charles shrank back. '"I must confess…I fear it may be the case" is what you said.'

'Yes, and I also said it was with a very heavy heart I did so,' Charlie countered.

'You should not have been listening in to a private conversation,' Lady Eleanor said primly. 'Eavesdroppers, it is well known, never hear any good of themselves.'

'Eavesdropping is one of the many things I was required to do to protect my country,' Jack said, rounding on her with a snarl. 'A duty

I discharged assiduously. Would you rather I had not?'

Her ladyship blanched, but Jack turned his attention back to his brother. 'Tell me I am not mad, Charlie.'

'Well, you must admit, you're not precisely stable, old chap,' Sir Charles said, accompanied by a feeble attempt at a smile, in an utterly misguided attempt to inject humour into the situation.

Jack recoiled, whirling around to face Celeste. 'And you! You must think it too, else you would not have asked the question in the first place. You, of all people! I thought...'

'Jack...' Celeste took hold of his arm and gave it a shake '...Jack, you must know that I don't think...'

He shook her off. He staggered against a gilt-leafed side table. The bowl of dried flowers which sat on it clattered to the ground and smashed. He stared at them all blankly.

Celeste took hold of his arm once again. 'Jack.'

He removed her fingers gently. 'Let me alone.' He straightened his shoulders and marched towards the door. It closed behind him gently.

Chapter Eight

'Why did you say that he was not stable?' Celeste turned furiously on Sir Charles. 'You could not have said anything more damaging had you tried. Jack has not lost his mind, but a part of him is afraid he might. *Eh, bien*, he asks his only brother for a little reassurance and what does he get?'

Sir Charles looked shocked to the core. 'I did not intend— I would never— With respect, *Mademoiselle*, you have been here a matter of days. Eleanor and I have been living with this situation for months. We have tried ignoring him, we have tried pretending nothing is wrong, and now we have tried confronting him. You saw the effect. I am most—most— I am extremely concerned about my brother.'

Lady Eleanor put a comforting hand on her

husband's arm. 'Sir Charles has only his brother's best interests at heart. This has been a terrible strain for all of us. I am as shaken as my husband by Jack's decline. We have the advantage over you, *Mademoiselle*, of knowing Jack before this—this change. You must believe me when I tell you it is drastic. And then there is our son.'

'Jack loves Robert, *Madame*—Lady Eleanor. That is precisely why he doesn't want to fill his head with the barbarity of war. You asked me how I *found* Jack. Well, I will tell you, for what it is worth. I think he is a deeply unhappy man, and also a very brave one. I think that he has seen and done things that none of us can even imagine. Things so horrific he cannot sleep for thinking of it. All this, he has done unquestioningly in the name of you and your country and your little boy. I think he deserves better than to be told by his own flesh and blood that he is mad. That is what I think. Now, if you'll excuse me, I'm going to find him.'

'But, *Mademoiselle*, Jack made it very clear he wanted to be left alone, I don't think…'

Ignoring Sir Charles, Celeste made her way out of the French window, and quickly across the stretch of lawn. She wondered if she had managed for the first time ever to get herself dismissed from a commission, but she could not, at this moment, bring herself to care. She did not know where Jack had gone but she had a pretty good idea where to start looking.

He was sitting on a rock, casting pebbles into the lake, his expression forbidding. Celeste was tempted, for a moment, to turn tail. Perhaps Sir Charles was right, and it would be best to leave him alone. She had no idea what to say. She had no idea what was wrong with Jack, but she had missed the chance once before, to try to comfort a person in torment, and she was not going to repeat the mistake by running away from a similar situation.

'Did Charlie send you to check on me?' he demanded as she sat down cautiously on the boulder beside him. 'Not brave enough to come himself, I suppose.'

'He thought you would be best left alone.'

Jack threw another pebble into the water. 'He was right.'

Celeste forced herself to remain seated.

Jack threw another pebble forcefully into the water. 'I won't harm myself, if that's what you're worried about. I would not inflict *that* on Charlie, on top of everything else, so you can leave with a clear conscience.'

He was angry. He was embarrassed, no doubt. He was obviously much more hurt than he cared to let on. He didn't mean it. Still, his barb hit painfully home. Celeste flinched.

Jack swore. 'I'm sorry. God, I'm sorry. That was a foul thing to say to you, of all people.'

'Yes, it was.'

Jack cast another pebble. 'Is that why you're here? Do you think I would...?'

'No. And nor does Sir Charles, before you ask.'

'Small compensation, when my own brother thinks I need to be locked up in Bedlam.'

'Your brother is *worried* about you. He doesn't know how best to help you.'

Jack threw the small bundle of remaining pebbles he had into the lake and jumped to his feet. 'Do you not think that if I knew of some cure for what ails me I'd have taken it by now? Do you think I enjoy being like this? Have you any idea what it's like for me to be so—so at the whim of emotions I can't control? Me! Discipline and order is what my life's been about until now. Men and information, that's what I deal in. I turn men into soldiers. I turn meaningless jumbles of letters and numbers into sequences and patterns. That's what I do, Celeste—that's what I did. Not any more. Now I can't make sense of anything.'

He turned away from her, pinching the bridge of his nose viciously between his thumb and forefinger. What he said resonated so strongly with her, she was tempted to tell him so, but what good would it do, to tell him that she too felt as if the world made no sense any more? 'I think you do understand some things, though,' she said. 'Whatever it was at dinner that made you sick, you knew it would. That's why you avoid dinner.'

'And would have avoided it again last night were it not for you.' He turned on her, his eyes flashing fury.

'That's not fair. I did not know you...'

'No, you didn't, but you smiled that winsome smile of yours, and you looked at me with those big brown eyes and you made it impossible for me to say no.'

She knew he was simply trying to hurt her, lashing out like a wounded animal, but the in-justice of this was too much. 'I did no such thing!' Celeste jumped to her feet. 'I don't have a winsome smile. I am not a fool. I look in the mirror, and I see I have the kind of face men find attractive, but I am not— I have never, ever, been one of those women who use a mere quirk of nature to manipulate people. *Never*.'

Jack swore again. 'I'm sorry,' he snapped, sounding anything but. 'Very well, you did not force me into that damned dinner, but if it had not been that, it would have been something else.'

'What do you mean by that?' Celeste folded her arms and glared at him.

'You,' Jack said. 'From the moment I first saw you, you've tormented me. Spying on me. Kissing me. Goading me. Tempting me. As if I didn't have enough to keep me awake at nights without torturing myself with visions of you, of us. I can barely keep my hands off you. I've never been that sort of man before. I've never lost my temper with Robert before. I've never come so near to spilling my guts on the dinner table before. And what is the common factor in all this? You.'

'That is completely outrageous! I could say the exact same thing of you. You make me feel as if I am some sort of—of insatiable temptress,' Celeste exclaimed. 'And look at me now, screeching like a fishwife. I never shout.

I never cry. I never have any difficulty whatsoever in keeping my hands and my lips and my body to myself. I am a calm person, I am a cold person, even, and yet with you…' She threw her hands into the air.

'You realise how ridiculous you sound,' Jack said.

Even through her temper, she did. Celeste bit her lip and tried to glower.

He sighed. 'How ridiculous we both sound.'

She took a tentative step towards him. 'I didn't come here to harangue you. I'm sorry.'

'I deserved it.' Jack managed a wry smile. 'You are most definitely not the kind of woman who uses her charms to get her own way. I went to dinner last night of my own accord. It was a sort of test. Which I failed rather spectacularly.'

Celeste took another step towards him. 'What happened, Jack?'

He stared out over the lake. He picked up a stone, then let if fall. 'It's just— There are smells. Certain smells.'

'The blood! You mean the blood from the meat?'

'No. No, it's not the blood. I've seen too much blood for it to be— Not on its own.' He picked up another stone and began to turn it over and over in his hands. 'I thought it might be. Eleanor is very fond of serving up roast beef, charred and bloody in the English tradition, so I do tend to avoid that, just in case...' He closed his eyes momentarily. 'But I would have been fine last night, I think, if it hadn't been for the stew she had specially made for you.'

'The Provençal dish?' Celeste's face fell. 'So it was my fault?'

'No. I did blame you, but I wasn't exactly rational. Don't ask me, I can't explain. Given my spectacular outburst back there. I'm not surprised Charlie thinks I'm mad.'

Celeste caught his hand. 'Jack, you know you are not.'

'I do know that much, actually.' He gently disengaged himself. 'You know, if Robert is hoping to catch a trout here, I reckon he'll be disappointed. I saw a heron take one this morning. If it's been here awhile, there will be precious little left.'

'I think they will be draining it very soon. You will have to find somewhere else to swim.'

'I'm thinking of going to London.'

Celeste swallowed hard. 'London?'

'I'm sick of kicking my heels here, and I'm

becoming an embarrassment to Charlie and Eleanor—they didn't even feel they could risk inviting their friends to dinner, for God's sake. And as it turns out, they were right.'

'Jack…'

'Celeste, I need to get away from here. And from you. You are far too much of a distraction—as I fear I am, for you. You need to concentrate on your painting, and I need to be doing something. I will take your locket and ring with me, if I may, do some digging, lean on my contacts a bit,' Jack said with a tight smile, 'I do still have some.'

'But you will be coming back?' she could not stop herself from asking.

'In a week or so. I promised I'd do my best to help you find answers. I have no intention of breaking that promise.'

'And I will be here. My commission will take me several more weeks.' Unless Sir Charles had her bags packed. Or more likely his wife had, Celeste thought, wearily contemplating the necessity for an apology.

'Good. That's settled then. So, if you could hand it over—the locket? I've still got the signet ring.'

'You mean right now?'

'I'm heading off first thing in the morning,' he said briskly. 'Turn around.'

She did as he asked. It was a good thing, Jack's wanting to go to London, she told herself. She did need to work. And he was right, he was too much of a distraction. She still, more than ever, wanted to resolve the issue of her mother's letter. She would not miss him at all. Not a bit.

His fingers were cool on the nape of her neck as he undid the clasp. If she leaned back only a fraction, she would feel his chest on her back, his legs against hers.

He turned her around, tucking the necklace into his waistcoat pocket.

'I am very grateful for all your help.'

'There's no need. I am glad to have a purpose again.'

'Still, I am grateful.'

Jack nodded. 'I should go.'

'Yes.'

'Early start.'

'Yes.'

He leaned forward to brush her cheek with his lips just as she stepped towards him to do the same. He caught her as she stumbled, his arms tight around her waist, her body pressed firmly to his chest. He looked down into her eyes, and she raised her mouth to his. Their lips brushed for the merest second. Enough for her to close her eyes. Enough for the attraction between them to spark to life and send them jumping awkwardly apart. For the second time in the space of a few days, they walked back together from the lake in silence.

London—two weeks later

Jack completed what had become his daily circuit of Hyde Park, then decided on impulse to walk through Green Park to St James's. He found a bench at the opposite end from Horse Guards, and sat back, closing his eyes and enjoying the early-evening sunshine on his face. The change of scene seemed to be having a positive effect on his melancholia. Only three times had he woken in the last two weeks after enduring the nightmare, though a good many of the other nights had been spent awake, his brain churning in an endless circle of questions.

Here in London, Jack could have easily stayed out on the town, but he'd never been a carouser, not even when he was a young colt.

Instead, he took the opportunity to catch up on his reading. There was a German mathematician called Gauss who had published several fascinating papers, which Jack was methodically working his way through. Complex stuff, and much of it in Latin, which kept him occupied through the long hours of darkness. He was having to pay extra for candles at his lodgings, and the piles of paper covered in scribbled equations were most likely interpreted by his landlord as evidence he dabbled in the black arts.

A barked order issued from the direction of Horse Guards shattered the silence of the park. Jack smiled wryly to himself. Someone was getting a rollicking. One thing he did not miss, the army's obsession with spit and polish. His slapdash approach to his own appearance, after all those years of having to appear immaculate, surprised him. He'd had his hair cut here in London, but he had felt no temptation to blow any of the considerable wealth he had amassed over the years on anything other than a couple of pairs of boots and some new breeches. To be bang up to the mark interested him not one jot.

Nor had he felt any urge to blow his cash on

wine, women or any other vice for that matter. London, even out of Season, offered many opportunities to do so. He'd attended far too many parties and balls in Wellington's entourage to find them anything other than a duty call. And women—Jack had always liked women, but for that reason, he'd never been interested in bawdy houses. Not that he condemned them, or judged the men and women who frequented them—a combination of war and absence made such places necessary to an army. But for Jack, the notion of sexual congress with a woman he did not know was repugnant.

Until he met Celeste, in the two years since that fateful day, all thoughts of intimacy were repugnant. His celibacy hadn't been a conscious decision at first. He had barely noticed the complete absence of desire, because he had at the time been between affairs. It was only later, when the opportunity arose and he—literally—did not. He'd dismissed it on that occasion as exhaustion. It was only now, thinking back, that he could see he'd simply—and without any regrets—taken to avoiding any social occasions where he would be confronted with his apathy.

He sat up on the bench, rubbing his eyes.

Away from Trestain Manor, alone in the city, awake during the long night hours, he had had plenty of time to think. He had no name for it, his condition, he doubted that any medical doctor would recognise it, but he could no longer deny its existence. Army life had kept it at bay. The pressure, especially after Napoleon escaped from Elba, to find ever more clever ways to keep one step ahead of the French, had forced him to work ever longer hours, deep into the night, not sleeping so much as passing out from exhaustion. It had been there, catching him unawares in his rare moments of inactivity, but only then.

Finding a new occupation was surely the key to containing his melancholia again. This mystery of Celeste's was merely a stop-gap, though it was a useful one, if only because it had been the kick up the backside he needed to stop putting up and start getting on with life.

Though it had been Celeste, rather than her unanswered questions, who had done the kicking, Jack thought ruefully. Celeste, with her sharp mind and her determination not to be cowed, as Charlie and Eleanor had been, by Jack's inexplicable behaviour. She was the reason he'd finally admitted to the problem. She was the reason the admission had led to action. She was the reason he was determined to find a way out of the morass he'd been sinking in.

He was grateful to Celeste. He was missing her like hell. He wanted her more than ever. Absence, instead of dulling his desire, had made it impossible to ignore. Well then, he must do the impossible.

Jack checked his watch and got to his feet. He was due to meet Finlay in an hour at a tavern over near Covent Garden for a spot of dinner. He wondered how she was faring with her painting. He pictured her in her studio, in that paint-stained smock, gazing critically at her day's work. Her hair would be coming out of its chignon by now. He pictured her, putting a hand to her throat, missing her mother's locket, and perhaps thinking about him.

He gave himself a mental shake, as he strode out of the park and made his way on to the Mall. Aside from the fact that Celeste had made it very clear she was not interested in any future but an independent one without ties and aside from the fact that admitting he had a problem did not necessarily mean there was a cure, there was one basic and fundamental reason why Jack had no right at all to dream of happiness. He might be able to manage his symptoms, but he could never rid himself of their cause, and he had no right to try. Like Blythe Marmion, he would carry his burden of guilt to the grave. And like Blythe Marmion, Jack believed her daughter deserved a lot better. Celeste was better off without either of them. What he needed to focus on was proving that.

Finlay had reserved a private room in the tavern, and was waiting for Jack when he arrived. 'Claret,' he said, pouring them each a glass. 'Not a particularly fine vintage, but not the worst we've had either. Dear God, man, we've drunk some awful gut-rot in our time.'

'Most of it that illicit whisky you insist on bringing back after every visit home to Scotland,' Jack said with a broad smile.

'I'll have you know my father is very proud of his wee home-made still,' Finley replied with mock indignation. 'Although I'm not so sure the excise man is quite so enamoured.'

'Still no uniform, I see,' Jack said.

Finlay laughed. 'Do you have any idea how curious these Sassenachs are about what a good Scot wears under the kilt? And to add to it, this mane of mine,' he said, referring to his distinctive auburn hair, 'makes them stare at me like I'm a specimen in the menagerie at the Tower.'

'More likely they're wondering how best to get you home and into their bed, if you're talking about the females of this city. And every other city we've visited, come to think of it.'

'Spare my blushes, man. You draw them in and I pick up the scraps is the truth of it. Used be, at any rate.' Finlay's smile faded. 'If only it was still that easy, to lose yourself in a lass—any lass. But we've both of us always been picky. A mite too picky, in my case.'

'Good God, don't tell me that you've finally met the one woman on this earth who isn't taken in by that Gaelic charm of yours?'

Finlay shook his head, the teasing glint gone from his dark-blue eyes. 'I know, it's unbelievable. And it is also of no consequence.'

Obviously, it mattered a good deal, but Jack knew his friend of old and forbore from questioning him. They were alike in that way, the pair of them, preferring always to keep what mattered most close to their chests.

'Any road,' Finlay said, picking up his glass, 'I'm on leave, and unlike some, I prefer to walk the streets of London without being accosted by all and sundry begging me to tell them what it was really like, the great triumph of Waterloo, and whether this was true or that, and have I ever met the great Duke. I leave the swaggering to the man himself. Though Wellington will need to get a bigger hat if his head swells any more.'

'You realise you're mocking England's saviour.'

'You realise that we fought at Waterloo for Scotland and Wales as well as England,' Finlay retorted.

Jack raised his glass. 'As you never fail to remind him at every opportunity.'

'The more he dislikes it the more I am minded to do it.' Finlay grimaced. 'Strictly speaking, my next opportunity should arise next Saturday. He's hosting some grand dinner before he goes back to Paris, and I'm expected along with a lady friend, and I've other much more important plans. I've tried excusing myself on the grounds I've no lady friend—or at least none fit for that company—but I'm getting pelters for not attending, let me tell you.'

'What are these other plans of yours, then?'

Finlay looked uncomfortable. 'They'll likely come to nought.'

But they were clearly very important, for Finlay, much as he might mock the pomp and ceremony of regimental life, was also very much aware of its importance to a career he'd worked bloody hard to forge. The parlour maid arrived with a loaded tray, before Jack had the chance to pursue this interesting train of thought.

The food was very good, and very much to Jack's taste, with roasted squab, game pie and a dish of celery. He made a better fist of it than Finlay, he was surprised to notice. His friend was distinctly out of sorts. Were they all, Wellington's men, changed utterly?

'So, to business.' Finlay pushed his half-empty plate aside. 'This ring that you asked me to investigate. I have to tell you, the ownership of it caused quite a stramash.' He placed Celeste's signet ring on the table. 'As you suspected, it's a regimental crest, though the dragon is misleading. Not Welsh, but the Buffs, from Kent.'

'The Third Foot.' Jack frowned. 'Do you happen to know where they were while the French were slaughtering each other in the Terror?'

Finlay pulled out a sheet of paper from his

pocket. 'Here you are,' he said, 'the official deployment records, though you won't be needing them.'

'You've found something of interest,' Jack said, recognising the familiar gleam in his friend's eye.

'Ach, did you expect any less of me?' Finlay picked up the signet ring. 'You see here, what looks like part of the marking of the dragon's wing? Take a closer look.'

Jack went over to the window, but the light had faded. 'No, I can't make it out.'

Finlay shook his head, grinning. 'Tut tut, Wellington's favourite code-breaker, and you've overlooked something vital. You should be ashamed of yourself, laddie.'

'Haud your wheesht, as my own Scots mother would say, and don't talk to your superior officer like that or I'll have you up on a charge.'

'Aye, you would an' all, if it weren't for the fact that you're not actually wearing the colours any more. Give it here.' Finlay lit a candle and held the ring close to the flame. 'See here,' he said, pointing to the tip of the dragon's wing. 'You have to know what to look for, but once you do, it's obvious. It looks a wee bit like that Egyptian writing we saw on the pharaoh's tombs, remember?'

Jack frowned, screwing up his eyes to examine the ring more closely. 'You're right. I see it now. What does it signify?'

'Aye, well, here's the thing.' Finlay put the candle down and took a sip of wine. 'I had to do quite a bit of digging on that one, and pull in a good few favours. Your man here,' he said, tapping the ring, 'was assigned to the Buffs as a cover. He wasn't your run-of-the-mill infantry man at all. He was a spy. A real spy, not your kind, that works out what to do with the secrets that are uncovered, but the kind that uncovers the secrets. An infiltrator, if you like.'

'Hell and damnation!' Jack stared at his friend in disbelief. 'Are you sure?'

Finlay nodded. 'Certain. If I wasn't a persistent bugger, I'd have hit a brick wall. Honestly, it's a whole other world that these boys inhabit. Makes yours look like an open book.'

'I had a bad feeling about this,' Jack said, picking up the ring and turning it over in his hand. 'How the devil did it end up hidden away at the back of a painting in the south of France?'

Finlay whistled. 'Is that where she found it, this wee painter lassie of yours?'

'She's not my wee painter lassie, she's my brother's landscape artist.'

'Mmm-hmm. You're going to an awful lot of bother for her.'

It was Jack's turn to look uncomfortable. 'You know me. I can't resist a mystery.'

'I do know you, a mite too well for your own comfort, I reckon.'

Jack snorted. 'I could say the exact same thing to you, Finlay Urquhart.'

Finlay lifted his glass. 'Well, here's to the bonds of friendship keeping both our traps shut.'

'I'll gladly drink to that.' Jack sipped his wine, then picked up the signet ring once again. 'Another dead end. I'm almost relieved. I'll just have to hope that Rundell and Bridge turn up something on the locket.'

'It's not quite a dead end, actually, though if you would rather...'

'Finlay, you devil, what else...?'

His friend grinned. 'Did I not say I'm a persistent bugger, and are you not the oldest friend I have in the world! Each ring issued to this elite squad was unique. The hieroglyph denotes a serial number assigned to each man. I've established that this ring belonged to one Arthur Derwent. Born 1773 to Lord and Lady Derwent, youngest of four sons. Commissioned aged sixteen. Served two years with the Buffs. And then, in 1791, his military record becomes a complete blank. Other than to record his death.'

'How did he die?'

'That, I can't tell you, Jack. There's nothing. Well, no, that's not true, the full story will be there, but I couldn't get at it. That's the strangest thing. Any time I tried to find out more, the door was slammed in my face. It's as if this chap never existed and the army wants to make sure it stays that way. All I know is that he died on active service. Don't know where, but I take it the date means something.'

'I don't know. Possibly, but without proof I'd be loath to speculate. Celeste—Mademoiselle Marmion—she's had enough unpleasant truths to deal with as it is without adding this to the mix. I can't talk about it, she only confided in me out of desperation—and to be honest, because I pushed her just a bit. She would be mortified if—'

'No, there's no need,' Finlay interrupted.

'I've enough on my plate myself without—
Never mind. I just wish I could have been of
more help.'

'You have been an enormous help and I'm
very grateful.'

'Nothing you couldn't have done yourself,
if you'd wanted. You know that, Jack, this is
much more up your street than mine. I know
you feel you're not one of us any more, but that
feeling, I promise you, is entirely one-sided.
The powers that be would welcome you back
with open arms.'

'No,' Jack said firmly. 'Those days really
are behind me.'

Finlay picked up the claret bottle and poured
the dregs of it into their glasses. 'Be that as it
may, there is one way of unlocking the key to
what it was the mysterious Arthur Derwent was
involved in when he died,' he said diffidently.

'You mean Wellington?'

'He's the one man in England with enough
clout to provide you with that information,
Jack. And I reckon he would if he thought there
was the slightest chance of you coming back
into the fold. In fact, knowing the man's eye
for the long game, he'd pull strings for you just
in the hope of it. But as I mentioned, he's away

back abroad next week so you'd have to be quick off the mark. Did I mention that I have an invitation to his dinner party going a-begging?'

'Which would also conveniently get you off the hook.'

Finlay laughed. 'A fortuitous side-benefit, nothing more. Anyway, I'm bloody certain Wellington would rather have you there than "Urquhart the Jock Upstart", as he never fails to call me. Seriously, Jack, if you want to unravel this puzzle any further, you're going to have to take the bull by the horns. Shall we get another bottle while you mull it over?'

Jack nodded abstractedly. Finlay embarked on one of his infamous anecdotes about life in the Highlands. His friend, who had had to fight harder than anyone to attain his current rank of major, took great pleasure in spinning fantastic tales of his 'wee Highland hame'. He recounted them in the officers' mess with the purely malicious purpose of insulting those who considered their blood too blue to mix with a commoner, but he was in the habit of recounting them to Jack first, in order to refine them for maximum effect.

Jack listened with half an ear. Though he was utterly appalled by the notion of facing not only Wellington but any number of his former comrades, part of him was already working out a strategy. Having failed what he'd come to think of as the venison test, part of him was still deeply ashamed. Dinner with Wellington would be the antidote he needed, and this time, he would make sure he could not fail. He would prepare properly. He would plan this like a campaign, with not one but two objectives, Celeste's and his own. It would be quite a coup to persuade the Duke to grant him access to this Derwent's file without making any actual promises. He'd need to think his tactics through very carefully. He found he relished the challenge.

'I'll do it!'

'You know you'll have to wear your regimentals?' Finlay cautioned him.

He had not thought of that. Jack swore, then braced himself. One more test. 'So be it.'

Only now did Finlay let his relief show on his face. 'I owe you, Jack,' he said, lifting his glass. 'I really do need to be somewhere else.'

Jack tilted his own glass and took a small sip, torn between anxiety and excitement. He had forgotten that tingling feeling, of being on the brink of something, of all the pieces of a complex puzzle not quite forming into a pattern, but promising that they might. He hadn't realised how much he missed it.

He couldn't quite believe what he'd agreed to, but he had no option now, and he was glad. No more enduring, he was ready to fight. For Celeste, and for himself. He'd better make bloody sure he didn't fail this time.

Chapter Nine

Celeste stepped back and assessed the completed painting of the Topiary Garden with a critical eye. She was still not completely happy with the quality of light, but the sun had moved from the top-floor room where she had set up her easel and she would be foolish to do any further tinkering until the morning.

She was drained and a little bit edgy, the way she always was when one of her paintings refused to be finished. The view from this window was one Jack had suggested to her the very first day she arrived here at Trestain Manor. Down there, and depicted on the canvas behind her, was the stone bench where they had first kissed. Sir Charles and Lady Eleanor would be shocked to their very respectable cores if she included that in her painting.

Though perhaps they saw more than they revealed. Perhaps the notion of his French artist kissing his soldier brother was one of those things which Sir Charles knew all about, but chose not to mention. Not because it was shocking, but because it was unimportant. A French artist could have no role to play in the future of a baronet's brother, save the obvious one as his mistress. Celeste perched on the windowsill. Why was it that being a mistress seemed so much more demeaning than being a lover? '*Bien*, it is obvious,' she muttered. 'A question of property, bought and paid for. Always, it comes to this, in France and in England. I will never be anyone's mistress.'

She would, however, very much like to be Jack's lover. In the two weeks that had passed since he had left for London, Celeste had been forced to accept that her feelings for him were a great deal stronger than she had ever experienced before. She missed him. The problem was, she missed him a great deal too much. She longed to make love to him. She knew he felt the same. One of the reasons he'd gone to London was because he was determined not to let that happen. Not that either of them had acknowledged the depth of their attraction, but they had not had to. That kiss in the lake had been evidence enough.

Sir Charles had made no reference to her intemperate outburst the day before Jack's departure. Another thing swept under the carpet, no doubt because the opinion of the hired artisan meant as little as the fact that the hired artisan had been kissing her patron's brother. Perhaps she was being unfair. Perhaps.

Jack had left his brother a note. It had been handed to Sir Charles at breakfast the morning of his departure, and the peer had been so surprised, he had read it aloud, quite forgetting Celeste's presence.

'So you see, my dear,' Sir Charles had said to his wife, 'he knows full well that his behaviour was somewhat extreme. I think we must take comfort in the fact that he feels well enough to venture alone to the metropolis.'

'I am not entirely convinced,' Lady Eleanor had replied, 'that he ought to be let loose in London in his fragile state of mind.'

Sir Charles however had fully recovered his optimistic spirit. 'We must regard that as a positive sign. He is no doubt looking to take up the reins of his life again. A cause for rejoicing, not worry.'

Turning away from the window, Celeste hoped that he was right. She wondered if Jack had made any progress with her locket or with that strange ring. She wondered how he was occupying his time. She could not imagine him shopping, or drinking in taverns or going to the theatre. Were there parks in London where he could walk? Was there a lake where he could swim? It was not only for the sake of his injured arm that he swam. His muscular body was testament to his love of exercise.

In an effort to stop herself thinking of that body, Celeste pulled a chair in front of her canvas. The untrimmed topiary had a fantastical look about it. It reminded her of something. She closed her eyes, willing her mind to go blank, a technique she had honed over the last couple of weeks, when memories had begun to pop into her head at the oddest times. Yes, she had it! Another illustration from the storybook her mother used to read to her.

There was no consistency to her memories, save that they were all from before the time she had been sent away to school. A swimming lesson. A description of a gown which made Maman smile at some secret memory. A sampler Celeste had worked on, depicting the English alphabet, which she'd had to hide from Henri. She could no longer deny that her mother had cared for her, but it made her determined efforts to disguise the fact all the more inexplicable. Celeste wondered, not for the first time, what Jack would make of it all. She laughed inwardly, not for the first time, at herself for wanting to tell him. There was, after all, something to be said for being understood, even just a little. It was not something she had reckoned on.

The sound of feet on the stairs outside the room made her heart give a silly little leap. No one ever came up here uninvited. It could not be Jack, because she'd have heard a carriage. Though the driveway was on the other side of the house. She jumped to her feet as the door opened, and her heart jumped again. 'It's you,' she said stupidly.

'In the flesh. May I come in?'

Celeste took a step back before she could throw herself at that very attractive flesh, trying to remind herself of all the very excellent reasons why she should not. Jack's hair was ruffled, his clothes were dusty and he was in need of a shave, but still her pulses fluttered at the sight of him as he crossed the room.

He took her hand in his, made to raise it to his lips, then changed his mind. 'I see you've been hard at work,' he said, nodding at the canvas.

'What do you think of it?' His opinion of her was not relevant to the success or failure of the commission, but it mattered all the same.

'Charlie will be pleased,' Jack said.

'Yes, but Sir Charles is easily pleased.'

Jack laughed. 'You know perfectly well it's good. You don't need me to tell you that.'

'No. But you *do* like it, don't you?'

'I do.'

Celeste smiled. Jack smiled back at her. Their eyes locked. She lifted her hand, as if to reach out for him, just as he did the same. Their fingers brushed. She turned away to sit on the window seat.

Jack leaned his shoulders against the fireplace. 'I have news. Rundell and Bridge, the jewellers, have confirmed that your locket was purchased through them. It was a private commission, and the maker's mark on your necklace belongs to a former senior goldsmith who has unfortunately retired to the country. However, they have written to him, enclosing a sketch of the item, and have promised to inform me as soon as they hear back from him. What they could tell me was that the stones were of the first quality. It's an extremely valuable piece.'

'*Mon Dieu*, then it is true what you said. Maman must have come from a wealthy family?'

'It seems highly likely.'

'Would it have been a terrible scandal then that she was *enceinte* and not married?' Celeste asked. 'Shameful enough for her family to disown her? I don't know, you see, not really. I mean of course, in France it is not any more acceptable than in England for any young woman to have a child without a husband, though it is naturally perfectly acceptable for a man to have a child without a wife.'

'Acceptable to some men, but we're not all the same.'

'You're right. I beg your pardon. I think you must have seen much of it though? Many women have a weakness for a man in uniform, and a man in a uniform who has been away from home for a long time—*bien*.'

'*Bien*, indeed,' Jack said wryly. 'I— Good Lord, why did I not think of that!' He had pulled a velvet pouch from his pocket. Now he reached inside and took out the signet ring with the military crest on it, and stared down at it as if he had never seen it before. 'I had a very interesting conversation with my friend Finlay Urquhart regarding this ring. It was most enlightening.'

By the time he had finished recounting his tale, Celeste's eyes were wide with wonder. 'So you think it's possible that this Arthur Derwent might be my real father? Can it be true?'

'It would explain why your mother was in possession of his ring. It's certainly plausible, though at this stage, nothing more.'

'So now we wait once more, on a letter,' Celeste said.

'Actually, there's something else we need to do first.'

He sounded odd. Nervous? He was staring down at his boots. Definitely nervous. 'There is?' Celeste asked.

Jack gave her a reassuring smile. 'Nothing terrible,' he said. 'At least—more tedious, really.'

'Yes? And what is this not-terrible, tedious thing that is making you so interested in your boots?'

Jack laughed, and joined her on the window seat. 'There's one man who can grant me access to information regarding Arthur Derwent,' he said, 'and by coincidence, he's hosting a dinner party at a house not fifty miles from here, on Saturday.'

'Oh. So you plan to call on him there?'

'I plan to attend the dinner party.'

'But you— But the last time you attended a dinner...'

'I almost fainted, I almost spilled my accounts, then the next day I blew up at my brother and his wife and fled to London,' Jack said drily. 'I haven't forgotten.'

But he had managed to mention it without either anger or embarrassment, Celeste noted.

'It was horrible bad luck,' Jack continued, 'the combination of the vegetable stew and the venison at Charlie's table. I was coping. And when I was in London I decided that I wanted to see just how well I could cope.'

'So it is another test?' Celeste pressed his hand. 'I think that is very brave. And a good thing. And I am very, very grateful too, but I don't want you to do this for me, if you think...'

'I'm doing it as much for myself as for you, Celeste. And for Finlay too. My army friend, the Scotsman I told you about. He has other business to attend to, and was eager to find someone to replace him.'

Celeste frowned. 'So there will be— Will there be other soldiers there?' Jack nodded. She eyed him suspiciously. 'This person you have to speak to about the secret file, he must be very important?' Another nod. It couldn't be! 'Jack, please, please don't tell me that you are going to dinner with the Duke of Wellington.'

He grinned. 'I'm not.'

'Thank God,' Celeste said, 'I could not...'

'I'm not,' Jack said, 'but we are.'

Celeste jumped to her feet. *'Non!'* She lapsed into a stream of incoherent French. 'No, Jack. You cannot mean it. Wellington! And this dinner— Will all the guests be soldiers?'

'Officers and their wives.'

'Jack, these soldiers—officers—will they be men who fought with you at Waterloo? The very battle which caused your—your...'

'My condition, for want of a better word,' Jack said shortly. 'My condition,' he repeated firmly. 'It wasn't at Waterloo that I— It has nothing to do with Waterloo.'

Celeste's jaw dropped. 'But I thought— Your wounds, your arm...'

'*Those* injuries have nothing to do with it. The event which—the circumstances which—that happened two years ago.'

'Two years ago. But how could you— You were still in the army—how did you cope?'

'With difficulty. I kept it under control because I had no choice.'

His eyes were troubled, but he looked at her unwaveringly. Though he had referred obliquely to what he called his condition, he had never before admitted to it so frankly.

'Whatever is wrong with me,' Jack said, pushing back his hair and squaring his shoulders, 'I've decided it's not going to rule my life. I must confront it, and the first step is this dinner which,' he said with a small smile, 'will also further your cause, I hope.'

Celeste felt for his hand. 'You are pretending it's not an enormous challenge, but I can't imagine...'

'Then don't. There's no point in going into battle thinking you'll die or that you'll lose— even when the odds suggest that you might,' Jack said. 'I don't want my aide-de-camp standing at my side like a frightened rabbit trying to decide which bullet to dodge, I want her watching my back. Do you understand?'

Celeste swallowed as the implications of what he was proposing began to sink in. 'Jack, I have never in my life attended such a grand function. I don't even know how to curtsy properly. I am base-born, my father apparently was some sort of spy, I'm French, and I'm an artist. I have no connections, no breeding…'

'Celeste, I don't care a damn about your connections or your parentage or your blood line. You're not a horse, dammit! I don't care who your mother was, or your father, and I don't give a damn about whether you were born on the right side of the blanket or not. You could be from Timbuktu for all I care.'

'But those other people…'

'Will see you for what you are, if you let them. A beautiful, clever, talented woman who deserves their respect and admiration for making her own way in life without compromise. I am willing to bet you'll be the only one of them at the table, what's more. What have I said to upset you?'

'Nothing.' Celeste sniffed. 'I don't know where Timbuktu is.'

'Africa.' Jack wiped a tear from her lashes with his thumb. 'Will you come with me?'

She twined her fingers in his. 'Yes. I won't let you down, Jack.'

'I know you won't.'

His kiss was the merest whisper, the lightest brush of his lips on hers, but it released a torrent of pent-up longing inside her. Celeste sighed. His fingers cupped her jaw. For an unbearable moment, she thought he would pull away. She knew it was what she ought to wish for, but she had only the will to wait, not turn away, because already her body was thrumming with anticipation. And then Jack sighed too.

They kissed deeply, the kiss of a passion too long pent up. Their lips clung, their hands pulled their bodies tight together, as if space, any space between them was too much. Their unbridled kisses made her head spin with delight, made her realise how much restraint they had shown until now. She clutched at him, her desire rocketing, trading kisses with kisses, her breathing ragged, her hands wandering wildly over his body.

'I want you,' Jack said hoarsely, kissing her mouth, her throat, her mouth again. 'I want you so much. I have never, ever wanted—not this much. Never this much.' His kisses grew deeper. She tilted her head back to deepen them further. Her hands wandered over his back under his coat, to the tight clench of his buttocks. He groaned.

They slid from the window seat on to the floor. 'You are so lovely,' Jack said, his hand tightening on her breast, drawing a deep moan from her. 'So lovely.' He sucked hard on her nipple through the layers of her gown, her undergarments. His hand cupped her other breast, his thumb stroking her other nipple.

'Yes,' Celeste said. 'Yes.' She stroked his back, his buttocks, she stroked the firm length of him through his breeches.

'Yes,' Jack said. 'Yes.' He slid his hand under her gown, past the knot of her garter. He reached the slit in her pantaloons and slid his finger into her. Instantly, she tightened around him. He stroked her, his eyes fixed on hers as he did. She flattened her hand on his shaft. He kissed her. Slid his finger farther inside her. Then slowly, tantalisingly, drew it out.

She undid enough of his buttons to slip her hand inside his breeches, and curled her fingers around the silky thickness of his shaft. He moaned. His breathing became ragged like hers. Slide and thrust, inside her. She was teetering on the edge already. Slide and thrust. She tightened in response. Jack was so hard in her hand. She tried to stroke him, but was constrained by the tightness of his breeches.

'Wait. Just—just hold me,' he said.

Slide and stroke. Slide and stroke. His gaze holding hers. She had never been so tight. And then he kissed her, and the thrust of his tongue and the stroke of his fingers was too much. She cried out, jerking underneath him, yanked into a hard, fast climax, shuddering as it took her, wave after wave, clinging to Jack, as if he would save her, her hand clutching at his shoulder, her fingers curled around his shaft.

Panting. And tears. Tears? He kissed her again, hard. She closed her eyes. Her lashes were wet. Tears? Her lips clung to his. She wriggled under him, trying to shift sufficiently to free him from his breeches. To give him what he had given her.

Jack shifted, gently removing her hand. 'Celeste, it's not—it's not that I don't want you.' His voice was harsh. The effort it took him to stop her was obvious. 'It's quite apparent that I do. More than I have ever—ever. But I can't. No, not can't. Dare not.'

He sat up, adjusting himself, fastening his

buttons, helping her to her feet, taking her hands, sitting down beside her on the window seat, stroking her hair back from her face. Then kissing her, so deeply and with such regret, she could not doubt the depth of his feeling. 'Dare not?'

Jack stared down at his hands. 'I haven't wanted to. Not since— Not for a long time. I told you that, I think. I thought that aspect of my life was over. And then I saw you.' He kissed her again. 'This, the way we are together, it is so much more than anything I've ever felt before. I'm afraid that I would want so much more from you than I've ever wanted from any woman before and I know...' He kissed her again to stop her speaking. 'I know you've made it very clear that your independence means everything to you, so I'm not presuming—'

He broke off, staring out the window, his jaw working. 'Even if you did,' he said finally, turning back to her, his face stricken, 'it wouldn't be possible. What happened two years ago makes it impossible for me to even contemplate— I don't deserve you, Celeste, and I'm afraid that if I gave in, if I allowed myself to—to make love to you, I would find it almost impossible to walk away, whether you wanted me or not. I have enough on my conscience without that.'

His smile was a grimace. His eyes were darkly troubled. 'There, I had not meant to say as much. You will think me presumptuous...'

'Jack, I think—I don't know what to think. It is the same for me—this, between us. You must know that. It frightens me. It makes me think—want—I don't know what.' She touched his cheek with her fingers. 'You seem changed. You seem— I can see a little of the soldier in you, I think,' she said with a lopsided smile, 'ready to go into battle.'

'It's what I'm doing, I suppose.'

'Won't you tell me what happened, Jack?'

He pulled his hands free, his expression set. 'No,' he said, 'absolutely not. No one knows, and I intend to keep it that way.'

She contemplated pressing him, but his tone made it clear it would be pointless, and she couldn't bear to be at odds with him again after this. He had changed. He was still vulnerable, and he was still in torment but he was, as he said, fighting back, though the cause of his torment remained buried, a festering sore. She shuddered at this stark imagery. She was learning herself that such sores needed to excised.

'I almost forgot.' Jack pulled her locket from the velvet pouch. 'Here. I had the jewellers clean it.'

The stones sparkled. 'I can't believe I ever thought it mere trumpery.' Jack fastened it around her neck. Her fingers closed over it. 'I have missed it.'

He kissed the nape of her neck. 'Celeste?'

'I do understand. I do.' She got to her feet, blushing. 'I don't know what I think, but I understand. And I am—I am very honoured that you have confided in me this much. It must have taken a great deal— We neither of us are very good at it.'

'We're both of us getting better, though.' Jack took her hand again, and kissed the palm. 'Don't mention anything about the dinner. I'm going to spring it on Charlie at breakfast so he'll have no option but to agree. Do you have a gown? I never thought to ask.'

Celeste smiled saucily. 'I am a Frenchwoman. Of course I have a gown.'

Jack laughed. 'I missed you,' he said, then turned away before she could answer. 'I'll see you at breakfast.'

'And I missed you too,' Celeste said as the door closed behind him.

'So the invite is from the Great Man himself? I thought Wellington was holed up in Paris.' Charlie pushed his empty breakfast plate to one side. His brother, as Jack had anticipated, looked suitably awestruck.

'He is only in England on a brief visit.'

'Ah. Did you hear that, Eleanor?' Charlie said, turning to his wife. 'Wellington himself has invited Jack to a dinner.'

'Jack and a partner,' Eleanor said, pouring herself a cup of tea. 'It is exceeding short notice to receive such an invitation.'

She was no fool. He forgot that sometimes. Jack buttered some bread and took a contemplative bite. 'The cards were issued a few weeks ago. My friend Finlay Urquhart has been holding on to this one for me,' he said. One of the principles of deception, always stick to as near the truth as possible. 'You remember Finlay, Charlie?'

His brother laughed. 'The Jock Upstart, isn't that what Wellington calls him? Indeed, I recall...'

'So who do you intend to take to this dinner with you?' Eleanor persisted.

'I rather thought I'd take Mademoiselle Marmion.'

Eleanor's breakfast cup clattered into her saucer. 'A painter. A *French* painter, moreover. To dinner with Wellington! Jack, you cannot possibly... Oh. Good morning, *Mademoiselle*. I trust you slept—There is no coffee. They have forgotten to bring— I will just ring the bell.'

'I'll do it.' Jack got to his feet, tugging the cord at the fireplace before holding Celeste's chair out for her. *'Mademoiselle,'* he said, resuming his seat opposite her, 'we were just talking about you.'

'Jack, you cannot— There must be someone more—'

'Eleanor.' It was the voice he used to cut through the excuses of a trooper who had failed to carry out his orders to the letter. Shouting, Jack had learned to appreciate, was not nearly so effective as this quiet, utterly implacable tone. Eleanor's jaw dropped. Jack bit back the urge to laugh. 'I have received a very flattering invitation to a dinner which the Duke of Wellington is hosting,' he said, turning to Celeste. 'I would be honoured if you would accompany me.'

Her eyes widened not from wonder, but from the effort she was making not to laugh. *'Moi?'* She turned to Eleanor, to Charlie, and then back to him with a very creditable attempt at surprised delight. He hadn't briefed her, and he hadn't needed to. Jack bit back his own smile. 'To dinner with the great Duke of Wellington. *Moi?* It is an honour that I surely do not deserve.'

'Actually—' Charlie surprised them all by intervening '—I think it's a capital idea,' he said, casting his wife an apologetic look. 'We all know that the Duke has an eye for the ladies, and *Mademoiselle*, here, is an exceptionally beautiful gal. Come now, Eleanor, you cannot deny it.'

Jack mentally cursed his brother's ineptness. To ask one woman to praise another's looks was to dice with disaster at the best of times. To ask one's wife to do so was to ensure that one slept alone for at least the next week. 'The Duke of Wellington is still, as far as I am aware, infatuated with Lady Wedderburn-Webster.'

Eleanor's eyes widened at the mention of the

notorious and by all accounts, fatally attractive lady. 'Is it true, Jack, that the child she bore is his? I believe that she was actually back in the ballroom only days after the birth. I was confined for six weeks after Robert, and a month after Donal.'

'As to that, I'm afraid I have no idea.'

'They say that she has not a single thought worth uttering in that flighty head of hers,' Lady Eleanor said. 'One would have thought that a man of Wellington's calibre would have chosen a more fitting and intelligent...' She stuttered to a halt, flushing, seeming to recall only at the last minute that she was talking about Wellington's mistress, and not his wife.

'Mademoiselle Marmion, you may recall, lives in Paris,' Jack said, bringing the conversation back around to the salient point. 'I thought Wellington would appreciate discussing his adopted city with one of its natives.'

'Excellent idea,' Charlie said, rubbing his hands together. 'The point is, my dear Eleanor, Jack must go to this dinner. There is no doubt that Wellington will be a man of huge influence when he returns to politics, as he surely must. And Jack, you know, must look to his future. He cannot afford to be turning such an invitation down, and it is too short notice to invite another lady to accompany him. Mademoiselle Marmion offers the perfect solution to the problem. It is settled then.'

Charlie beamed. Eleanor smiled frigidly. Celeste looked down at her plate of bread and butter, biting her lip. Mission accomplished! Picking up his fork, Jack cut into an egg and took a bite. It was cold, but surprisingly good. He cut another piece.

Celeste made an excellent accomplice. He'd spent much of the night imagining how it would have been if he had not somehow plucked the willpower to stop yesterday. He almost wished he hadn't been so strong-minded. When he woke up, his morning swim had been a necessity for a very different reason than on any other day. Jack set down his fork. It hadn't been *that* dream. He had not had *that* dream for—he frowned—more than a week?

'Is something wrong, Jack?'

He turned to Eleanor, who had posed the question. 'Not at all. I was merely contemplating having another egg,' he said.

'Then let me fetch it for you,' she said.

She got hurriedly to her feet to do so, rather than summon a servant or allow him to help himself, obviously keen to encourage his returning appetite. Her concern touched him. It struck him that before he went to London, it would merely have irked him. He wondered guiltily how many other such small acts of kindness he'd misconstrued. 'Thank you,' he said with a smile as she handed him the plate.

Eleanor blushed. 'You are most welcome, Jack,' she said.

He made a point of taking a bite of egg and nodding his appreciation. 'By the way, I brought Robert back a present from London.'

'A present? That is exceedingly thoughtful of you. May I ask what it is?'

Eleanor's face lit up, and Jack felt another twinge of guilt. He couldn't remember the last time she'd smiled at him like that. 'It's a box of soldiers,' he said. 'Actually, rather a large box. Models of the armies who fought at Waterloo. I thought he could invite his little friend from the village round later, and I'd set it out for him, just as it was. Explain how the battle unfolded, that sort of thing.'

'Jack!' Eleanor clapped her hands together in delight. 'Jack, that is most—most— I must say, I am quite flabbergasted.' She turned to

Charlie. 'Did you hear that, my love? Robert will be delighted.'

'I am sure he will be, but—are you sure about this, Jack? I mean, you've been rather keen to avoid the subject, and…'

'And now I see that it was wrong of me,' Jack said smoothly. 'Robert ought to understand both sides of the story. To read some of the accounts in the press, you'd think that we—Wellington had an easy triumph. In fact the victory meant all the more for our—his having such a worthy adversary in Napoleon.'

'Well then, provided that Wellington still triumphs,' Charlie said with a rumble of laugher. 'Indeed, Jack, that is most— You won't mind if I sit in? I'd be fascinated to hear your thoughts for myself.'

'Not at all.'

'I must go and tell Robert at once,' Eleanor said. 'Will two o'clock suit you? He will be— Charles, my love, come with me. We should both be there when he hears the exciting news. You will excuse us.'

Jack finished his egg. Celeste poured herself another cup of coffee. 'Mission accomplished?' she asked with a quirk of her eyebrow.

He laughed at her choosing his own words. 'I think so.'

'And these toy soldiers, would they happen to be another test?'

Jack pushed his chair back. 'Sometimes the trouble with a beautiful, clever and talented woman is that she is rather too perceptive. I must go, I have a battleground to prepare.'

Chapter Ten

Four days later, Celeste gazed out of the window of her guest bedchamber at Hunter's Reach, the country estate in neighbouring Surrey where Wellington was hosting his dinner—although in actual fact it was Lord and Lady Elmsford, the owners of the house, who were the nominal hosts.

The house had been constructed during the reign of Queen Elizabeth, built in the classic 'E' shape which was a common tribute to the Virgin Queen. Celeste's room was on the third floor on the north wing of the house, facing towards a long sweep of carriageway. Jack had been clearly on edge when they arrived a few hours ago, as much on her behalf as his, but she had managed to reassure him that she was more than capable of playing her part. Though as Celeste watched the stream of carriages arriving, she felt less certain with every passing minute.

Moving restlessly to the mirror, she studied her reflection critically. Her evening dress was of white silk, the overdress gauze woven with sky-blue leaves of flossed silk, trimmed with net and satin. She had had it made in Paris on a whim a month after her mother died, a fruitless attempt to console herself with something utterly frivolous which she would never have the opportunity to wear. She had no idea what impulse had made her bring it with her to England, but she was vastly relieved that she had. Her long evening gloves were also new, as were the sky-blue slippers which matched her gown. Her fingers went automatically to the locket, glittering at her throat. 'I wish I had you here to advise me, Maman,' she whispered. 'You would know all the protocols regarding how deep I should curtsy to each rank of attendee.'

She had refused her host's offer of a lady's maid, never having had one, and kept her *coiffure* simple, in a topknot held by a ribbon to match her gown, with a few artful curls. Now, peering nervously at the result, Celeste worried that it was overly simple for such a grand occasion. She had no shawl, and could only hope that the throng of guests would warm the cavernous rooms downstairs. Another thing she could not understand about the English, the way they made a virtue of the cold. Staring at the empty grate in her bedchamber, she wondered if there was some unwritten rule that fires were not to be lit until the first snowfall.

A discreet tap on the door startled her. 'Jack. Thank goodness. I was not sure if I was expected to make my way down myself. *Sacré bleu!*'

He was wearing the tight red military dress uniform with its high, gold-braided collar. His jaw was clean-shaven, tanned against the gleaming white of his starched shirt and neatly tied cravat, just visible beneath the coat. His hair was swept back from his brow. The gold braid ran in a broad line down the front of his uniform, which fitted snuggly at his waist, where a heavy gold sash was tied. More gold braid on his cuffs, and more on the short tails of the coat, made him look quite magnificent. White gloves, white, very tight breeches, and boots polished so highly that they could have acted as a mirror. 'You look exactly like your portrait!'

'I seem to remember you thought I looked like a pompous ass.'

'You said that. I said you looked like a Greek god, peering down on us mere mortals.' Her smile faded a little as she studied his face. 'I know as your aide-de-camp I am to be all stiff upper lip, but am I permitted to ask how you feel in uniform?'

'Damned uncomfortable.' Jack coloured. 'Fine. Odd. I feel like an imposter. But fine. This is my dress uniform. I never— The only bad memories it has are of dinners such as this one, with too many egos recounting their own particular tales of bravery, and far too many toasts.' He bowed low over her hand, brushing his lips to her glove. 'I have been remiss. Mademoiselle Marmion, may I say that you look utterly radiant.'

'Lieutenant-Colonel Trestain, may I say in return that you look exceedingly dashing.'

He smiled faintly, tucking her hand into his arm and making for the stairs. 'Are *you* nervous?'

'Not at all.' Jack raised his brow. 'Only a little. Mostly of Wellington. Will he look down that famous nose at me because I am French?

Then there is your English politics. I can't tell the difference between a Tory and a Wig.'

'Whig. Frankly, neither can they,' Jack said drily. He led her to a first-floor balcony which overlooked the Great Hall. 'You have nothing to worry about, you know. They are just people.'

Celeste gripped the wooden banister, peering down at the glittering crowd through the huge iron light-fitting, shaped like a carriage wheel, which was suspended from the ceiling. 'People with titles, dripping in jewels, who talk as if they own the land.'

Jack laughed. 'That's because many of them do. Where is your Revolutionary spirit?'

'Beheaded,' Celeste said, her eyes fixed on the crowd. Most of the men were in red, a positive battalion of senior British military personnel. If it was daunting for her it would be even more so for Jack, who was doing this for her. She waved her hand at the swarm of Redcoats beneath. 'Do you know all of these officers?'

'Most of them.'

She studied his face anxiously, torn between awed admiration at his courage, and concern lest he fail this challenge he had set himself. Was he really prepared for this? No matter, this was not the time for doubts or questions. Jack wanted his aide-de-camp to watch his back, not cower like a frightened rabbit. She stiffened her shoulders, preparing to do battle. *'Allons, mon colonel,'* she said, tucking her hand into his arm. 'I won't let you down. And if I do make some terrible gaffe, you can blame it on the fact that I am French, since I am sure that is what everyone will be thinking in any case.'

The Duke of Wellington was receiving his guests at the foot of the stairs. He had the aloof carriage and expression of a man who at the same time disdained and expected reverence. He was immaculately dressed, his scarlet coat giving the appearance of having been moulded to his fine shoulders. The famous nose was not nearly so hooked as the caricatures portrayed, Celeste noted, though his eyes were every bit as hooded. And every bit as observant. The mouth was unexpectedly sensual. As he treated the woman in the queue in front of them to a charming smile, Celeste understood why his Grace had his pick of the ladies.

'Trestain. You are looking well. Regimentals suit you.'

Jack, Celeste noticed, instinctively straightened his shoulders as if he were being inspected which, she supposed, he was. 'Your Grace. May I introduce Mademoiselle Marmion.'

'A pleasure, *Mademoiselle*,' the great man said, bowing over her hand. 'I understand that you are an artist. If your paintings are as pretty as you then I am sure you are much in demand.'

Flustered, Celeste nodded, casting an enquiring look at Jack, but he looked just as surprised as she.

'You must not think that because I no longer have you in my service, that I am entirely bereft of spies to gather the latest intelligence on you, despite the exceedingly short notice the Scots Upstart provided me with,' Wellington said to Jack with a diffident smile. 'I confess, I was surprised to hear that you had been tempted out of hibernation. It gives me some hope that we may yet tempt you back into harness.'

Wellington turned to Lord and Lady Elmsford. 'You will know Lieutenant-Colonel Trestain as my code-breaker,' he said.

'It is an honour, sir,' his lordship said, 'I believe your work has been invaluable to his Grace. He tells me you are much missed.'

Jack's smile was tight. 'No one is irreplaceable,' he said. 'His Grace excepted, naturally.'

The Duke of Wellington smiled thinly at this sally, though Celeste suspected he was of the opinion that it was true. The man had an ego the size of France. He was also, she reminded herself, a master strategist, and he clearly wanted Jack to return to his service. It hadn't occurred to her until now that the Duke, if he did grant Jack access to Arthur Derwent's file, would expect to be paid in kind. Surely Jack was not contemplating a return to the army?

'A code-breaker! I am very fond of acrostics myself,' Lady Elmsford was saying to Jack, 'though no doubt you find such puzzles embarrassingly simple.'

'You would be surprised to know how many codes are based on similar principles,' he replied. 'Unless you wish his Grace to try to recruit you too, I would keep that talent under your hat.'

Jack had not expected quite so many of his fellow officers to be here. He ought to have checked the guest list with Finlay, but then, if he had, there was a chance it would have discouraged him. Now, smiling and exchanging pleasantries with familiar faces, he was not precisely glad he was here, but he would be when it was over.

Celeste's grip on his arm was like a vice. His aide-de-camp was much more nervous than she was letting on. In this rather daunting gathering, she was no seasoned trouper, but more akin to a young ensign bravely carrying the colours. He smiled down at her reassuringly, feeling his own spirits rise. He had not had his nightmare since returning from London. He had worked his way through the entire battle of Waterloo, skirmish by skirmish, in the presence of two small boys and his brother, without faltering once. Now here he was, in his regimentals, engaging in reminiscent chat on that same subject, and his palms were not even sweating.

One of the late Lieutenant-General Picton's men was recounting, for Celeste's benefit, the legend of the Frenchman, dressed as a English Hussar officer, who descended on a British-occupied village, pretending to be on an information-gathering mission from Lord Uxbridge. She was hanging on his every word, her eyes wide, like a child being told a fairy story. Jack had heard these stories so often, they had ceased to mean anything to him, but now he listened afresh, it really was amusing, for the French spy had been so convincing, he'd actually managed to order the British soldiers about, though he disappeared in jig time when their commanding officer turned up.

Waterloo made its appearance as he had expected, in several more conversations, but each time Jack tensed a little less. Not even four months ago, the battle had taken place, but it seemed a great deal more distant. Listening to the men who had been his friends and comrades for so many years, he felt a detachment he had not expected. Their world was no longer his.

A wave of sadness for what he had lost threatened to envelop him. He reminded himself that it was not lost but voluntarily surrendered. A sharp nip on his arm made him look down at Celeste. The eloquent look she drew him made it obvious that she was in dire need of rescue. The lascivious look on the face of the guards captain entertaining her with tales of his own heroism made it clear what she needed rescuing from. He was not the first to seem smitten with her. Jack hadn't exactly forgotten how beautiful she was, but he'd forgotten the impact she made when first encountered. Until now, Celeste herself had seemed oblivious of the admiring glances, raised quizzing glasses and downright leers. Or perhaps she was accustomed to it? Jack slipped his hand around her waist and drew her in to his side. She smiled up at him and slipped her hand back through his arm.

The dining room at Hunter's Reach was like a very much larger version of the one in Trestain Manor, with exposed oak timbers and extensive panelling. To Celeste's relief, Jack was seated next to her at dinner. Aside from that one moment when she'd had to pinch him, he seemed to be handling the occasion effortlessly. It had been strange, seeing him mingle with those other soldiers. There was no doubting that he was one of them. She had learned more in the last two hours about his life in the army than he had told her in— Was it really less than six weeks since they had first met? The respect and admiration he drew from his fellow officers did not surprise her, but the awe in which a number of them held him did. They spoke of him as if he were a magician, recounted some of his successes as if they were achieved by a form of sorcery. She had thought Sir Charles's claim that Jack was famous had been born from brotherly affection, but it seemed even Sir Charles had no idea of the extent of Jack's abilities.

It struck her afresh how much he had given up when he resigned his commission. Perhaps he was thinking the same thing? The test, as he called it, began to make more sense now. Despite having insisted that his soldiering days were over, perhaps he was still hankering for them after all. He had sounded completely convincing, but that could be because he was trying very hard to persuade himself.

In the company of these senior militia men gathered round the huge table, Jack was a changed character. More intimidating, in a way. She looked at him, chatting smilingly with the overly forward and overly endowed woman on his right. He certainly looked relaxed and in control but she couldn't help remembering what he'd said about putting on a front to go into battle.

As the first course was carried in by a small battalion of footmen, Celeste dragged her eyes and her thoughts away from Jack to the man seated on her left, one of the few in the room not wearing a red tunic. He needed little encouragement to talk about himself and the pivotal role he had played in the introduction of something called the Corn Laws which seemed, confusingly, to have very little to do with bread. When Celeste finally managed to complete a sentence without interruption, the man declared he hadn't realised she was a Frenchie, and embarked upon a description of his recent pilgrimage to the Devon coast to view HMS *Bellerophon*, in which Napoleon was being conveyed to exile on Elba. He seemed to think that Celeste was personally acquainted with the Emperor, and consequently was inclined to take umbrage on behalf of the entire English nation.

The arrival of the next course was the signal for all heads to turn almost as one. Celeste bit back a smile. All heads save one, that was. The woman on Jack's right was still talking. She could not see his face, but the woman was quite unmistakably casting lures. That she was beautiful could not be denied, with blue-black hair almost the colour of Jack's own, huge blue eyes, and an expanse of creamy skin on display. Her eyelashes fluttered. Her hands also. The pink tip of her tongue kept touching the plump indentation in the centre of her upper lip in a brazen gesture of seduction. Even as Celeste watched, she managed to lean over, display her bounteous cleavage, whisper something in Jack's ear and drop her napkin on to his lap at the same time.

Celeste committed the cardinal sin of leaning across Jack's arm. 'You will excuse me, Madam, but I have something most particular to say to Monsieur Trestain.'

'That was rude,' Jack said, though he was smiling.

'No doubt you thought her very beautiful.'

'No doubt that is what you think I thought.'

Celeste narrowed her eyes. 'I think her gown is vulgar. The décolleté is indecent.'

'Only a woman would say so. There is no such thing as a décolleté that is too low, as far as we men are concerned.'

'Nor a bosom that is too full,' Celeste replied tartly.

Jack burst out laughing. 'I cannot believe you said that.'

'I meant only to think it.'

He grinned. 'You know, despite the fact that you are not parading your quite delightful bosom about like a—a houri in a sultan's harem, you must be perfectly well aware that you, Mademoiselle Marmion, have turned every male head in this room.'

'Though not yours,' Celeste said before she could stop herself.

'Oh, mine was turned the moment I first saw you on the banks of the lake.'

He meant it teasingly, but she remembered him then, as she had first seen him, naked, scything at that awkward angle through the water, and heat flooded her. 'I could not take my eyes off you,' she said.

'That,' Jack said, 'is a feeling which is entirely mutual.'

His eyes darkened as he leaned towards her, and she moved too, as if drawn by some invisible force, only the clatter of a spoon on a glass making them leap apart, as his Grace the Duke of Wellington got to his feet and announced a toast: To England, Home and Beauty.

Jack watched impatiently as the port made a slow circuit of the table for the second time. Without Celeste by his side, he was distracted, worrying how she would fare in the company of the ladies. He had always found the endless toasts in the officers' mess tedious, always found the need to disguise the fact he wasn't actually emptying his glass each time tiresome, and tonight was no different, although at least when they were toasting the ladies and the king and their host and hostess and this patron and that patron, there was no opportunity for any other topic of conversation.

A final raising of glasses to the king, and to Jack's intense relief Wellington pushed back his chair. He had managed, in the few moments between the ladies departing and the port arriving, to make his request to be granted access to Alfred Derwent's file. Wellington had raised his eyebrows, looked as if he was going to ask the nature of Jack's interest and then thought better of it, before consenting somewhat grudgingly to have it sent to Trestain Manor. He made it clear that the file contained highly confidential information and it was most irregular for Jack to have sight of it. The Duke then reminded him, in no uncertain terms, that having granted such a great favour, he would require Jack to repay it at a time of his choosing. What that might entail, Jack would worry about when it happened, which of a certainty it would, for the Duke always got his pound of flesh.

Celeste was not, as he had feared, sitting alone and neglected when the gentlemen left the dining room, but at the centre of a huddle of the younger wives. He stood on the periphery, listening with some amusement, for she was confiding in these most fashionable well-heeled ladies, where to shop for the best bargains in Paris. All of the places she mentioned were in unfashionable areas with which none of her listeners would be familiar. The ladies were, however, enthralled. One of them was actually writing notes down on the back of a visiting card. 'And as to undergarments, Mademoiselle Marmion?' a petite blonde whispered, and Jack decided it would be politic to make himself scarce.

He was standing next to a suit of armour, thinking that men in mediaeval times must have been considerably shorter than they were today, when Celeste rejoined him. 'How you ladies do love a bargain,' he said.

'You were listening!'

'I left before you shared the secrets of your undergarments.' Jack looked sheepish. 'That didn't sound quite how I intended.'

Celeste blushed. 'You should not have mentioned it at all. A lady's undergarments are not a fit topic for a gentleman to discuss at a military dinner.'

'Actually,' he retorted, 'you would be surprised at how often the subject comes up.'

'Jack!'

'Celeste.' He raised her hand to his lips. 'You have performed magnificently tonight. Thank you.'

'It is I who should be thanking you.'

'As to that, I have spoken to Wellington. He has agreed to send me Arthur Derwent's file.'

'Knowing his reputation, and what you have told me of the Duke, I'm sure there was a forfeit to be paid.'

'Have I told you that you are very astute as well as beautiful?'

'Yes. Jack, I'm being entirely serious. I would not have you compromise yourself or your principles for me. Are you contemplating going back into the army?'

'No, but there's no harm in letting Wellington think I am.'

'You lied to the Duke of Wellington?'

'Certainly not! I merely withheld the body of truth. Celeste...'

'Lieutenant-Colonel Trestain! Well, I'll be

damned. Didn't expect to see you here. Your name wasn't on the guest list that I saw.'

Jack's blood ran cold as the man grabbed his hand and pumped it vigorously. 'How do you do, Carruthers. I am here in Major Urquhart's place.'

'Ah, Urquhart, the Jock Upstart. I do remember seeing his name. I completely missed dinner. Carriage threw a wheel on the way here, but I thought I'd best show face, keep on his Grace's good side.'

Jack turned to Celeste. 'May I introduce Colonel John Carruthers,' he said. 'Mademoiselle Marmion is— She is an artist. Painting some landscapes of my brother Charlie's estate.'

'Delighted,' Carruthers said, looking at Celeste with indifference, the first man all evening to do so. He had never been much of a ladies' man, Jack remembered. A bluff, old-school but highly respected soldier, he was the type of man who called women fillies, and no doubt rode them as hard and selfishly as he did his horses. It made him unpopular with some of the men, Jack recalled now, his callous attitude to his mounts—the equine kind, that is. Callous treatment of women now, that was deemed, ironically, to be a less heinous crime by a number of officers. One of the many things Finlay found repugnant about the mess. One of the many things Jack and Finlay agreed on.

'…don't you think?'

Jack started. Carruthers was looking at him expectantly.

'Indeed, Monsieur Trestain was saying to me before dinner that he would not be surprised if the Duke became your Prime Minister,' Celeste said, drawing him a meaningful look. 'He will be a Tory, no? And not a Wig? I mean Whig.'

'I heard you'd resigned,' Carruthers said to Jack. 'I must admit, I was surprised. Even in peace time there's a need for a chap with your skills. Trestain here was a bit of a legend, Mademoiselle Marmion, as I expect you've heard a hundred times tonight.'

Sweat broke out on Jack's back like a squall of summer rain. His hands were clammy. '*Mademoiselle* has had a surfeit of our stories this evening,' he said. 'More than enough.'

Carruthers nodded. 'I'm sure. Difficult to believe though, after all these years, that we're really at peace. Do you think it will last?'

'Oh, I think so. Yes.' Jack nodded furiously, relieved that Carruthers had been diverted. Now if he could just close the whole conversation down and escape. He wiped his brow surreptitiously. The room had become stiflingly hot.

'You know, it was a bad business, that fiasco in the north of Spain.' Carruthers's voice broke into Jack's thoughts, his tone sombre. 'I haven't seen you since that day, but I think of it often. Don't talk about it of course. Had to be hushed up, as you know only too well.'

Jack's heart began to race. 'I don't think…'

'A rotten trick, using women and children in that way, like some sort of shield. Not the sort of tactic I could ever imagine an English army indulging in.' Carruthers shook his head gravely.

He could see them. The huddle of women. The children clinging to their skirts. The silence. The smell. Dear God, the smell. Jack took a deep breath. Another. Another. All he had to do was get away from Carruthers. Or shut him up. 'I don't think this is a fit subject for Mademoiselle Marmion's ears,' he said. His voice seemed to boom, but either he was mistaken, or Carruthers didn't notice.

'No, no, you're quite right.'

'Good.' More deep breaths. He wiped his

brow surreptitiously. He caught Celeste eyeing him with concern, and straightened his shoulders. She pinned a smile to her face and turned her attention back to Carruthers, though she also slipped her hand on to Jack's arm. 'I think, if you'll excuse us…' Jack said.

'You know, I've always wondered,' Carruthers burst out, 'where the devil did the enemy forces go? Your intelligence seemed so watertight. And yet they seemed to melt into the landscape. It preys on my mind, keeps me awake at night sometimes, that we didn't capture them.'

Jack's jaw dropped, shock abruptly dispersing the fog in his head. 'That's what keeps you awake at night? Our failure to capture those men? Not the slaughter of innocents?'

'Casualties of war, Trestain, that's what they were. Of course, I wish it hadn't happened but—as an officer, the fact the mission failed is what pains me most.'

Jack began to tremble violently, not because he was in danger of fainting, but because he wanted to smash his fist into Carruthers's face. He was icy cold with fury. Sweat trickled down his back. He could still see them, those huddled casualties of war, struck dumb with fear. 'Innocents,' he said in a low growl.

'Oh, I doubt that very much,' Carruthers said. His brows snapped together. 'Dammit, Trestain, that is the kind of loose talk that the British army will not tolerate. That is the very reason why that whole episode was—well, I should not have brought it up. I see that now.'

Jack's fists clenched. With immense difficulty, he uncurled them. Lights danced before his eyes. He wanted to wipe that pompous, callous look off his senior officer's face. It took him every inch of willpower to hold out his hand. 'You will wish to talk to his Grace. He is over there, holding court. Don't let us detain you.'

Carruthers hesitated only briefly, before giving his hand a brief shake. 'Your servant, *Mademoiselle*,' he said and departed.

Jack stood rooted to the spot. His eyes were glazed. Sweat glistened on his brow. Here, Celeste had no doubt, was the story at the root of his condition. He was glowering at Colonel Carruthers, as if he wanted to run him through with his sword. Though he was not wearing one, his hand was hovering over where, she presumed, the hilt would lie.

'Jack.' He stared at her as if he didn't recognise her. 'Jack!' She yanked hard on his arm. 'We should leave. Now. I am no expert on etiquette but I am sure it is poor form to attack a man—a superior officer—in the middle of a regimental dinner.'

He blinked, but her words seemed to penetrate. Celeste began to walk, keeping a firm hold on his arm, towards the first door she could find, slamming it closed behind her. Jack slumped against the wall. She gave him a shake. His eyes were blank again. 'Jack!' Another shake, to no avail. Muttering an apology, terrified that at any moment someone would open the door, Celeste gave Jack a hard slap across the cheek.

'What the hell?'

'Walk. Now.' Celeste grabbed his face between her hands, forcing him to look at her. 'We have to get you to your room. Do you understand?'

He blinked. He nodded. Then he began to walk, heading down the long corridor at a pace so fast she had to run to keep up with him. Up a set of stairs. Along another corridor, another set of stairs. She had no idea where they were going, but Jack seemed certain. Panting, she followed him until the next set of stairs opened on to a familiar corridor. His bedchamber was directly across from hers.

He threw open the door and dropped on to the bed, his head in his hands. He was shivering violently. Celeste pulled the feather quilt from the bed and wrapped it around him. 'You had better go. Thank you, but you—you should go.'

'Don't be ridiculous, I cannot leave you like this.'

He clutched the quilt around him. 'I will be much restored directly—the worst is— I will be fine.'

She touched his brow. It was soaking with sweat and icy cold. She cursed the resolutely empty fire grate. There was a box beside it. Perhaps that contained coals. She opened the box, but it was empty save for a tinderbox, which she used to light the candles on the night table.

His shivering grew more violent. The front of his shirt was soaking with sweat. 'You need to take your coat off, Jack.'

He stared at her, his expression unnervingly

calm while his body shook. 'I can't believe it. How can he think like that? Those women and children. So callous. Casualties of war, he called them. As if they were killed on a battle-field. Innocents! I can't believe it.'

Celeste knelt at his feet to take off his boots and stockings.

'I wanted to smash his face.'

'That was very obvious.' Celeste uncurled his fingers from the quilt and tugged him to his feet, easing him with some difficulty out of his coat with its complex fastenings. He stood motionless, neither helping nor hinder-ing her, racked with sporadic, violent shivers. She quickly undid his cravat. His shirt was soaking with sweat. She struggled, for the fab-ric clung to his skin, but eventually managed to pull it over his head. Deciding against re-moving his breeches, she pulled back the bed-covers and ushered him into bed. He lay flat on his back, his eyes wide open, staring up at the ceiling.

'The irony is, Carruthers is in the right of it. Casualties of war, that's how the army sees them. That's what will be written in the file that no one will ever be permitted to look at. Carruthers is right. What mattered is not the slaughter of innocent civilians, but the failure of the mission.' He turned his face towards her, his expression pleading. 'I was a soldier for thirteen years. You'd think it would be easy for me. I've told myself it was my duty to see it their way, Celeste, that I'm letting them down, that I'm not the man I thought I was, for failing in that duty, but it makes no difference. I can't. I can't. And if Carruthers knew the full story—but he doesn't. No one does. No one except me.'

He struggled to sit up. Celeste pushed him back, holding him down, his torment racking her with guilt and compassion. She spoke soothingly, as one would to a child. 'You must rest, Jack. You must try not to torment yourself like this.'

'God knows, I've tried, but it refuses to go away. I dream. And I see them. Like ghosts. Living in my head.' His fingers closed like a vice around her wrist. 'It was my fault. The village. The women and children. I didn't double-check my information. I didn't validate it, cross-reference it as I always did. But they said they couldn't wait, there was no time and because Wellington's code-breaker was infallible they acted. Except I'm not. It was my fault,

Celeste. My fault. Oh, God, all mine.' His grip on her wrist loosened. She thought she had never seen a man look so haunted as he turned away, and a racking sob escaped him.

Overcome with pity, feeling utterly helpless, Celeste sank on to the bed beside him and curled into his back, wrapping her arms around him. His shoulders heaved. She could feel his muscles clenched tight in his efforts to control himself. She wanted to tell him it would be all right, but how on earth could she? She could not imagine what horrific images he had in his head, but the ones that Carruthers and Jack had between them managed to instil in hers were bad enough. Here was the dark secret which had scarred Jack for life. Here, laid bare for the first time were the results of that pain, the silent agonies he had kept hidden from everyone. She pressed herself closer against him, wrapped her arms more tightly around him, as if she could somehow stop him from shattering into a thousand pieces.

She pressed her mouth against the nape of his neck. His skin was burning now, where it had been icy only a few moments before. The sobs were quieting now. He was no longer shaking. She kissed him again, closing her eyes, wishing that she could give him something, anything, to ease his suffering.

He pushed the quilt back, putting his arm over hers. The muscles in his back rippled when he moved. His skin was still hot, but dry. She pressed her cheek to his shoulder.

'I'm sorry.' Jack's voice was muffled, but it was Jack's voice.

'Don't be. Please, don't be.' Relief brought tears to her eyes. Stupid. She had nothing to cry about. Her heart ached for him.

He pressed his lips to her fingers. 'You saved me.'

'No. You saved yourself.' She gave him a little shake. 'You were lost for a moment, Jack, but then you saved yourself. You were angry.'

'I wanted to kill him.'

'But you didn't run away. You were not sick. You were in no danger of fainting. I didn't save you, Jack, you saved yourself.'

'But you were there. My aide-de-camp. You didn't let me down.'

'No, but if it were not for me, you would not have been here, Jack.'

'I would have. I told you. For me, as well as for you. Don't you feel guilty about that. We've already enough guilt between us to sink a ship.'

He kissed her fingers again. His mouth was warm. Soft. 'Thank you.'

'It was nothing. Please don't. Oh, Jack, I was so—and you did it. You did it. You passed your test. Such a test. I had no idea. None. I can't imagine— I was so worried about you—and I didn't know what to do.'

'You watched my back, just as I asked you to. You got me out of there in one piece. Thank you,' he said, stroking her hair.

'You're welcome,' she said as he tilted her chin up. She said absolutely nothing as his mouth descended hungrily on to hers.

Chapter Eleven

Jack closed his eyes, drinking in the sweetness of her lips, the lushness of her mouth, savouring the soft, pliant contours of her body as Celeste wrapped her arms around him. 'You got me out unscathed,' he said again.

'You saved yourself.'

He had. His anger had saved him. It was not his condition that had sent him into a tailspin, but his railing against it. He had saved himself, and Celeste had been there at his side to rescue him. He had only a hazy memory of the journey from the Great Hall to his bedchamber, but he knew he wouldn't be here without her help. He ached with longing for her. He wanted her so much. He needed her so much. He had not the strength or the will to resist her any more. He kissed her deeply. He trailed kisses over her eyes. He licked the tears from her salty cheeks. He pushed a damp tendril of hair back from her brow, and kissed the flutter of pulse at her temple.

She pushed at the bedcovers, which were tangled between them. He kicked them away. Her eyes were like gold in the candlelight. Her hair was pale as milk. He kissed her again. Such heady kisses she gave him back, filling him with a longing that seemed to come from deep within him.

He kissed her neck. He kissed the swell of her breasts. He cupped them through her gown. She shuddered. She flattened her palms over his chest. Skin against skin. Naked skin. He wanted to meld himself to her. He wanted to drown in her, and damn the consequences. He ached to have her wrapped around him, to dive into her and to lose himself there for ever. Safe. Lost. The kind of oblivion he was no longer capable of resisting.

He kissed her again, his tongue tracing the shape of her mouth, his hands tracing the shape of her breasts. He was ready, more than ready, but he wanted more. He did not want it to end. He wanted to show her how much she mattered to him, how much he wanted her, how very much.

He kissed her mouth lingeringly, then eased himself from her, putting his finger to her lips when she protested. He moved down her body, pressing kisses all the way before parting her legs to kneel between them, raising her skirts.

He kissed the skin between her stocking and her undergarments, undoing her garters. He kissed her slim calf, her ankle, before taking her stocking off. He could see the rise and fall of her breasts. He could hear her shallow breath. He took off her other stocking. He leaned over her to kiss her mouth again. Then slipped his hands under the delightful curve of her rear, and eased off her pantaloons.

When he covered her sex with his mouth, she cried out. He stilled her, laying a hand on her stomach to ease her back on to the bed. Then he licked into the hot, wet sweetness of her, and the cry she gave this time was guttural.

He took his time. Tasting. Licking. Sucking. Stroking. Kissing. He took his time because he wanted to show her how very much he wanted her. Her breathing was ragged, like his own. The taste of her, the scent of her, the softness of her, made him so hard. He felt her tighten, sensed the change in her breathing, fastened his mouth on her as she swelled, and held on to her as she came, her fingers clutching at his shoulders, her heels digging into the mattress, saying his name over and over.

Celeste lay shattered by a climax so intense she thought she might faint, and at the same time, she thought she might fragment into a thousand pieces. She could hear herself moaning, panting, pleading, and she could do nothing, wanted to do nothing, save yield. She was utterly sated, and yet at the same time, even as the pulsing eased, her body was already demanding a different, more primal satisfaction.

Instinctively she pulled at Jack's shoulders, her back arching under him. He covered her body, rolling her on top of him and kissing her. He tasted of her. The solid ridge of his erection nudged between her legs. His hands tugged at the strings of her corsets. When they were loose enough, she flung them off. With a sigh of satisfaction, he pushed down the top of her shift to reveal her breasts, rolling her on to her back again to kiss them, lick them, taking her nipples into his mouth, sucking, nibbling, sucking.

She could barely think. She was aflame, burning with the need to have him inside her, wantonly, shamelessly egging him on with her hips and her hands and her mouth. The muscles of his back rippled under the flat of her palms. She slid her hands down, inside the waistband of his breeches. His buttocks tautened. He let her go only to rip the fastenings of his breeches open and cast them off. He sat astride her naked body, only for the second time, and for the first time—gloriously naked and thickly erect. She reached out to touch his silky hardness, forgetting all her doubts and all his too, in the need which consumed them.

His kiss changed. Deeper. Slower. He touched her slowly too, his hands on her shoulders, her back, feathering down her spine, then back to her breasts, cupping, stroking, slowly but surely making her tense, tighten, throb, on the brink of another climax, and also, rather curiously, on the brink of tears. She touched him. The hollow in his shoulder where the musket ball had hit him. The hard wall of his chest. His nipples. The curve of his rib cage. The dip of his belly. She curled her fingers around his shaft. One slow stroke. He inhaled sharply. Another.

His hand covered hers. He shook his head. 'Need to— Not that. Too much.' He kissed her again, and rolled her under him, masking her body with his. 'Sure?' he asked.

For answer she wrapped her legs around him and kissed him hard. 'You will be careful, Jack?'

'Of course. I promise. Of course.'

The first thrust was tentative, parting her carefully. The next was surer. She clenched around him, clinging on to her self-control, not wanting to let go yet, though it was already building. Jack's breathing was laboured. The sinews on his arms stood out like ropes. He thrust again, more confidently, higher, deeper. A harsh groan escaped him. She clung to him as he lifted himself, then cried out as he thrust again, and she met him this time.

She sensed his straining for control. She clung desperately to hers. Not yet, not yet, not yet. But their bodies found a rhythm of their own that could not be resisted, thrusting and arching, harder and faster, higher, tighter. He slid his hands under her bottom, tilting her up, and she cried out as she opened up, as he pushed inside her, feeling the waves of her climax take her, digging her heels into his buttocks, her fingers into his back, saying his name urgently over and over as she surrendered, sensing him thicken as she came, another thrust, another that she met wildly, before he withdrew at the last second and his own climax took him, dragging a guttural cry from him as he shuddered, pulsed, shuddered.

The tears might have been sweat on his cheeks. She kissed them away. He wrapped his arms around her, pulling her tight against him. Their skin clung, heat and sweat, rough and smooth. Her own tears tracked unnoticed. She was in another world, floating with bliss, mindless, and at the same time, every nerve was on fire.

But as the final waves of her climax ebbed, the fear was already making its insidious way to the front of her mind. *Dare not*, Jack had said, because he was afraid he would find it difficult to walk away. He had not considered that she might have the same difficulty, but she was already fairly certain that she would.

She had never been in love. She had always thought herself indifferent to love, or even incapable. But then, she'd thought herself indifferent to so many things that had subsequently proved not to be the case. She could see it, sense it, waiting to pounce on her. If she turned her back it would creep up on her. She felt as if she were standing on the top of one of Cassis's white limestone *calanques* and looking down at the turquoise sparkle of the sea. Tempting. Glittering. Lethal.

The urge to flee was very strong. Whatever it was that propelled her to such dizzying heights would also be the end of her if she let it. She would be powerless in its sway. She would be incapable of doing other than its bidding. It might make her wildly happy, but she was pretty certain it would also eventually make her deeply miserable.

Celeste began to ease herself free of Jack's embrace. His arms tightened around her. He opened his eyes. He smiled at her, a sated, satisfied smile that squeezed her heart and destroyed all her resolution. She smiled back. Then his smile faded. He let her go gently, but he let her go.

Jack sat up, pushing his hair back from his forehead. Ought he to feel guilty? He looked at the woman lying on the bed beside him, and felt nothing save this fierce need to hold her, keep her, always. She touched him to the core. The strength of his feelings almost over-whelmed him, but it was the sheer force of them that made him realise he had to make sure that it ended here. In another life, if he was another man, he could allow himself to care. In another life, she would love him back. In another life, he would deserve that love. But he had only this life, and he must endure its vagaries. He could never be happy, while Celeste deserved every happiness. He had to make sure that she understood now, before it was too late, how hopeless it was. He had to save them both from the pain of dashed hope, and there was one sure-fire way of doing that.

'Celeste, there is something we must discuss.'

Her hair trailed over her shoulders, pale against the warmth of her skin. 'There is no need,' she said dully. 'You were right. We should not have— It was a mistake.'

'A mistake we can't repeat,' he said. 'Must not. I need to explain why.'

But even though he knew he had to speak, he found it almost impossible. Nothing to do with the embargo which the army had placed on the subject, everything to do with what he was about to destroy. Jack closed his eyes, leaning his head back against the headboard. 'It was my fault,' he said. 'That's the most important point to understand.' He opened his eyes. 'It was my fault, and nothing I can do will ever change that.'

He sat up, pushing a pillow behind his back. Celeste curled her legs around her, angling herself in the bed to face him. She looked as grim as he felt. 'You heard the gist of it from Carruthers.' He frowned, forcing himself to think back, though he had gone over it so many times, there was really no need. 'We were marching north, aiming for Burgos in Castile. Wellington—he was Wellesley then—wanted to move our supply base from Lisbon to Santander. I got wind that a band of elite French soldiers were hiding out in a small hilltop village. We had been monitoring them for a while. They were responsible for all sorts of surprise attacks on our flanks, a real thorn in our side. We suspected a leak from one of our own informants. There were a hundred very good reasons for us wanting to rid ourselves of them, and I was under a great deal of pressure—but that is no excuse.'

Jack pushed his hair back from his brow again. He was damp with sweat. 'I shouldn't have let on. I should have kept it to myself until it was verified, but I didn't and once it was out, action followed quickly. They were like ghosts in the night. We'd lost them a few times. It was deemed too risky to wait. I should have protested more forcefully. I should have demanded that we wait so that I could check, cross-check, as I always did.'

'Jack, you did protest though?'

'Not enough. No one listened.'

'But you did…'

'Celeste, it doesn't matter what I tried to do, what matters is what happened. We sent our men into that village thinking it was a fortress, based on information I provided. Carruthers was the commanding officer. He took no chances. He went in hard, all guns blazing.' He was cold now. He clenched his teeth together to stop himself shivering, clenched every muscle in his body to stop himself shaking.

'Jack, this is too painful for you. Please stop.' Concern was etched on Celeste's face.

He managed a weak smile. 'Not so long ago, you'd have been prodding me in the chest and demanding that I go on.'

She took his hand. 'I couldn't imagine then

what ailed you. I didn't know then quite how much pain you were in.'

'My pain is nothing. I need to tell you. I need you to know what no one else does. I owe you that much.'

I owe you that much. And then it would be over, whether she wanted it or not—and she was a good deal more ambivalent about that than she'd realised. But what she felt didn't matter at the moment. What mattered was Jack. She was terrified of what he would tell her, and terrified of what his telling her would do to him, but she knew, with utter certainty, that he had to get it off his chest. Celeste felt for his hand. Her own was icy. 'Very well. Go on.'

He gave a little nod. 'I knew in my gut that something wasn't quite right. That was why I insisted on being allowed to accompany Carruthers. I wasn't part of the attack, but I went into the village immediately afterwards.' He faced her determinedly. 'Women and children, Celeste. Spanish women and children, whose men fought on the same side as us. But there were no men. Not a sign of the French. Not a trace that they'd been there. We will never know if they were forced to co-operate, to keep silent, or whether we were entirely mistaken. They were dumb with fear, the few that had survived the onslaught. Carruthers's men had attacked the village with all the firepower at their disposal. It took them a while to realise their fire wasn't being returned.'

Goose bumps rose on Celeste's skin. She could see it in her mind's eye. The village. The women. The children. The dead.

'It's what I dream,' Jack continued. 'It's so vivid. My boots crunching on the track. The sun burning the back of my neck. I lost my hat. There was a chicken. It ran right in front of me. I nearly tripped over it. I could hear Carruthers shouting orders, I could hear his men sifting through the carnage, but it was as if I was walking alone through a montage. So quiet. So still. There really is such a thing as deathly silence.'

He was still looking at her, but his eyes were blank. It filled her with horror, and a pity that was gut-wrenching, the more so because she knew she could do nothing to help him.

'After a battle, what you smell is smoke and gunpowder. There was a pall of it so thick on the battlefield of Waterloo, that you could hardly see a yard in front of you. In the village,

I know it must have been the same, but I remember it as clear blue skies. The smell—the smell—' Jack broke off, dropping his head on to his hands, pinching the bridge of his nose hard. 'I was ravenous, I hadn't eaten properly for days. There was a stew cooking on a fire. Peasant stuff. Broth. *Herbes de Provence*. It made my mouth water. And then I—then I—that's when I became aware of the smell of the blood and the—the charred flesh. That's when I was sick. And that's when—when—when I—that's when I saw her.'

Jack's shoulders shook again. He dropped his head on to his hands again and scrubbed viciously at his eyes. Celeste could hear him taking huge, ragged breaths, counting them in a low, muttering, monotonous tone. She wanted to hold him, comfort him, but he was rigid with his own efforts to regain self-control. She felt helpless again, and more desperate than ever to help him. She scrabbled in her mind, through the morass of horror that he'd told her, trying to think of something, anything that would help, but her brain was frozen with the shock of it, unable to conceive of what it must have been like for Jack—what it must still be like.

She tugged his hands away from his face.

'I can't imagine,' she said pathetically, 'I can't even begin to imagine.'

'I don't want you to. I wouldn't wish what is in my head on anyone.'

'The smell. The venison, that broth, that was what happened at dinner that night at Trestain Manor?'

'Yes.' Jack gave a ragged sigh.

'But there is more, is there not?' Celeste forced herself to ask. 'You said that Colonel Carruthers did not know the worst.'

'He doesn't.' Jack began to shake again. 'I've never spoken of it. I don't know if I— No, I can. I can. I can do it.' His knuckles gleamed white. A pulse beat in his throat. 'There was a girl,' he said. 'A young girl. I don't know, twenty, no more. She was standing over me— when I was being sick— I don't know, I didn't hear her, but when I looked up, she was there. Dear God.' Sweat beaded his brow. He mopped it with the sheet. 'She had a pistol in one hand. She was pointing it straight at my head. There was a bundle in her other. Clutched to her chest. A bundle. I thought—I thought it was rags. I don't know what I thought. I was— It was— I was— It was her eyes. Blank and empty. Staring at me. Through me. I was sure she was going to shoot me. I had no doubt she was going to shoot me. She had that look—of having absolutely nothing left to lose. I didn't move. I didn't speak. I felt this—this strange calm. It wasn't that I didn't care. I didn't feel anything except, this is it. This is it. And I waited.' Jack turned to her, his eyes wet with tears. 'I waited. And she turned the pistol to her own head, and she pulled the trigger. And it happened so slowly, so very, very slowly, and I did nothing, until I heard the crack, and I saw her crumple, and the bundle of rags fell, and it was her dead child.' Jack dropped his head on to his hands. 'Dead. Both of them, And it should have been me. It should have been me.'

Sobs racked his body. Celeste held him, rocking him, her own eyes dry, too shocked for tears, numb with horror, wordless with pity. She held him until his sobs stopped, until he pushed himself free and turned his back on her to throw water over his face from the bowl, pull a dressing gown over his damp body. He sat down in the chair at the window. 'So you see,' he said slowly, 'I know all about the torment of futile questions. What if I had kept the information to myself? What if I had checked it more thoroughly? What if I had not insisted

on going along? What if I had remained with
Carruthers? What if I'd not been sick? What
if I'd tried to take the gun from her? What if
I'd tried to reason with her? I know what it's
like, Celeste, to have the possibilities tear at
you until you can't sleep and you can't eat. But
the difference between us is that my guilt is
entirely justified. That poor, bereft young girl
took her own life and it's my fault. Tonight,
with your help, I've proved I can manage the
symptoms. But I can never be rid of the guilt.
And that's the price I will pay for ever. You
see, don't you?'

What he said felt quite wrong. She saw a
man torturing himself, determined to go on
torturing himself because he thought he deserved no better. She saw a brave man, fighting
to control his demons, while at the same time
determined to carry that burden with him. She
could see what he was trying to spare her, but
she couldn't see that their cases were so very
different. What if this? What if that? Why was
he so set on relieving her of guilt, and so determined to cling on to his own?

Celeste stared at him helplessly. One thing
was clear. Whether she wanted it or not, there
was no future for her and Jack because he

would not allow it. That was what he was telling her. Let me go, and spare us both the pain. She could do that. Jack had more than enough to bear already, and she— No, she could not allow herself to want a man who would not permit himself to want her. Not even Jack. Sadly, exhausted, defeated, she nodded, and began to pick up her clothing.

'Celeste,' Jack said as she made for the door. 'Celeste, I need you to know that tonight— I can imagine ever wanting…'

'Do not say that.' She turned on him, suddenly angry. 'Don't tell me how wonderful it has been, and how unique, and perfect and— and—do not tell me. You think I want to be always thinking of that, in the future, when you are not there and I am taking comfort in some other man's body?' She couldn't imagine it, but she forced herself to say it, because what did he expect! 'I am sorry,' she said gruffly. 'I know how much it cost you to tell me that. I can't begin to imagine what you are going through. I am sorry if it is selfish of me to be thinking—and I wish I could help you as you have helped me—are helping me—but I can't. I can't tell you what was going through that poor girl's mind, any more than you can tell me what was going on in my mother's. But you are set on absolving me, Jack.'

He made no answer. She supposed it was because there was no point. Outside, the night was giving way to a grey dawn. Celeste let herself quietly out into the corridor.

It was over. He had made certain it was over. Jack sat in the post-chaise beside Celeste the next day, subdued and silent, trying to persuade himself that he'd done the right thing. His confession, so long held at bay, had wrung him dry, but instead of making his guilt more raw, it seemed to have simply numbed him. The pain came from looking at the woman seated next to him, and seeing the dullness in her eyes, and knowing he was the cause. The pain came from knowing that he had wilfully destroyed something precious. The pain came from knowing that every day brought him closer to the day that would be the last day of their acquaintance. The only way he could manage it was to vow to himself that he would find her answers before that day arrived. That should be enough. He'd make it enough.

As soon as the carriage drew up at the front door, Celeste gathered up her reticule, picked her hat from the seat where she had discarded it in a futile attempt to pass the journey by sleeping, and made her way into the house, no doubt eager for the privacy of her bedchamber.

Wearily, wishing he could do the same but knowing his brother would be agog to hear all about the dinner, Jack was not surprised to be told that he was expected in the morning room at his convenience. It was the least he could do, and it was churlish of him to resent it, he told himself. Dresses and uniforms, toasts and a few choice anecdotes would do it. He'd managed to fool every one of the dinner guests into believing that Lieutenant-Colonel Trestain was alive and kicking, and none of them meant as much to him as Charlie. Charlie, his brother, his own flesh and blood, who had taken him in without question, and who had put up with Jack's moods and his silences and his absences.

And Eleanor too, his long-suffering sister-in-law. She would appreciate a course-by-course account of the meal, if he could only remember what it had consisted of. Opening the door and summoning what he hoped was a cheerful smile, Jack decided he'd just have to make it up as he went along.

* * *

Three days later, Celeste was in her studio, putting the final touches to her painting of the lake. The next painting, a view from the hill of the manor and the village, was already sketched out. She had been working long hours since returning from Hunter's Reach, partly in an effort to stay out of Jack's way, and partly in an attempt to stop thinking about that night. There was no doubt now in her mind that she would be a fool to wish for the impossible, but there were times, moments of weakness, when that was exactly what she did.

Jack's distinctive tap on the door made her jump. One look at his expression made her heart plummet. 'What is wrong?'

He put the tray he'd been carrying down and poured two glasses of cognac. 'Sit down.'

'Jack, what is it?'

He pulled a letter from his coat pocket and handed it to her. 'This arrived in the post this morning. It's from Rundell and Bridge. I'm so terribly sorry, Celeste, but it seems one part of the trail has gone completely cold.'

Her fingers shaking, she pulled out the contents and scanned it quickly. It was only after a second, more painstaking reading that the full import of the words sank in. She picked up the glass of cognac and took a large sip, coughing as the fiery spirit hit the back of her throat. 'And so you are proved correct,' she said to Jack, who was watching her anxiously. 'Maman was indeed a gently bred English lady. "Blythe Elizabeth Wilmslow, only and much beloved child of the late…"' Her lip trembled. She took another, more cautious sip of the cognac and picked up the letter again. '"The late Lord and Lady Wilmslow." So my mother's parents are both dead.' Her fingers went to the locket, which had, according to the letter, been commissioned by them for her mother's twenty-first birthday.

'I'm very sorry.'

Celeste took another sip of brandy. A hot tear trickled down her cheek. She wiped it away. 'I can't think why I am— It's not as if I knew them, these Wilmslow people.'

'They were your maternal grandparents.'

'No, they would never have acknowledged me—because I am illegitimate.' She sniffed hard. 'I always knew that. I don't know why it's harder to accept now that I have the names of these— My mother's parents. Wilmslow. It is a very English name.' Another tear trickled down her cheek. She scrubbed it with the edge of her painting smock. 'It is stupid to feel sad for the death of people you don't know. Especially since, unlike Maman, they did not die prematurely.' She consulted the letter. 'Only three years ago, my mother's father passed away, and then two years ago, her mother. Yet not once did she mention them. Even though they were still alive and living here in England until very recently.' She sniffed again. 'Perhaps there is a family trait that encourages estrangement.'

'Celeste, you know that's not true.' Jack took her glass from her and lifted her hand to the locket. 'Your mother was "the only and much beloved child" it says in the letter. This extremely expensive piece of jewellery is proof of how much her parents loved her. And you must surely see that what is inside is proof of how much your own mother loved you.'

'Despite all evidence to the contrary?'

Jack nodded. 'Despite that.'

He put his arm around her shoulder. Celeste closed her eyes, enjoying the solid feel of him, letting her tears trickle through her closed lids. The cognac fumes were clouding her brain but something in the letter was nagging away at her. She jerked upright and scrabbled for it again. 'It says here that the Wilmslows' estate was inherited by a third cousin because Blythe Wilmslow died without issue. But when her parents died Maman was still alive. I can understand that they would not know about me, but why would they believe Maman dead?' She jumped to her feet. '*Alors*, why can nothing be simple! Why cannot a question lead to an answer instead of more questions?'

She gazed at her completed painting of the lake. She was pleased with it. The light was just right. Late afternoon, the shadows playing on the water. And here, on the edge, was the hawthorn bush where she had hidden to watch Jack swimming that very first morning.

She turned back round. There he was, sprawled as usual, his long legs stretched out before him, no coat, no cravat, his hair rumpled. He looked tired. Only a few nights ago, she had lain in his arms. Only a few weeks, and she would be finished her commission and return to Paris. Without answers. Without Jack.

'And so it ends,' Celeste said, trying not to let her voice quiver. 'As you said, the trail has run cold.'

'There is another trail.'

'The file? Why did you not say it had arrived?'

'I was worried it would be too much.' Jack rolled his eyes. 'I know I have no right or need to manage you, but it's a habit that's rather engrained into officers, this managing. Are you ready?'

'That sounds ominous.' Celeste sat back down beside him and poured herself another inch of cognac. Jack had not touched his. She lifted the glass and took a sip. 'I'm ready.'

'Right. Well, in 1794 Arthur Derwent was sent on a secret mission to France to rescue a number of well-to-do Englishmen and women from the Terror, including one Blythe Wilmslow. Three out of the four people on his list returned safely but Blythe did not, and nor did Arthur. According to the file, they both died in Paris that same year, 1794.'

Celeste's mouth fell open. She set her cognac glass down untouched. 'You must be making this up. It is too fantastical. A spy despatched to carry out a daring rescue of my mother. It is like something from a lurid novel.'

'I assure you, it's in the file in black and white. France was an extremely risky place to be for a member of the English aristocracy at that time. The dangers were all too real.'

'Maman's parents, this Lord and Lady Wilmslow, they must have been besides themselves with worry. I don't understand, Jack—if France was so dangerous for Maman then why did she stay?'

Jack shook his head. 'You're right, it doesn't make sense, but there's nothing more in the file. We can, however, deduce one rather important fact.'

'Jack, I am an artist, not a code-breaker. What is this important fact?'

'For good or bad, Arthur Derwent could not possibly have been your father. He went to France in 1794. You were already four years old.'

Celeste clutched at her brow. 'You must think I am an idiot.'

'On the contrary. You have an enormous amount to take in, that's all.'

'But then why did my mother have this man's signet ring? Did he really die or did he too disappear, like Maman seems to have done? And when did Henri come into the picture?'

Jack shrugged. 'I don't know the answer to any of those questions, but I know where we should start looking. It's just a hunch. No, it's more than that. Call it an educated guess.'

'What is?'

'That the answer lies in France. In your mother's house in Cassis.'

Chapter Twelve

South of France—October 1815,
one month later

Celeste stood on the deck of the small blue-and-white fishing boat as they made their way into Cassis harbour after the short sea journey along the coast from Marseilles. A weak morning sun glinted off the familiar white cliffs. The sea was the same colour as the central stone in her locket. The sun dappling the water, the tang of salt, and of this morning's catch, mingled with that herby scent she could not define but was the essence of the south, combined to fill her senses.

It was strange to be speaking her own language again, more strange to hear the rough dialect of Provence. She had forgotten how very beautiful it was here, and how much she loved the sea. Dread had been her primary emotion on every visit she could recall as an adult, and there had been blessed few of them. The last time, it had been to bury her mother. Today, she thought to herself with a sad smile, she was here to try to finally bury the past along with her.

The fishing boat bumped against the harbour wall. The fisherman jumped on to the jetty and tied up. Jack lifted their few bits of luggage out of the boat before helping Celeste out.

As he paid the man, talking easily in his excellent French, Celeste stood on the jetty, looking up at the village which ran along the edge of the shore. It had never felt like home, but today there was a sense of homecoming. She was excited to be here. She was a little daunted. She was afraid that despite Jack's assurance that there was always something which had been overlooked, that they would reach another dead end.

He was still talking to the fisherman. His face was tanned from their days at sea, for he had spent much of their journey to Marseilles up on deck. He had explained their trip to Sir Charles as army business in such a way that his brother immediately assumed it was also cloak-and-dagger business. With the advantage of Celeste having met Wellington, he mendaciously informed his brother that the Duke himself insisted that she accompany him on this mysterious mission as part of his cover. Sir Charles was entirely unconvinced, but refrained from saying so, content to indulge Jack in the hope that whatever the purpose of his trip, it would aid his recuperation.

The arrangements for their travel had been made and executed so efficiently that Celeste could almost have been persuaded that Jack really was taking her on a secret mission. He had been, for the most part, the rather intimidating commanding officer she had witnessed at Wellington's dinner. It effectively created a distance between them, which Celeste knew was the point. That night at Hunter's Reach had been their beginning and their end. She could only surmise that his determination to expedite her quest was rooted in his desire to put an end to their time together. She tried very hard to persuade herself that he was acting in her interests as well as his own. She tried, with considerably less enthusiasm than she once would have, to persuade herself that she was as set upon remaining the one and only architect of her own future.

'Ready?'

Celeste grimaced. 'As I will ever be, I suppose. Jack, do you really think you will find something?'

He nodded. 'I told you, there is always something to be found if you know where to look.'

She wandered over to the edge of the pier and gazed out to sea. 'Such a—a tangle of revelations have brought us here. I still find it difficult to make sense of any of it. My mother was so reticent. She was like a mouse, scuttling about, hoping no one would see her. You know, I'd even forgotten how beautiful she was until I looked at the miniature in my locket. She always covered her hair with caps, and her clothes…' Celeste wrinkled her nose. 'Black, black, brown and black.' Her face fell. 'Why did I never notice that, do you think?'

'Because she didn't want you to?'

'You are right. How she hated questions, Maman. Almost as much as she hated being noticed.'

'I would imagine that you would have caused a great deal of notice when you were growing up. Even as a child, if the picture in the locket is true to life, you were ridiculously lovely.'

Celeste flushed. 'It is just a trick of nature that makes my face appear beautiful you know. Symmetry...'

'I don't much care what it is. You have the kind of face and figure that turns heads wherever you go, as that dinner of Wellington's proved.' Jack touched her hair. 'This alone must have got you noticed here in the south. The people here are generally very dark.'

'I don't remember.'

'Yes, but you were sent off to school when you were ten, weren't you?' Jack said, looking much struck. 'And to Paris, where you would not exactly blend in with the crowd, but nor would you be quite so distinctive.'

'What do you mean?'

'Your mother patently came here to disappear. A daughter who would have every lad in the village setting his cap at her would hardly be conducive to anonymity.'

'That's ridiculous, Jack.' Celeste rolled her eyes. 'Though no more ridiculous than the idea of Maman being forced to go into hiding in the first place. And I suppose it is a little bit more palatable a story to swallow than that she wanted to be rid of me.'

'I thought you had accepted by now that that simply wasn't true.'

'Oh, I think she loved me in her own way, but her own way was to make sure she didn't show it. I don't understand why.' She brushed a tear away angrily. 'Now you will think me a pathetic creature.'

'I think you many things, but pathetic is not on the list.' Jack dabbed at her cheeks with his kerchief. 'The wind and the salt air are the very devil for making one's eyes run.'

Celeste managed a watery smile.

'I'm sorry,' Jack said. 'I have been so set on getting us here, that I have not thought about what an ordeal it will be for you.'

'Not an ordeal. It's just a house.'

'Stuffed full of painful memories. Perhaps it would be best if you went to an inn, if there is such a thing here, and I can search the house.'

'Jack, I am not precisely looking forward to going back to the house, but I do need to go. I'm sure if there's anything to be found that you will find it, but you can't lay my ghosts for me.'

'When we first met, you were adamant that there were no ghosts to lay.'

'When we first met, I was very sure about a good many things, and I have been quite wrong about almost every one. English cooking. English weather. Englishmen.'

Surrendering to the urge to touch him, she flattened her palm over the roughness of his cheek. He caught her hand, pulling her tight up against him. 'Celeste.' His lips clung to hers for a long, tantalising moment, then he dragged his mouth away. 'If you knew how much I have to struggle not to— If you knew.'

The feelings she had been working so hard to control made her snap. 'If it is such a struggle, Jack, then perhaps we are wrong to deny it.'

'We know we're not.'

'*You* know we are not,' she said sadly, turning away. Out at sea, the sky was darkening. A wind had blown up. The tide was on the turn. The fisherman who had brought them here was already on his way, the boat scudding along the white-crested waves, heading back to Vallons des Auffes. Celeste pulled her cloak around her. 'We should go,' she said to Jack brusquely, picking up a portmanteau and striding ahead of him, along the jetty and into the village.

* * *

The house stood apart at the far end of the meandering street, at the opposite end of which stood the village church. The key was where it had always been kept, under a large plant pot to the side of the door. Celeste struggled to turn it in the lock. The salt water made everything rusty here. Jack edged her aside and pushed open the door. She steeled herself, but the only smell was of dust. She took a tentative step into the hallway. 'It's cold,' she said, turning to Jack.

He put down their bags and closed the door behind him. It creaked, just as it had always done. She'd forgotten. No, obviously she had not forgotten. She had rolled the carpets up when she was here the last time. Her feet echoed on the boards as she made her way to the sitting room. Her stomach was churning. As she opened the door, she realised she was half-expecting her mother to be there, sitting at the table by the window, making the best of the morning light, painting or embroidering or drawing.

'Always doing something,' she said to Jack. 'My mother. Her hands were never still.'

The furniture was covered in cloths, as she

had left it. The grate was empty. The spaces on the walls where her mother's paintings had hung were clearly marked. As she stepped into the room, her nose twitched. The dusty smell of watercolours assailed her, mingling with the dried lavender her mother kept in a bowl on the hearth. The bowl was empty. The watercolours were in Celeste's Paris studio.

She went over to the window. The surface of the table was covered in tiny droplets of paint. She could make out every colour. She ran her fingers over a bump of muddy brown, her failed attempt to mix red, she remembered. 'Henri was furious,' she said to Jack, 'though Maman made more of a mess than I ever did.'

His chair was over there in the corner. Maman's faced it. She had had a stool. It wasn't here now. She'd never been back long enough to merit anything more comfortable. A few weeks ago, she would have sworn that this was because she was not welcomed. Now she recalled many times when she sought any excuse not to come.

'You should start on your search while the light is still good,' she said to Jack. 'Let me show you the rest of the house.' She led him quickly through the dining room to Henri's study where the glass-fronted bookcases covered the walls. 'I was never permitted in here,' she told Jack. She led him down to the kitchen and scullery. Then back up to the top floor. The fifth stair creaked as it always had.

'Henri's bedchamber.' Celeste threw the door open. 'Maman's bedchamber.' Another door thrown wide. The bed was stripped, the mattress rolled. Her feet fixed themselves automatically on the very edge of the threshold, as if the invisible barrier was there still, even though her mother was no longer here to forbid her to enter. Celeste stepped boldly in and threw open the cupboard. Maman's few remaining clothes were here. Thick woollen skirts and jackets. Her heavy black boots.

She could not have described that very particular smell that was her mother. Wool, powder, roses, but there was something else. She closed her eyes. It was still there. Faint, but there. 'Essence of Maman,' she said softly to herself. A fleeting image of herself howling in pain, of two hands swooping down on her, and then that smell as she buried her face in her mother's neck and was comforted.

She blinked. Jack was watching her carefully. 'Memories,' she said, closing the cupboard. 'Don't look so concerned. They are not all of them bad.'

But some of them were. The last room was her childhood bedchamber. Thinking only that this had been her sanctuary, Celeste opened the door almost without thinking. It swung wide, the panel slamming into the coffer which was positioned behind it. Positioned in that precise place to obscure the corner of the room, where a small girl could crouch down, hidden from the open doorway, and where that small girl could cry inconsolably because there was no one to care that she cried, or why.

In a daze, Celeste entered the room, curling herself into the tiny space, wrapping her arms around her waist. 'They never beat me. They never touched me. Neither cruelty nor love, but indifference is what they gave me, and forced me to give them in return. That was what was so hard.'

Jack lit the fire in the kitchen because it was the one room where there were no bad memories. They set out the picnic they'd brought with them from Marseilles. He had little appetite, though Celeste ate with her usual enthusiasm. The wine was rough and young. He drank only a little, contenting himself with watching her. She seemed different. Despite the tears she had shed, she seemed happier. He remembered the first time she'd broken down in front of him, how appalled and embarrassed she had been. She still hated to cry, but she no longer fought quite so hard not to. This afternoon, when she'd been curled up like a child in the corner of her bedchamber remembering God knows what misery, she hadn't been embarrassed by his presence. She had shared her ghosts with him as she led him through this loveless place, not hidden them.

An odd melancholy gripped him as he watched her carefully spreading tapenade on a piece of bread. As she always did, she studied the morsel carefully, as if she was thinking of painting it, before popping it into her mouth. She wiped her mouth with a napkin before taking a sip from her wine glass, something else he had observed was an ingrained habit.

'You're not hungry?' she said, looking up from preparing another morsel. She inspected it carefully, gave a satisfied nod and smiled at him. 'Try this.'

The olives were rich and salty with anchovy. The bread was heavy with a thick crust. Jack nodded, smiled, because she was looking at him so anxiously. 'Delicious,' he said.

'Tomorrow I will go to the church and put flowers on the graves,' Celeste said. 'Maman is buried beside Henri. They think she drowned, the people here. They don't know that she— No one else knows about the letter.' She handed him a thin slice of the blood sausage topped with a small square of hard goat's cheese. 'Try this.'

He ate obediently, aware that she was feeding him as if he were a child or an invalid, but happy to indulge her for the sake of watching her. There would not be many opportunities to watch her in the future. A few more days. A few more weeks. Too many to endure, and not nearly enough. He had already decided he wouldn't be going back to Trestain Manor while she finished Charlie's commission. Seeing her like this, conquering her ghosts, he had the strangest feeling, as if she was walking away from him, disappearing into the distance while he stood rooted to the spot, watching her, unable to follow.

Jack shook his head, mocking his own flight of fancy. Celeste handed him a neat quarter cut from a tart of roasted tomatoes and artichoke hearts. 'I'm sorry I was so—so emotional today,' she said. 'It must have been embarrassing for you.'

He pressed her hand abruptly, perilously close to breaking down. 'It was— I am honoured that you allowed me to— I was just thinking how horrified you would have been, only a few weeks ago, by my witnessing— I am honoured.'

'You look so sad, Jack.'

'No.' He cleared his throat, took a sip of wine, coughed. 'I did not like seeing you so sad, that is all.'

'I was sad here, when I was little. I had forgotten how much I cried. I thought I never cried. But I'm not sad now. Today I remembered that it was not all so very bad.' Celeste gave one of her very French shrugs. 'Not so very good, but not always so very bad. Thank you for making me come here.'

'I had no idea, Celeste, that this house held so many terrible memories. I was fortunate enough to have had a very happy childhood.'

'Though you were deprived of Hector the horse?' she teased. 'Don't feel sorry for me, I've done enough of that myself over the years, and you know, I think I have been a little bit self-indulgent. I was never hungry or cold. I have never been in want of a roof over my head. I was never beaten, and I've never been reduced to selling myself for money. Selling my artistic soul a few times,' Celeste said with a chuckle, 'but nothing else.' Her smile faded. 'In Paris, you would not believe the poverty which is taken for granted. Sometimes, I wonder what on earth our so-famous Revolution was for. These people don't see much evidence of *égalité*.'

'These are the people that armies rely on in times of war, sad to say,' Jack said. 'I doubt France is much different from England. Or Scotland,' he added with a nod to Finlay. 'Napoleon said an army marches on its stomach. I reckon more than half our enlisted men signed up to fill their bellies. Skin and bone, some of them are when they join, and riddled with— Well, what you'd expect from men who have spent their lives in rookeries where they sleep ten to a room, and you have to haul water from a pump fifteen minutes' walk away.'

'You seem to know a deal about it.'

'When you eat, sleep, march and fight with the same men for months on end, you tend to learn a lot about them,' Jack said. 'Besides the fact that I helped write hundreds of their letters, and paid the occasional visit to the families of some of the men who died in battle.' He grimaced. 'Once, to check on a man—a very good man—who had lost both legs.' Jack pursed his lips. 'I remember at the time he said it would have been better for his family if he had died. I told him he was wrong, that they would rather have him alive at any cost. I had no idea how patronising that was of me, until I saw— Well, I've not forgotten it.'

'Since Waterloo, the streets of Paris have been filled with men who fought with Napoleon. I don't know what will become of them.'

'London is no different.' Jack took a sip of wine. 'Victors or vanquished, the soldier's fate is often the same. That is the true price of peace. Something ought to be done.'

'I will paint them, and you will have engravings made of my work, and you will use them to show all the people with money and influence—your Parliament, your brother, the Duke of Wellington—and they cannot fail to see that something must be done.'

'It's a good idea, though I doubt Wellington will wish to have anything to do with it. Too embarrassing for him to be faced with the evidence. I know,' Jack said, amused by the indignant expression on Celeste's face, 'they were his army. Without them he would not have had his great victory.'

'Nor his great ego,' she interjected.

Jack laughed. 'You have his measure very well. It has to be said though, it was his great ego that won us the battle. He never once faltered in his belief that we would triumph, and there were times, believe me, when many other of his officers did.'

'Not you?'

'No, not me. The man is a pompous, conceited, philandering egotist, but as a soldier, as a commanding officer, he is second to none. Not even Napoleon.'

Celeste's brows shot up. 'You admire the man you spent all those years at war with?'

'As a soldier.'

Jack looked down at his plate and discovered he'd eaten the tomato tart. His glass was empty. Celeste had folded her napkin neatly on her own empty plate. He got to his feet and moved the shabby settle closer to the fire, stoking the embers with more of the wood which he'd found neatly stacked in one of the small outbuildings. They sat together, watching the flames and sipping the last of the wine. 'I don't think I'd make a very good politician,' Jack said. 'I am a man of action. Or I used to be.'

Celeste's hand found his. 'You still are. If it were not for you, I would still have been trying to work up the courage to enlist the help of one of those Bow Street running men. You have solved the mystery of Maman's locket and discovered the names of her parents. You have traced this Arthur Derwent, and you persuaded the great Duke of Wellington to tell you top-secret information that I would never have known existed, never mind obtained permission to read. Which puts me in mind of something I have been meaning to ask. Has he called in his favour and asked you to return to his service? Could you do so without returning to the army?'

'Half of his staff have done so in diplomatic roles. The embassy in Paris is full of my former comrades. This most likely sounds paradoxical, given my former role, but I never practised or approved of deception. I may be wrong, but my impression is that deception, flattery and downright lies are at the heart of the diplomatic service.'

Celeste laughed softly. 'In that case, I can think of no one less suited.'

'I wish that were true, but you know it's not.'

'Jack, you could not be more wrong. It is the fact that you are honest, and that you have a conscience, and that you will not accept the lies of the army and of Wellington that makes you different from that Colonel Carruthers and all the others.' Celeste turned sideways on, gently forcing him to look at her. 'You are the one who is right, not them. What you saw, regardless of how it happened, it was a terrible thing, and it will always be with you. As it should be. But that is a very different thing from taking on the burden of blame.'

'It was my fault, Celeste. I thought I'd made it plain.'

'It may have been. It may not have been. I might have saved my mother from drowning herself if I'd listened to her. I may not have. You are so very set on proving that I could not have, so very set on sparing me the guilt that you are so very determined to keep to yourself. Are the cases really so very different?'

'Yes,' he replied automatically, 'of course they are. You know they are.'

'I know you think they are. Just as I know you think this—us—is hopeless.'

'Don't. Please don't. I can't bear it.'

'Jack.' She touched his cheek. 'Jack, you don't have to.'

'I do.'

'Then I must bear it too.'

Only then did he realise that she had hoped. Only then did he realise that it was already too late. He loved her. There was nothing that could be said, and so without access to words Jack did the only thing he could do to tell her, just this once, how he felt. He kissed her.

Celeste melted into his kiss without a thought of denying him, her lips clinging to his, her arms twining around his neck. It had been there for days, weeks, ever since that night they had made love, that knowledge. It had been growing more insistent throughout this day. This house and its ghosts had stripped her of the last of her armour, leaving her defenceless. Tonight, in the domestic intimacy of the one room not populated by ghosts, by the flickering light of the fire as they ate and talked, it had taken hold of her. She loved him. She was in love with him. She was in love with Jack Trestain.

She kissed him to stop the words babbling out. She was in love. 'Jack,' she said, because it was all she could trust herself to say. 'Jack.' She loved him. She kissed his eyelids. She loved him. 'Jack.' She loved him.

'Celeste.' He kissed her again. 'Celeste.' His voice was ragged. 'Oh, God, Celeste, I want you so much.'

He caught her face between his hands and kissed her passionately. Then he groaned. 'We shouldn't.'

Panicking, she kissed him again. 'We can. We must.'

He hesitated for only a second before his mouth claimed hers once more. His kiss was hot and hard and all she had craved since the last kiss, and all she would crave when this became the last kiss. She closed her mind to this and concentrated on remembering. She loved him. The silkiness of his hair. The way he let it grow too long over his collar. She loved him. The hollow in his throat. The peculiar gouge in his shoulder where the musket ball had been cut out.

She pushed him gently back and got to her

feet. She loved him. She turned to allow him to unfasten her gown and her corsets. She slid both to the ground, standing before him in her shift and her stockings. She loved him. She slipped her shift from her shoulders. She loved the way his skin tightened when he was aroused. She loved the feel of his hands, gentle on her breasts, and that circling thing he did, and the soft pluck of his lips on her nipples that made her blood tingle.

She undid his waistcoat. She pulled his shirt over his head. She knelt at his feet and took off his boots. She loved him. She leaned over him to kiss him again, grazing her nipples on the rough smattering of hair on his chest.

She loved the way he looked at her. She loved the way his hands were always drawn to cup her bottom the way he did. She undid the fastenings of his breeches and helped him to kick them away. The firelight danced on their skin. She loved him. She kissed him. He tried to pull her on top of him, but she shook her head. She loved him. She knelt between his legs, licking and kissing her way down his chest, his belly. She felt the sharp inhale of his chest as she brushed the tip of his shaft with her mouth.

She looked up, willing all that she felt to be there in her eyes, and then she began to make love to him with her mouth and her tongue and her hands, trusting her instincts to teach her what she had never done before, nor desired to do.

She loved him. His hands were on her shoulders. In her hair. He was saying her name urgently. His chest was heaving. She licked and she kissed and she stroked. Satin skin sheathing hard muscle. He jerked against her. Swore. 'Not yet,' he said, 'not that, Celeste. Delightful—dear God, delightful as it is. Please.'

Please. She let him pull her to her feet. He spread the blanket from the settle on the hearth, pulling her down with him. He kissed her. Firelight danced on her skin. Heat pooled between her legs. He rolled under her, lifting her on to him, and she sank down on to the thick length of him.

She was slick. She was tight. She tilted her body to take him in higher. Jack moaned, his hands on either side of her waist. She circled her hips, pulling him deeper. He shuddered. He cursed. His fingers curled around her breasts. She loved him. Celeste tilted back her head, and began a slow lift and slide, lift and slide, lift and slide, until she could hold back no longer, crying out as her climax shook her, the pulsing of her muscles triggering the same pulsing in his as he lifted her free. 'Jack,' Celeste said with a sigh, 'oh, Jack.'

Afterwards, they lay entwined in front of the fire, watching the flames turn to embers, the embers to ashes. Celeste dozed fitfully. As dawn broke, she rose, carefully, reluctantly, with aching sadness, disentangling herself from the man she had given her heart to. He was sleeping. She stood for a moment, looking down at his beloved face, his tousled hair, in the grey light of dawn, before quietly gathering up her clothes and creeping up the stairs to her childhood bedchamber to ready herself for a visit to Maman's and Henri's graves.

The sky was overcast, the sea a froth of white. Clutching her cloak around her, the hood pulled over her face, Celeste made her way down the main street of the village to the churchyard. She sat by the graves for a long time, closing her eyes and allowing the memories, good and bad, to wash over her. There were still many more painful than pleasant, but she made no attempt to filter them. They were

all hers, every one of them. She allowed herself
to cry for the first time for the simple loss of
her mother. Looking at Henri's stark grave, she
felt no sorrow, only pity for the very unhappy
man she saw now he had been, and anger too
that he had taken whatever ailed him out on
the innocent child she had been.

'As you did too, Maman,' she said, kneeling
down and spreading her fingers wide on the
stone. 'I love you,' she whispered. 'I can tell
you that now that you are not here to prevent
me. I love you and I wish—I am still angry, a
little, with you for not allowing me to. So I do
want very much to be able to understand, because I do want, very, very much to be able to
forgive you. And myself.'

Leaving the churchyard an hour later,
Celeste found herself reluctant to return to the
house. Stopping at the café for a breakfast of
café au lait and freshly baked rustic bread, she
watched the last of the fishing boats set sail,
and the sky, in the way it did at this time of
year, change from grey to pale blue. As she
approached the house, her footsteps began to
drag. She did not want Jack to tell her that he'd
been unable to find any clue as to her mother's

connection with Arthur Derwent. This was her last chance to find her answers, and she needed them more than ever. She didn't want to have to live with thinking so badly of Maman.

More selfishly, she did not want to have to learn to live with the not knowing, and the guilt which nagged and niggled at her every time she thought of her mother's last visit to Paris. She remembered all those weeks ago— goodness, a lifetime ago—asking Jack how the families of the men who had taken their own lives coped without answers. She furrowed her brow, trying to recall what he had replied, and realised that he had not. He had spared her the truth, that in most cases there were no answers. He would never know for certain why the girl chose to kill herself. He would never know if his being there made any difference. He would never know how close he had come that day to his own death. The girl had spared him. If only Jack would spare himself.

Celeste walked on past the house to the end of the village and the coastal path. The series of limestone cliffs known locally as *calanques* embraced the vivid blue of the Mediterranean like welcoming arms. Some were deep-water bays, some more gently shelving sandy coves.

Here was the one where the deep fissures formed a cave she had once been taken to on a boat trip. It had been summer. She remembered diving from the boat and swimming into the dark, dank cavern. She closed her eyes, trying to picture herself. Twelve? Thirteen? So she had been home from school for the summer. Another memory she had suppressed.

The gentle breeze whipped her hair across her face. She had not bothered putting it into her usual chignon, but had tied it back with a ribbon. In the summer, the heat made walking along the *calanques* unbearable. Scrub fires were common. Surrendering to impulse, Celeste found the narrow footpath that zigzagged down the cliff to the sandy bay beneath. Sitting on the white sand, watching the waves lap at the steeply shelving beach, she finally allowed her mind to turn to last night.

She was in love with Jack. A smile played on her lips, thinking of the wonder of their lovemaking, only for it to fade into sadness as she faced the sheer wall of hopelessness. Her own journey into her past had peeled from her the years of hard-earned indifference, exposing her to the storm of emotions she'd weathered since first reading her mother's letter. This new

Celeste could be hurt. She cried far too much. She felt guilt and anger, but she also felt love for the first time in her life. That too would cause her pain, because the man she loved could not come to terms with the horrors lurking in his own past.

Thinking back to that night when Jack had told her about the massacre in the village, the horror of it struck her afresh, but she could not, as she had done until now, quite equate Jack's story with Jack's determination to make himself miserable. '*Mon Dieu*, that is exactly what he is doing, just exactly like Maman!'

She picked up a handful of the soft sand and watched as it trickled through her fingers. Guilt. An emotion with which she had become very familiar, thanks in a way to Jack himself. He had known from the beginning how inextricably mixed were suicide and guilt. His desire to save her from that guilt was, she saw now, her thoughts racing, one of the reasons he had been so eager to help her from the first. But why must Jack's guilt be any different from hers?

And then there was the problem of Maman and the guilt which drove her to spurn her daughter's love, and to reject her parents. Lord and Lady Wilmslow thought their daughter was dead. Who had told them this? Could it have been Maman? Ridiculous. Yet Jack had seemed certain only yesterday that Maman was hiding here in Cassis.

Questions and more questions and yet more, whirling around her head like a sandstorm. But there, at the centre, like the sun, was her love for Jack. Only an hour or so ago, she'd knelt at her mother's grave and told her that she loved her. All those years she had been forced to suppress her feelings.

'Not again,' Celeste said decidedly. 'Never again. Even if it is hopeless. Even if this terrible, dark secret of his stops him ever accepting it. I'm going to tell him before he leaves me for ever. After we come to the end of this other dark secret of Maman's—however that might end. Then I will tell him.

'I will tell you, Jack Trestain, that I love you, whether you want to hear it or not,' Celeste shouted at the now cloudless sky. Throwing off her clothes, and plunging into the bay, gasping as the water stung her Parisian-pale skin, she struck out strongly into the waves.

He retched violently, spilling his guts like a raw recruit, in a nearby ditch. Spasm after

*spasm shook him until he had to clutch at the
scorched trunk of a splintered tree to support
himself. Shivering, shaking, he had no idea
how long the young girl had been looming over
him. She raised her hand and pointed the pistol
at his head. In her other hand, clutched to her
chest, was a bundle of rags. Her eyes were va-
cant. Jack waited, certain that this was his last
moment. The girl turned the gun. So slowly,
yet he did not comprehend what she was doing
until he heard the sharp crack.*

Jack sat up, gazing dazedly around him,
the sweat cooling quickly on his naked skin.
The room was freezing. The blanket in which
they had slept was knotted around his legs.
There was no sign of Celeste. In the scullery,
he cranked the pump of the huge sink. Only
then, as he ducked his head under the icy water,
did he realise what he'd dreamt. The girl. The
gun. Her face. His feeling of utter inertia. Just
as he'd described it to Celeste, but never before
had he dreamt it.

Pulling on his crumpled clothes, he checked
his watch and was astonished to discover it was
past ten. Outside, the sun was making an attempt to part the clouds. He lit the fire, filled
the kettle with water and set it on the hook

which hung from the chimney, having decided, after one look at the complicated stove, that it was beyond him. There were coffee beans in a box in the larder. They smelled dusty, but he ground them anyway. Still no sign of Celeste, but her cloak was gone from the hook at the front door. He remembered now that she had been intent on visiting her mother's grave.

He could not decide whether it was progress or not, this extension to his dream. A direct result of his conversation with Celeste last night, that was certain.

You are so very set on sparing me the guilt that you are so very determined to keep to yourself. Are the cases really so very different? Were they?

The coffee tasted as dusty as it had smelled, but he drank two cups and ate some of last night's stale bread. He had always assumed himself at fault. He had never once questioned that. Yet he had from the beginning seen Celeste's case in completely the opposite way. Was he wrong?

'Wishful thinking,' he muttered, 'and you know bloody well why, Trestain.'

He put his empty coffee cup carefully down. Love. He closed his eyes, but it didn't go away.

He loved her. Last night, he had made love to her. He was a bloody fool. He loved her. Jack swore. Then he frowned. That didn't change the fact he had no right to love her, and he was not fit to love her. But, dear heavens, how he loved her.

Jack pushed his chair back, making it screech on the flagstones. 'To work,' he muttered. 'Answers are what she needs, she told me so last night. And since I can't provide her with anything else, the very least I can do is make sure that she has those.'

He was in Henri Marmion's study when Celeste arrived back several hours later. Her hair was wet. Her skin was flushed. Her eyes sparkled. Jack's heart gave the most curious little flip. *Here she is*, a voice in his head whispered insidiously. *Yours*.

He was already halfway across the room when he caught himself and came to a sudden halt, feeling decidedly foolish and a little bit sheepish and rather angry with himself. 'Has it been raining?' he asked gruffly.

'I've been swimming.' She smiled at him. 'And thinking.'

'Right.' Did she want him to ask what she'd been thinking? 'You look—different.'

Her smile widened. 'Yes? That is because my hair is sticky with salt and my clothes are full of sand and my skin is red with the sun. And because I have made some very important decisions.'

'What decisions?'

'I will tell you, but not yet.' She hesitated, then put her hands on his shoulder and kissed his cheek. 'That is for last night. And because I know you don't want to talk about it, then I won't, but I want you to know that I will always, always remember.'

His arms went round her waist of their own accord. 'Celeste…'

Her expression became serious. 'Do not tell me you regret it, Jack.'

'Never,' he said fervently.

'Bien.' She slipped from his embrace and looked around the room, taking in the open doors of the bookcases, the stacks of books on the desk. 'What on earth?'

'I thought yesterday that this little library must have cost a small fortune to amass. Look at these,' Jack said, pointing to a row of thick volumes bound in tooled leather. 'A full set of the *encyclopédies*, no less.'

'I feel so stupid,' Celeste said, running her hand along the shelves. 'I was never permitted into this room, but even when I was here in January, I didn't think— It is like the school fees, no? Where on earth did the money come from?'

Jack grinned, producing the letter with a flourish. 'At last,' he said, 'I think I might be able to answer one of your questions. I found this hidden away inside a copy of the *Odyssey.*'

Celeste gave a little squeak. 'Jack! What is it?'

'A letter from a Madame Juliette Rosser of Boulevard de Courcelles, Paris. *Madame* encloses a draft for the usual amount,' Jack said, 'and expects a receipt by return of post.'

'And that is it?'

'It is enough.'

'But—what shall we do?'

'Isn't it obvious? We go to Paris.'

Chapter Thirteen

Paris—one week later

As the carriage came to a stop, Celeste smoothed a wrinkle out of her gloves. Her jade-green walking dress was simple but very well cut, the matching, short pelisse with long, narrow sleeves fitted to perfection. Her brown boots matched her gloves. The ribbon on her hat matched the strings of her reticule. Even in the rarefied surroundings of the exclusive Boulevard de Courcelles, which overlooked the elegant Parc Monceau, she hoped she would pass muster.

Jack too was dressed elegantly, in knitted pantaloons and Hessian boots, his tailcoat fitting tightly over his shoulders. Unlike her, he did not seem nervous. No uniform, but today he was Lieutenant-Colonel Trestain. Rather than intimidating, for once Celeste found it reassuring.

'Have you been able to find out anything about this Madame Juliette Rosser?' she asked.

'The Rossers are a very old family. *Madame* is related somehow to the Comte de Beynac, whose main estates are in the south-west near Cahors, where you thought Henri originated— which may or may not be a coincidence. This is the Comte's hotel, though I gather Madame Rosser has been in residence for many years, through most of the Terror, unusually. She is one of those grandes dames of Parisian society whom everyone fears and few are permitted to actually visit.' Jack smiled ironically. 'It seems we are most honoured. Or rather you are, since we must assume it is the Marmion name which gained us this audience.'

'I don't know why, but I thought that a woman named Juliette would be young.'

'Just because the most famous one of all died young doesn't mean that none of her fellow Juliettes survived past twenty.' Jack covered her hand with his. 'You are nervous, and no wonder, but remember, this might prove to be another dead end.'

'You don't believe that, do you? You have

one of your famous code-breaker hunches, don't you?' His smile was non-committal. Most certainly, he was the Lieutenant-Colonel today, Celeste thought. Caution personified.

The door of the carriage was opened. She stepped out, and the butterflies in her stomach multiplied a hundredfold as she eyed the ornate portico of the Hotel Beynac. Behind these huge double doors might very well lie the answers to her questions. Which would mean the end of her journey. Which would mean, more than likely, and most importantly, the end of her time with Jack, for she could not imagine him returning to Trestain Manor.

So be it. Celeste's heart would be broken, but she would at least tell Jack that she had a heart and that it belonged to him and always would. He would not love her, but she would not let him deprive her of her love for him. She would not be miserable. Well, for a time perhaps, but misery was better than indifference, and she was done with indifference. She would find a way of being happy. She absolutely would!

The door swung noiselessly open. Jack took her arm, smiling down at her reassuringly. Her heart turned over. Celeste gritted her teeth and walked passed the liveried footman, her head held high.

* * *

Madame Juliette Rosser was exceedingly tall, exceedingly thin and exceedingly old. Her white hair was piled high on top of her head. She had the kind of cheekbones on which, Jack thought, a knife could be sharpened, and the kind of long, thin nose that could cut paper. She was dressed in the height of fashion, in a black-silk afternoon gown with an overdress of grey—and very expensive—lace.

The Hotel Beynac was also dressed in the height of fashion—also very expensively, though it had the kind of elegance which could only be achieved by a combination of money and power. The furnishings were new, but the tapestries were old, and the array of objets d'art which adorned every surface looked worthy of the Palace at Versailles. Which might well indeed have been where some of them had originated.

As he made his bow low over Madame Rosser's liver-spotted hand, Jack was aware that her gaze was fixed on Celeste. She nodded absently at him, but when Celeste made a deep curtsy showing, Jack thought proudly, not a trace of her considerable nerves, Madame Rosser raised the eyeglass which hung from her neck on a gold chain and slowly inspected her from head to foot.

Celeste tilted her chin at the woman. 'I trust I pass muster.'

Jack bit back a smile. Madame Rosser, to his surprise, gave a crack of laughter. 'Yes, there can be no doubt about it,' she said.

'Excuse me, *Madame*, but no doubt about what?'

The woman raised her thin brows haughtily. 'Why, that you are Georges' daughter. I assumed that was why you were here.'

Celeste's hand went to her breast. 'Georges?'

'My nephew. Georges Rosser, the Comte de Beynac.' The thin eyebrows were raised even farther as Celeste's jaw dropped. '*Sacré bleu*, I don't believe it. The little English milksop actually kept her mouth shut all these years. You had better sit down,' Madame Rosser snapped, 'and you too, Mr Trestain,' she added in English.

'I can speak French passably well,' Jack said, helping Celeste on to a gilded sofa covered in wheat-straw satin.

The old woman ignored him and picked up a hand bell, which was answered so quickly Jack suspected the butler must have been standing outside the door of the huge first-floor drawing room. 'Cognac,' she snapped, 'and then you may go, Philippe. We are not to be disturbed.'

'I am not going to faint,' Celeste said, though Jack thought she looked as if she might very well. 'I don't need a cognac.'

Madame Rosser sat down on the chair opposite. 'Perhaps not,' she said, 'but I most certainly do.'

'They were betrothed in 1788, Georges and your mother,' Madame Rosser began. 'Blythe Wilmslow was not the match my family wished for such a prestigious title as the Comte de Beynac, but my nephew was one of those fellows who had read that dreadful man Rousseau's *la nouvelle Héloïse*. Foolish boy, perhaps if he'd claimed a better acquaintance with Rousseau, he could have persuaded that madman Robespierre he was on his side. Rousseau, you know, was much admired by Robespierre and Saint-Just,' Madame Rosser said. She took a sip of cognac and sighed heavily. 'Perhaps you don't know. You are so young. You can have no idea of what Paris was like then, during the Terror. Every knock on the door sent one's blood running cold. There was no rhyme or reason, by

then, for many of the arrests. A slighted neigh-
bour. An old score being settled. Mourning too
openly for a guillotined husband. Anything.'

She slumped back in her chair, closing her
eyes and rubbing her temples. Celeste looked
helplessly at Jack. 'If this is too much for you,
Madame...' she said tentatively.

The old woman's eyes snapped open. 'No. I
do not like talking of those times, but it must
be done. You have a right to know what blood
flows in your veins, though you have no entitle-
ment to claim it, or aught else. I sincerely hope
your motive for coming here is not based on
avarice. If it is you will be sorely disappointed.'

'All I require from you, *Madame*, is the
truth, nothing more,' Celeste said firmly.

The old woman took another sip of brandy,
visibly bracing herself. 'Then you will have
it. Your mother and my nephew were betrothed. Blythe Wilmslow was in France on the
Quatorze Juillet, when the Revolution began.
Her parents wished her to return to England,
but...' Madame Rosser shrugged. 'We all
thought at the time that the Revolution would
come to nothing.

'They were here with me in Paris when
Georges' arrest put an end to any hope of a

marriage. I told Blythe that she should go back to England, but of course,' Madame Rosser said sarcastically, 'the little English miss was too much in love and too foolish to leave Paris without Georges.' *Madame* took another sip of brandy. 'And too much in love and far, far too foolish to refrain from surrendering to her grand passion. You, Mademoiselle Marmion, were conceived in the *conciergerie* where my nephew awaited trial.'

'I think, if you don't mind, I would welcome some of that cognac now,' Celeste said faintly.

Jack jumped to his feet to pour her some, holding the glass while she drank, for her hands were shaking. 'You might have employed a little more tact in imparting such shocking news,' he said angrily.

Madame Rosser eyed him disdainfully. 'I am not aware that it is any of your business, Mr Trestain. What exactly is your role in all this?'

Celeste raised her brows haughtily. 'I am not aware that it is any of your business, Madame Rosser.'

Jack laughed. *Madame* pursed her lips. 'You are the image of your mother, save for the eyes, which you have from our side of the family, and where also, I think, you get that...'

She shrugged. 'Insouciance. All very well in a Rosser of Beynac, *Mademoiselle*, but not so acceptable in one conceived in a prison and born on the wrong side of the blanket.'

'How dare…?'

Celeste grabbed Jack's wrist, shaking her head. 'I would be obliged if you would finish your story, *Madame*, in plain speaking, and I will remove my tainted blood from your presence. For good, before you ask.'

Madame Rosser nodded. 'In plain speaking, then, *Mademoiselle*, your mother was trapped in Paris, for by then the borders were closed. I could not have her here in her condition, but I made sure she was safe, and I paid for the doctor to attend her lying-in. Of this, her parents knew nothing. Then out of the blue, an Englishman turned up looking for her.'

'Arthur Derwent.'

'Yes. That is him. How did you know?'

'Maman had his signet ring.'

'He was sent here covertly to take your mother and three other prominent Englishmen home. She stubbornly refused to go. She wept and wailed and batted those big eyes of hers at the poor man, and said she would be compromised if she returned with a child and no husband. He was young, and an honourable man too. But he was also one of those rash young men rather too fond of glory. He agreed to attempt to rescue my nephew from imprisonment. It had been done. It was not the impossible he attempted, but it was ill-fated. He was shot dead by one of the guards. A few days later, my unfortunate nephew was sent to the guillotine. Whether that was a result of the botched escape attempt we do not know. I expect Derwent gave your mother that ring for safekeeping. I would imagine it would have been awkward for the English if his identity were to be discovered. He never returned to reclaim it.'

Madame Rosser sighed wearily. 'With Georges dead, your mother was something of an embarrassment, but I too have a sense of honour. Henri Marmion's family have served the Rossers for centuries. It was fortunate that he was in Paris at the time. Your mother was like you, a very beautiful woman, and one who had that...' She snapped her fingers, then looked pointedly at Jack. 'As I suspect Mr Trestain can vouch. *Bien*, it took only the lure of being able to call such a beauty his wife and the promise of an annuity small enough to be insignificant to me, large enough to be very significant to Henri. Blythe took a little more persuading, but she had no other option in the end, save to do as I bid. She was not married to Georges, but she was English, and she had borne his child. There was a great chance she would be arrested. And so—that was it.'

Madame Rosser got to her feet and pulled the gold cord which hung from the ceiling by the fireplace. 'I trust I have answered all the questions you wished to ask? You will accept my condolences for the loss of your mother,' she added coldly without giving them a chance to answer. 'When my last bank draft was returned, I made enquiries and discovered she had died. Drowning, I think.'

'Suicide,' Celeste said calmly, getting to her feet. 'Unlike you, Madame Rosser, it seems my mother had a conscience.'

'I may not have a conscience, but I do have a sense of duty, *Mademoiselle*.'

'You may rest assured that your duty is now done. I require nothing further from you. I thank you for your time, *Madame*, and I bid you good day.' Celeste dropped a shallow curtsy.

'The allowance, *Mademoiselle*, my nephew would have wished me to—'

'You cannot buy my silence. I have adequate means of my own. Good day, *Madame.*'

Celeste walked from the room without looking back. As the door to the salon closed, Jack caught her arm. 'You were magnificent,' he said.

Jack, torn between fury at the callous treatment Madame Rosser had meted out and admiration at the way Celeste had dealt with it, bid the driver take them back to her studio post-haste. She shook her head when he tried to talk to her, and when he made to escort her through the courtyard door, she told him that she needed time to think, and asked him to call on her later in the evening.

When he arrived back at the apartment a few hours later, she looked relatively calm. 'Go in,' she said, 'I will be only a moment.'

The door to her studio stood wide open. A huge room with tall windows opening out on to the roof, and even at this time of year and at this time in the evening, the impression of light. Canvases were stacked against the walls. There were three easels, a huge cupboard, a long trestle table and a number of crates which he supposed must contain her mother's work.

The windows of her main living room also opened out on to the roof. Two large comfortable sofas faced each other across the hearth, draped in a multitude of coloured shawls and cushions. A small table contained a bottle of wine and two glasses. A larger table and chairs sat in front of one of the windows. A dresser stood against one wall, but the rest of the room was painted in the palest of green, the only decoration being the canvases on the walls.

Faces. Lots and lots of faces. Not a single landscape in sight. There were children playing on the banks of the Seine. There were studies of old women and washerwomen. There were men playing boules. Old men smoking pipes. An organ grinder. A soldier in a ragged uniform with only one leg. A woman in a café with a glass of what he presumed was absinthe.

'They are not very good, but they are mine. Not that anyone would commission this kind of thing, even if I wanted them to.'

Celeste was wearing a long, flowing garment of scarlet silk embroidered with flowers, tied with a sash around her waist. 'How are you?' Jack asked. 'After this afternoon, I'm surprised you're still in one piece.'

'I was not when I arrived back here, which is why I wanted you to come back later,' she said ruefully. 'I didn't think I had any tears left to cry but I surprised myself once again.'

He smiled, because she wanted him too, but he was not convinced. 'You handled it perfectly. I wanted to grab her by the throat, but you looked down your nose at her in exactly the way she looked down that nose of hers, and it was a much more effective put-down.'

'For two whole minutes. That woman is impermeable. Like stone. Would you like a glass of wine?'

Without waiting for an answer, she poured them both a glass, setting them down on a small table by the fire. She sat down on the sofa, tucking her legs under her. Jack sat at the other end. She took a sip of wine. It reminded him of Madame Rosser, the way she sipped. Steadying herself. Bracing herself. For what? She seemed on edge. And no wonder, considering what she had just been through, Jack told himself. But she was watching him—oddly.

'When I went for my walk on the *calanques* that morning in Cassis, I realised that you

and Maman had a great deal in common,'
Celeste said.

'I don't see how—'

'For example, there is your sense of duty,'
she interrupted. 'My mother promised that
horrible woman never to tell anyone the story
of my origins. After the Revolution was over,
there was no possible threat to her life or to
mine, yet she said nothing. She was by then, as
far as the world was concerned, a respectably
married woman. She could have gone back to
England, but she allowed that woman—pre-
sumably it was she, that scheming, Machia-
vellian *salope* who will not claim me for her
grand-niece, I presume it was she who informed my mother's parents that she was dead,'
Celeste said bitterly.

Jack, who had in fact come to pretty much
the same conclusions himself, wished now that
he had given vent to some of the many pithy
things he'd wished to say to Madame Rosser.
'I'm so sorry this has turned out so badly,' he
said.

Celeste looked surprised. 'But no. I cannot
doubt now that Maman loved me, for she went
to such pains to keep me. I am sure if she'd
wished it, Madame Rosser could have arranged

for me to be given away. Maman must have loved my father a great deal to risk so much for him. And he—as she said in her letter, he would most likely have loved me too, because he obviously loved Maman. You are wondering that I am not more upset? I told you…'

'I'm wondering what it is you're really thinking, because I get the distinct feeling you're not saying it,' Jack said frankly.

Celeste smiled. 'You are right, but I will. Only I— It is difficult.' She took a sip of her wine. 'It is complicated. I am sad, of course, but I understand Maman so much more now. I will never know for certain if I could have made a difference that day, when she came to me here, but I do know now the source of the guilt which made her life unbearable, and I know I could never have changed that. It was her decision, her life. I think— I hope that I will learn to accept that in the future.'

'So you have your answers finally?' Jack asked.

'I have my answers—or all the answers I'm ever going to get,' Celeste agreed. 'You have done what you promised, and I am very grateful because without you—I don't know.' Her voice quivered. She closed her eyes, her fingers clenched tight on the cushion she was holding against her. 'Jack, I have things I need to say before you go.' She tilted her head and met his gaze determinedly. 'I know you will go, I know that. But I need to— You need to— I need you to listen before you do, because I love you.'

And so after all her careful rehearsing, she had blurted it out! Celeste held her breath. Jack simply gazed at her as if she had shot him. Had she expected him to throw his arms around her and tell her he loved her too? Angrily, Celeste was forced to admit that she might indeed have hoped this. 'Don't look so surprised,' she snapped, 'you must have guessed.'

'I did not dare.'

'Well, I do,' Celeste said, crossing her arms over the cushion. 'I love you, and I'm telling you because I decided in Cassis that I won't let you do what my mother did to me.'

'Your mother?'

'Yes, you know I too am a little tired of talking about her, but she is— You and she have so much in common, Jack. She wouldn't let me love her either.'

He flinched. 'Celeste, don't say that.'

'I love you, Jack, and you can't stop me.'

'Celeste, I...'

'No.' She shook her head stubbornly. 'You have to listen first. I have thought it all through, so you have to listen. Only now I forget what I was saying.'

'Duty,' Jack said.

'Yes, yes. There is Maman doing her duty by Henri and Madame Rosser, even though she has to hurt me. And I can understand that now a little, but why, I ask myself, was she so determined to continue with the situation when it was making her miserable? Now I know the answer to that too. She felt guilty. She had been the architect of the death of one man, and she no doubt blamed herself for having failed to rescue the man she loved, and every day she could look at me, and see the evidence of what she had lost, and—so you see, guilt. She didn't feel she deserved to love me. She certainly didn't feel entitled to be happy, and so she chose to be miserable.'

'Chose?'

Celeste nodded firmly. 'Chose. I think it was her penance.'

'And you think that is what I am doing?'

She flinched at the cold note of anger in his voice. 'I don't think you choose to be miserable, but you don't try to be happy either. And I do think that you see your life as a penance, as Maman did.'

'You don't know what you're talking about.'

'But I do. I know perfectly, because no matter how many times you say it is not, our cases are the same.' Celeste tried desperately not to panic. Jack looked as if he was on the verge of leaving. What had seemed so clear was now becoming jumbled in her mind. 'I love you,' she said, resorting to the one thing that had not changed. 'Jack, I love you so much. You've done so much to help me, why won't you let me help you?'

'Because you can't. Because nobody can.'

'Because you won't let them!' Frustrated with herself for making such a hash of things, and with Jack for refusing to listen, Celeste spoke without thinking. 'You told me right from the start that it was a mistake, digging up Maman's past. You told me that it would hurt me. I didn't believe you. I was wrong. It has hurt me so much, but you must have seen, Jack, did I not tell you in Cassis, how much it has helped me too? I am not the person I was, and I'm glad. I'm not the Celeste who built this great big wall around herself and pretended that she was happy there was no one inside her castle with her. Now I laugh and I cry and I love, Jack. I am in love with you and I'm not going to pretend otherwise.'

'Celeste, I can't—'

'Jack, you can. Listen to me,' she said urgently. 'Listen. The thing my mother felt most guilty about was being alive, when my father and Arthur Derwent were dead. She didn't kill them, but she felt responsible. And she paid with her misery. You did not kill that girl, but you act as if you did. You are giving up your own life in payment, Jack, can't you see that, just as Maman did. You did not kill that girl. She took her own life, Jack, when she could have taken yours. She spared you.'

'Spared me?' He stared at her, incredulous.

'Yes, spared you. You thought it was your last moment. You thought she was going to kill you. You accepted it. You did nothing. If you had, perhaps she would have pulled the trigger on you. Perhaps she was testing you. Perhaps your lack of resistance proved to her that you regretted what had happened, that you accepted her right to kill you. I don't know.'

'I will never know.'

'No, you won't. Like me, you will never

know exactly why. Like me, you will never know if you could have stopped her. But if I can learn to live with that, why cannot you? She spared you, Jack, and you are acting as if you wish she had not.'

He jumped to his feet. 'You're wrong.'

'No, I'm not.' Celeste grabbed his arm. 'If our cases were reversed, if I told you I couldn't let myself love you, that I had to spend the rest of my life atoning by being unhappy, even though you were desperately in love with me, what would you do?'

'I do love you.' Jack turned blindly for the door. 'I do love you. It's the only thing I'm sure of.'

'Jack!' He was out of the apartment before she could catch him. She heard the pounding of his feet on the stairs and ran after him as fast as she could. The door to the courtyard was swinging open. Celeste stepped out into the Paris street in her bare feet, darting uselessly in one direction and then the other, but he had vanished into the night.

He ran blindly at first, as fast as he could, careless of where his feet took him. Curses followed him as he collided with another man, but he ran on, oblivious, with Celeste's words pounding in his head.

I love you.

You can't stop me.

I love you.

I won't let you do what my mother did to me.

I love you.

If I can learn to live with that, why cannot you?

I love you.

Jack turned a corner too tightly and staggered into a wall. The pain that shot through his injured shoulder brought him to his senses. He was in a dark alleyway strewn with rotting vegetables. A market, he surmised. Looking around at the dark holes of he gaping doorways, he felt that he was being watched. His senses on full alert, he walked casually towards the pinprick of light which he hoped would prove to be a main thoroughfare.

It was a barge passing on the river. The alleyway led directly down to the Seine. Across on the other bank, he could hear singing, but here, all was quiet. He walked, keeping one eye out for trouble, until he reached a well-lit street. And then he walked until he reached an area he recognised. And then he walked on and found himself back at the apartment he had fled from several hours before.

He was sick of running. Celeste loved him. And he loved her. Jack leaned against the courtyard wall, staring up at the starless sky. Celeste loved him, and she was determined to keep loving him, no matter what. She deserved to be happy.

While he deserved only misery? Was he actually wallowing in his guilt, as she had suggested? Was he choosing unhappiness as atonement, as Blythe Marmion had done? No, there was no comparison between them. None.

And even if there were—which there was not—the cases were still different. Celeste's mother had been unhappy, but she had been perfectly normal. Her guilt did not manifest itself in nightmares and temper flashes and forgetting where she was and—all the things he was learning to control. All the things Celeste had helped him to understand. He had passed the tests he had set for himself. It was not a canker, as he'd imagined it for so long, a parasite which fed on his guilt—it was part of him, his condition. Another battle scar, and like the hole in his shoulder, he was learning to live with it.

Which brought him back to guilt. *If our cases were reversed, if I told you I couldn't let myself love you even though you were desperately in love with me, what would you do?*

He would still love her. He would tell her he loved her, and he would keep telling her until she believed him and until she accepted that she had no reason at all not to love him back. He wouldn't walk away. Even though that was what he was expecting Celeste to do? To sit back, and accept his decision and to live with it? Was that arrogance or was he back to wallowing in his guilt?

Guilt stopped Blythe Marmion loving Celeste. Jack did love Celeste. But Jack could never make Celeste happy because Jack didn't deserve to be happy. Because it should have been Jack who died, and not the girl.

But the girl had spared him.

Celeste had all her answers now, and not many of them were pleasant, yet tonight she'd seemed surprised when he suggested it had turned out badly. He remembered what she'd said in Cassis, about laying ghosts. He remembered wishing he could do the same. He remembered concluding, as he always concluded, that it was impossible. But if Celeste could do it, why couldn't he?

What if he was wallowing? What would the girl say to that? He had always assumed that she was torturing him with her suicide. He had always believed it was revenge for her child's death, for all the deaths. *Remember this, soldier. Never forget this, soldier.* What if she simply couldn't bear to go on?

What if she was sparing him?

What if he allowed himself to love Celeste?

The idea filled him with such happiness, he felt light-headed. It felt—it felt right.

What if he lost her? What if he walked away, and she stopped loving him and she found someone else? He couldn't contemplate it. He couldn't imagine it. He had, he realised with horror, assumed that she would always be there, waiting for some indeterminate point in the future when he might feel entitled to claim her. He cursed himself under his breath. Arrogant, stupid, fool. What was he waiting for? The future could be now, if he was willing to take a chance. If she was still willing to take a chance.

Jack looked up at the apartment building. 'Dammit, there's only one way to find out.'

* * *

'Oh, Jack!' Celeste fell on him, wrapping her arms around his neck. 'Oh, Jack, I have been so worried. I am so sorry. I should not have said— I only meant to help you.'

'You did.' He pulled her tightly against her, holding her so close she could hardly breathe. 'You did.'

She leaned back to look at his face. 'What has happened?'

He laughed. 'You,' he said and kissed her. He tasted of the Paris night. He kissed her hungrily. 'I love you so much,' he said. 'I don't know if I can forgive myself for what happened in the village that day, but I do know I'd never forgive myself for losing you. I can't believe how close I came to that, Celeste. Oh, God, Celeste, I love you so much.'

He kissed her again, more wildly, and the heaviness in her heart shifted. He loved her. She framed his face with her hands. 'Is it true? You really love me?'

'I really do love you, more than anything. That's the easy bit,' Jack said, kissing her again. 'I love you, and I don't want to waste another moment of my life without you. You were right. About the guilt. About atoning. About all of it. I was spared. I don't know why, but I was spared, and it's time I claimed my life back. I don't know how I'll do it, Celeste, but I want to try. I love you, and I'd be a bloody fool to pass up the chance of happiness with you.'

'And you are not a bloody fool.' She beamed at him. She didn't think she had a smile wide enough for him, so she kissed him. 'I love you.'

'And I love you. I don't know what that means for us, Celeste. I have no idea what our future will be, but I can promise to love you always, and to try.'

'Jack, *mon coeur*, that is all I want.'

There would be a time for explanations, but it was not now. Celeste led him into her living room, where the fire burned and the uncurtained windows showed them the night-time Paris sky. They kissed, the deepest, thirstiest of kisses, as they shed their clothing, claiming each other with their mouths and their hands. They kissed, and they touched, and they sank on to the rug in front of the fire and they made love. There would be a time to discuss the future, but what mattered now was that they had a future, and it started here.

Epilogue

Trestain Manor—two years later

' "It was with some interest that we attended the exhibition of paintings which is currently being displayed at the town house of a certain celebrated member of the ton." ' Sir Charles looked over the newspaper at his wife. 'Well, we all know who that is a reference to. I wonder how Jack managed to persuade him?'

Lady Eleanor finished pouring the tea. 'My love, when I think of the amount of money Jack has persuaded the great and the good to part with for this enterprise of his, convincing his lordship to hang Celeste's pictures in his salon would have been an simple matter.'

Sir Charles laughed indulgently. 'Very true. Though I confess, they are not the sort of pictures I'd want hanging in my salon. I much prefer those landscapes she used to paint. Very pretty, they were,' he said.

'Yes, one could think of many words to describe her recent works, but pretty would not be one which springs to mind,' Eleanor said with a shudder. 'Those portraits which she made of the Waterloo veterans, for example. Why must she choose the— Well, frankly, Charles, the shabbiest and the most pathetic of men. As I recall, one had no legs, and another— His face. I could not get the image of that poor man's face out of my mind for days.'

'Which was rather the point, don't you think?' her husband said drily. 'That particular set of paintings was, I gather from Jack, almost solely responsible for raising the funding needed to establish the hospital in Manchester.'

'Jack would say that. I have never seen a man so besottedly in love. Or so proud of his—his wife.' Lady Eleanor put down her tea cup. 'You know, it is such a relief to finally be able to address Celeste as Mrs Trestain. I don't know why it took them so long to get married.'

'There was the small matter of her origins, though I believe that dear Celeste was rather more concerned about that than Jack.'

'She is the daughter of an English lady and a French count. *Such* a romantic story. It is a pity they were not married, but look at the FitzClarences. Being base-born never did them any harm.'

Sir Charles patted his wife's hand. 'Would that everyone saw it your way, my dear, but Celeste's French family will not even acknowledge her.'

'Well, her English family are very happy to own her. Now that she is finally Jack's wife, of course. Do read me the rest of that piece, my dear.'

Sir Charles cleared his throat. '"The portraits are painted by Mademoiselle Celeste Marmion, who has, we understand, lately taken on the name of Mr Jack Trestain, formerly Lieutenant-Colonel Trestain, known to many of us as the Duke of Wellington's renowned code-breaker." Wellington will not like that. He has made it very publicly known what he thinks of Jack's fund-raising.'

'To his detriment. I never thought I would say this of the man who saved England, but I think his attitude towards those poor men who fought for him, indeed laid down their lives for him, is shameful.'

'Absolutely. It is enough to make one consider turning Whig,' Sir Charles said. He waited for his wife to laugh at his joke and, slightly unnerved when she didn't oblige, once more returned to the newspaper. '"Contrary to what we have come to expect of Mademoiselle Marmion's work, this latest selection of paintings is bucolic, a mixture of landscapes and portraits, all of which were made in the north of Spain. The funds which Mr Trestain hopes to raise from the sale of the paintings are to be directed towards one village, in recognition of the support which the Spanish peasants gave the British army in the latter years of our war with France."'

'It is rather an odd thing to do, is it not?' Lady Eleanor asked, frowning. 'Why this particular village?'

'I am sure it is merely a case of it being representative,' Sir Charles replied, folding up the newspaper. 'Symbolic, don't you know. Shall we take a trip up to town next week? We can take a look at Celeste's latest exhibition, and we can have dinner with the pair of them. Jack is in fine form and excellent company these days. He is quite restored.'

'I like to think that we played some small part in his recuperation.'

'I rather think Celeste must take the lion's share of the credit for that. And Jack himself. I must say I'm immensely proud of what he's achieved, even if it is considered beyond the pale by some of my acquaintances.'

'One can only hope that marriage has moderated their billing and cooing. I was positively embarrassed, the last time we met.'

'My love.' Sir Charles got up from his seat and kissed the nape of his wife's neck. 'Nurse has taken Robert and Donal and the baby out for a picnic. I was rather hoping that we could indulge in some billing and cooing ourselves.'

'Charles!' Lady Eleanor exclaimed, looking shocked.

He pulled her to her feet and kissed her.

'Oh, Charles,' Lady Eleanor said in a very different voice as she allowed him to take her hand and lead her out of the breakfast room.

* * * * *

Historical Note

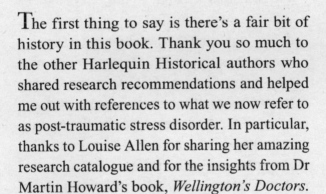

The first thing to say is there's a fair bit of history in this book. Thank you so much to the other Harlequin Historical authors who shared research recommendations and helped me out with references to what we now refer to as post-traumatic stress disorder. In particular, thanks to Louise Allen for sharing her amazing research catalogue and for the insights from Dr Martin Howard's book, *Wellington's Doctors*.

Four books in particular were of immense help in the gestation of this story—and all four are now looking as dog-eared and exhausted as I feel, having written it!

Christopher Hibbert's *The French Revolution* is an excellent all-encompassing account of the Revolution from its early days right through the Terror until Napoleon stepped in. It gives a real sense of what it must have been like in the last days of the Terror, when Celeste's mother was hiding in Paris and, as Madame Rosser attests, arrests became quite indiscriminate. The case she mentions of a woman guillotined for grieving too openly for her husband is a true one.

Richard Holmes's *Redcoat* tells the story of the British army from an ordinary soldier's point of view. It's stuffed full of fantastic anecdotes, including stories about interminable mess dinners and endless toasts, which mirror the dinner Jack and Celeste attend. Finlay, of whom we shall see much more in the next book in this miniseries, came to life as a direct result of my reading in *Redcoat* that almost no enlisted men made it up through the ranks of Wellington's army. Who could resist a man who beats the odds—and the ingrained snobbery too?

If you only read one book about Waterloo I'd highly recommend choosing Nick Foulkes's *Dancing into Battle*. This is not a blow-by-blow account of the battle itself, but of the men who fought it, their wives and children, and the gossipmongers who watched from the sidelines.

It's irreverent, funny and, unlike many historical tomes, a very easy read.

Lady Richmond's famous ball, which is mentioned in this book, gets the full treatment here, as does the Duke of Wellington's relationship with the fatally attractive though apparently quite empty-headed Lady Wedderburn Webster, which so enthrals my Lady Eleanor.

The story of the French spy who passed himself off as one of Lord Uxbridge's men also originates from here.

And then there's my favourite example of the British stiff upper lip: when Lord Uxbridge was wounded, he said to Wellington, 'By God, sir, I've lost my leg.'

'By God, sir, so you have,' the Duke replied.

George Scovell, an engraver's apprentice, was Wellington's real code-breaker, and if you want to know more about him try Mark Urban's book *The Man Who Broke Napoleon's Codes*. As to Jack's dark secret—though the setting and timing, near Burgos in 1813, is historically accurate, the event itself is an invention wholly of my own. In fact it owes rather more to the Vietnam War than the Peninsular one, when the Vietcong used innocent villagers as shields, as may or may not have happened, in Jack's story.

A lot of reading and research, but luckily I have another book to write on the same subject. Finlay's story is next. Though how that will turn out at this moment in time I have absolutely no idea!

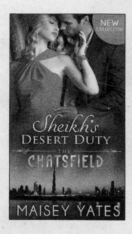

215_INSHIP2

MILLS & BOON®

Seven Sexy Sins!

 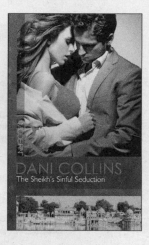

The true taste of temptation!

From greed to gluttony, lust to envy, these fabulous stories explore what seven sexy sins mean in the twenty-first century!

Whether pride goes before a fall, or wrath leads to a passion that consumes entirely, one thing is certain: the road to true love has never been more enticing.

Collect all seven at
www.millsandboon.co.uk/SexySins

MILLS & BOON®

& HISTORICAL

AWAKEN THE ROMANCE OF THE PAST